SAVING TIME
JENN LEES

COMMUNITY CHRONICLES BOOK 3

To Graham Frank Fancourt.

17/2/1938-21/6/2016

Thank you, Unc. You know why.

Contents

Chapter One

North Western Highlands of Scotland, 2061

S unlight glinted on the sea loch, like diamonds strewn across sapphire-blue velvet. The sun-warmed wind blew across the waters of Loch Ewe, rippling shimmers of light on this summer's day. Murdo MacDonald squinted against the glare while the wind bristled through his greying beard as he rounded his boat on his side of the Isle of Ewe.

His white-washed crofter's cottage came into view beside him and to the left, positioned on the island that sat in the middle of this wide expanse of sea water. Ahead was the neck of the sea loch and past it the open ocean. Opposite his home, a large, narrow, dark vessel bumped gently against the white-posted pier of the oil depot at Drumchork. Abandoned for years, the depot's store of fuel long since depleted. The submarine filled his sights and Murdo sighed in resignation.

"So, there ye are. I've been waiting for ye."

Cutting the small boat's motor, he drifted, staying by the shoreline of his island and well away from the submarine.

Watching in silence.

The hatch of the submarine opened. A little at first, then gradually to its fullest extent, clanging open on the metal surface of the submarine. A man in a khaki uniform emerged; his bald head and face were a dark sunburned-red. The submariner continued his journey across the vessel's hull, scanning his surroundings as he went.

Murdo ducked further into the cabin of his small motorboat. He would avoid any contact. His brother had drilled into him the dangers of exposure to radiation. His eldest brother—oh so many years ago.

Others followed behind the first submariner, their skin a similar red slough. Vomiting and short periods of rest punctuated their slow journeys across the vessel's deck, onto the pier and then along the old road.

Murdo's mouth dried.

So, it had begun.

***

Achnasheen, North Western Scottish Highlands

Rory pulled his stallion up sharp. It was times like this, after climbing the horses up a mountain, that he gave thanks for his father's foresight in breeding from Highland Mountain horses. Rory's stallion panted and snorted, sides white with foam, jangling tack as he tossed his head. Leather saddles creaked beside him, alerting Rory to his team's arrival at the summit of this mountain, Bhienn Fionn.

On top of the Munro, the peaks of lower mountains—those less than three thousand feet—surrounded Rory and his crew. The fresh wind blew the grass flat over grey rock-covered hills and funnelled its way down to Loch Maree, which reflected the bright blue sky and nestled itself between the elevations of the Finnach mountain range. Rory gazed out at this land—his place on this planet—took a breath of the Highland air and smiled to himself.

This was where his soul sang. Whatever went on in the wild world out there, he was content to be here—and nowhere else.

Below him was the old village of Achnasheen and the roads leading into it from the west and east. Loch Finnach was to the north. Rory looked past Loch Maree. Far in the distance was Loch Ewe, the sea loch leading out to The Minch, the body of water between the mainland of Scotland and the Isle of Lewis.

Aye, where I stand is an ideal lookout.

"Wow, it's so clear we can see for miles," Kendra said from her horse beside him.

Her bow sat over her shoulder, and she'd strapped her quiver full of arrows at her side. Her long, dark hair tied in its usual plait fell over her weapon. She was astute, amiable, and good in a fight. He'd trust her with his back any day.

"Excellent visual today. It will be here, then." Rory slung his father's long range rifle over his shoulder then slipped out of the saddle.

The wind caught Rory's dark red hair and blew it across his face. It was long enough now to tie back. He lifted his saddlebags, easily taking the weight of the supplies in them.

Callum dismounted and followed suit, his Beretta in its holster, and his Buck knife in its sheath hung from his belt. Callum wore clothing made by the community: hand-woven wool cloth shirts and buckskin leather leggings. Everyone did, as manufactured clothing was a thing of the past and a rarity. Rory regarded his identical twin brother's tightly cropped hair, vivid blue eyes, and tall, muscled frame. They were the same, but not the same. Mandy knew it for certain now.

Things had been strained between himself and Callum, but not for long. A bond such as theirs was hard to disrupt, even with matters of the heart. It was eight months since Rory had returned from the past with the beautiful young woman, hoping to have a relationship with her after rescuing Mandy from the slave-trade.

But no.

The same, but not the same. Mandy had found her love in his twin.

Rory brushed thoughts of Mandy aside and began to focus on the task at hand—setting up a temporary camp to prepare for constructing a permanent strategic outpost. He and George Stobbart, the head of the Militia, had decided to extend their security due to the persistent raids of the many bandit groups that roamed nearby and were now becoming bolder. They would build another closer outpost halfway between here and home, the Invercharing Community.

Xian dismounted his horse, landing without a sound. Bouncing. The agility of this young Chinese man amazed Rory. Xian had taught Rory some Gung-Fu in the twelve months since he'd joined the Community. Rory loved it. Its strict discipline had given him a sense of security and its free-flowing forms in the exercises were relaxing and invigorating at the same time.

Therapeutic even.

He'd needed *therapeutic* after returning from the past. He often woke in a cold sweat with the vivid memory of Dad's death, as if he were reliving it. They were like visions: Mum holding Dad close, his blood covering them both. Dad whispering into her ear as his life left him.

Don't go there now. Focus on the task at hand.

"So, we collect rocks then?" Xian asked.

"We'll dry stone our fort," Rory clipped his answer.

"And you know how to do *that*, don't you Rory?" Rory's younger brother, Brendan, stood with his head cocked.

Sandy-haired and blue-eyed, he took after their father, Scott.

"Well, we copy what they've done along the road there." Rory gestured to the road below the mountaintop on which they stood. "Should nae be difficult."

"My dad always said it was an art form," Kendra said.

"We'll be *artists* then." Rory shook his head.

He was a soldier. There were many skills people had to relearn since the stock market crashed just over forty years ago. The ensuing chaos and disruption to twenty-first-century life had removed most modern technology from people's lives. It had forced them back to basics. Never knowing this technology himself, it always amused Rory when his younger brother Murray, Brendan's twin, tried to restore the old computers which had originally arrived with the early members of the Community.

The rest of his team dismounted and gathered the grey rocks that lay scattered on the ground at the top of this mountain. They would also use the rocks which formed a cairn left by hill walkers in the past. No one walked hills for pleasure these days.

"Um..." Brendan had the binoculars as it was his turn to be the lookout.

"*Um* what?" Rory's head flicked toward him at his tone.

Hesitating, Brendan looked away from the lenses and glanced at Rory. Brendan's expression sent the chill of a cool mountain breeze to Rory's guts. Rory dropped the rocks he held, strode over to Brendan, then grabbed the high-powered binoculars from his hands.

"Where?" His voice was terse, expecting to see riders—bandits—but there was nothing.

"Directly ahead." Brendan pointed.

Rory followed the line of his arm. A narrow valley ran the other side of Bhienn Fionn. A long loch sat at the base of the mountain opposite and a dilapidated road cut the valley through the middle. Amongst the grass of this undulating glen lay a blob of darker green, vaguely human in form. Immobile.

"Okay. I need a volunteer to ride—" Rory began.

"I'll go." Kendra's voice floated past his ear as she made her way to her horse and slid into the saddle. "I'll let you know if you need to come."

"Keep an eye out—" he began.

"For bandits. I know." Kendra flicked her long black plait over her shoulder.

Kendra rode down the mountain and Rory turned to the task at hand—dry stoning. There shouldn't be too much of an art form to it. They needed to build a walled lookout soon. Rory shovelled the area they would build in and dug down to bedrock, which wasn't far. The structure would sit on this solid base. Rory soon discovered rocks have a mind of their own and need to fit together if they are going to stay together. Callum seemed to have the knack. After an hour of his brother's careful selection and placing of stones, the beginnings of a circular wall had emerged.

"Kendra's waving." Brendan lowered the binoculars and held them out to Rory. "She wants us to go there."

"Right, you stay here, Brendan, and mind our equipment. Keep your weapon handy," Rory said. "You guys come with me." Rory directed the order at Callum and Xian.

The fact Kendra wanted him meant it was serious. She wasn't one to be melodramatic.

They picked their way down the steeper side of Bhienn Fionn, then galloped in the direction of Loch Maree where Kendra now waited on her horse. The khaki-clad form lay in the grass nearby.

Rory slipped his leg over the saddle and jumped off his horse.

"No. Don't go any closer," Kendra shouted from her horse. "It's not good."

"I'm no' afraid of a dead body, Kendra." Rory continued toward the inert human.

"No! Rory please, stop." Kendra's tone held alarm.

Rory stopped mid-stride. "Why?"

"I'm not sure but I think he died of radiation sickness," she said.

"What makes you think that?" Rory blinked, trying to concentrate, and not let the implications of this stir up any alarm.

"He's got no hair. Not even eyebrows or eyelashes." Kendra pointed to the man's face. "And his skin is so red. Like really, really, bad sunburn but, well, it's never *that* sunny here to cause such sunburn."

"Why are you standing back?" Callum made to go toward the dead man. "It's not contagious, is it?"

"No! Seriously. Don't go any closer." Kendra held up her hand, signalling for Callum to stop. "He's radioactive. I think. Oh, I wish Chris was here, she would know more—being medical. I remember your mother talking about it, a long time ago."

Callum stepped back to Rory, now both were well away from the dead man.

"He's Asian," Kendra said.

"Where's he from?" Rory asked Xian.

"I don't know." Xian set his hands on his belt next to his gun holster and his short sword. "Why are you asking me?"

Rory rubbed the back of his neck. "Look, I'm no' meanin' to be racist or anything but I've never been far out of these Highlands, let alone out o' Scotland. But you came from a more cosmopolitan place than me, Xian. Can you shed some light on what we're dealing with here?" Rory peered closer at the body. "Is there a badge on his uniform? It might be a flag of his country. If we had the binoculars, I could—"

"There's someone up there," Kendra shouted as she looked at the cairn on the top of Bhienn Fionn.

Rory spun. A group of figures were up on the peak with Brendan. They were moving rapidly, and it wasn't friendly. Cold clutched Rory's spine as he strode to his horse and flew into the saddle. He'd left the youngest alone, believing his proximity would be a deterrent to any bandits.

I was wrong.

Callum and Xian had followed suit, and they soon kicked their horses to a gallop. They made their way up to the would-be fort but the climb, being steep in places, slowed them down and the top of the Munro was empty by the time they crested the final rise. Weapons and food stores were gone.

No Brendan.

Rory's heart sank, his mind spinning. He peered down the mountain, over the far side near the cairn. There was nothing.

"They *must* have gone that way," Callum voiced Rory's thoughts. "We would've seen them on our way up otherwise."

"Aye. So down we go." Without hesitation, Rory kicked his stallion down the steep descent. The bandits had his baby brother, and they wouldn't get away with it.

The others followed, stones and dirt flying. Skidding a zig-zag route down the side of the mountain, Rory led them to the forest that edged its base, and halted.

Still no one in sight.

"Ssh. Listen." Rory pointed to the trees.

Horses' whinnies within the forest reached them. Here and there a human voice drifted out. The bandits were in the distance but still among the trees.

"Quietly now," Rory ordered. "They may have a base camp. We'll sneak up on them. No going in guns blazing. It's our wee brother in there. The bandits won't hesitate to shoot back. They have all our spare ammo, after all. *Nobody's* to be shot today."

Rory dismounted and tied his horse to the tree at the edge of the forest. The others did the same.

Rory crept toward the human sounds in the forest, his crew stayed close by with their weapons at the ready. The bandits were amateurs, announcing their presence with whoops and yells.

What? Did they expect us not to follow them?

It disgusted Rory. His stomach churned at the possibilities of what they could do to Brendan. He quickened his pace.

They were soon within sight of the bandit's makeshift camp. Rory ducked behind the nearest tree, confident of his team doing the same. He peered around the side of the Scots pine's trunk and counted five men and a woman. The group of desperates had tied Brendan to a sapling near the campfire in the centre of their hide-out.

The bandits were busy sorting the food supplies and ammunition they'd taken from the top of the mountain. No one watched the hostage.

Distracted. Now was the time to attack. Rory would make his plan known.

Silent weapons.

Rory turned to Kendra to indicate she use her bow. She'd already notched an arrow.

Xian had his throwing knives in his hands and his sword at his side ready as always. And the man himself was a silent weapon.

Lethal. Deadly.

Rory unsheathed his Buck knife and placed the British Army standard long range rifle on the ground next to him. He was more comfortable as a sniper, but ammo was in short supply. Besides, a silent surprise would give them the best chance of success. Callum held his Beretta and would wait till Rory gave the signal to shoot.

Xian indicated he would go forward and start the rescue.

Rory nodded.

Xian, silent as a cat and just as graceful, slipped his way through the trees to stand near the group whooping their delight over their bounty. Xian's wrists flicked, and corresponding expressions of shock appeared on the faces of those bandits now pierced by his knives. One to the ribs of a man, and one to the shoulder of the woman.

The others scattered, grabbing for guns and knives in their retreat to their mounts. Whinnies of horses and the cracking of broken branches punctuated their flight as they rushed out of the forest.

With the bandits' attention now away from Brendan, Rory snuck around to the other side of the camp near the campfire. Brendan opened his mouth to speak. Rory put a finger to his lips to shush him. He would attract any bandits not occupied by Xian. Rory reached forward with his hunting knife to cut Brendan's bonds. Footsteps came behind him. Rory's hackles rose.

Rory turned to meet a fist on its way to his belly. He tightened his core, absorbing the blow. He regained his balance as his focus sharpened. Heart thudding. Rory lunged with his knife at his assailant's abdomen. The man's forearm blocked Rory's thrust, bone on bone. Grating. The man grabbed Rory's wrist to disarm him of his hunting knife. Rory kicked out between the man's legs and to the side. His opponent now balanced precariously on one leg. An easy knock over. The bandit crashed to the ground. Flat on his back. Continuing the forward motion Rory landed with a knee on the man's chest. With a thump, it forced the wind out of the bandit.

In the heat of the moment, a surreal calm surrounded Rory. He'd never been so close to a bandit, nor at the point of decision in which he now found himself.

Should I kill him?

The Chief Council members line up in a row and face this same man Rory now holds on the ground beneath his knee.

They look at the bandit, expressions stern.

One speaks.
"...for the crimes of kidnap and robbery we sentence you..."

The vision and flash of calm faded as thudding returned to Rory's temples. The man struggled. Rory punched hard onto the man's mouth. Teeth ground onto lips. Rory's knuckles flashed a sharp pain. The man's eyes closed as he lost consciousness.

Rory took a long pull of air. Fights were over in a second, but the adrenalin hung around a while longer. He held his hunting knife with a trembling hand.

On the other side of the camp, Xian spun and rose in the air as the side of his foot connected with the temple of a man twice his height. The man crashed to the ground. All the other bandits had fled except for the woman with one of Xian's throwing knives in her shoulder. She sat on the ground, wailing.

Callum and Kendra emerged from the trees and walked toward him as he cut Brendan's bonds.

"Everyone okay?" Rory directed his question to each member of his crew.

"Didn't fire a shot," Callum answered first.

"I loosed an arrow or two. Better go find them." Kendra slumped away.

"Just check those amateurs are no' coming back," Rory ordered.

Over the other side of the camp, the woman's wails continued as Xian squatted by her and tied her arms behind her back, causing an increase in her volume.

"You okay, Xian?" Rory called to him.

"Pardon?" Xian cupped a hand behind his ear. "I can't hear you over the noise."

"You bastards will pay for this!" the woman said through her wails.

"No, *you* and your friends will pay for this," Rory said.

He made his way over to Xian after using Brendan's cut bonds to tie up the man he'd rendered unconscious. The man with the knife in his ribs lay sprawled near Xian.

Dead.

Rory tossed the other bonds to Xian, who tied the hands of the man he'd knocked out.

"We better take all of this stuff back to the Community." Rory pointed to the goods strewn around the bandit's campsite. "All our equipment's gone from the cairn, so it's here somewhere. And get you and your friends some medical attention," he said to the woman who now held her shoulder in silence.

Callum had retrieved their horses, and Kendra marched their prisoner to hers. Kendra removed the knife from the woman's shoulder and applied a pressure bandage she's got from her saddlebags. The woman's gasp followed by her scream assaulted Rory's ears.

"Just in case she has any guts about her," Kendra said. She pushed the semi-conscious woman up and onto the saddle where she would ride behind her, then added. "And decides she'll stab someone with the knife on the way home."

Rory suppressed a smile.

That's what you'd do, Kendra.

The unconscious man was coming around. Rory had placed him belly-down across his saddle—not a comfortable position. Rory could muster no compassion. The bandit had taken his wee brother hostage and stolen their gear; he didn't deserve comfortable.

Rory mounted behind his captive and walked his horse out of the screen of the forest as a quiet buzz in the sky came closer.

"Blast those bloody drones," Rory yelled. "Have we no' had enough o' them? The Government is nosey enough to bother us with these, but not to come and see us themselves!"

Rory slipped his long range rifle from over his shoulder and rested its butt against his right shoulder, holding its weight with his left hand. Not that steady, but it would do. He took a breath and aimed, let the air out slowly, and squeezed the trigger. The drone exploded, and its pieces showered to the ground.

***

The high gates of the Invercharing Community came into view. A fence surrounded the Community Compound's buildings, greenhouses, and vegetable gardens. The high mountains that skirted the valley were grass-green dotted with a patchwork of brown bracken fern and heather coming into purple flower. The wider end of this otherwise narrow glen in between two mountain ranges provided broad meadows for crops and grazing. Sheep roamed the hills, cattle sat on the vivid green grass chewing cud, and horses wandered and frolicked in fenced areas near the main buildings. On the closer hills, windmills spun lazily, generating the power that supplied their compound's frugal requirements. Beside each windmill farm, the usual sentinel stood watch, guarding the precious power source. The Community wasted nothing, utilising every resource to the furthest degree. In his saddlebags, Rory had the empty shells they'd found in the bandit's camp. The younger members of the Militia would aim to make more bullets from the less damaged ones.

"If the guard in the watchtower has done his duty and reported to the medical team we're arriving with injured," Rory said to Callum riding beside him. "There's goin' tae be a stir in the medical centre."

"And we're a wee bit early. The other crews will still be out settin' up the outposts." Callum pulled his horse to a halt.

Christine rushed out the front gate, her light-blonde hair tied back and her expression full of concern. On seeing Kendra riding in unharmed, her shoulders relaxed, and a smile brightened her usually stern face. She approached the injured man Rory had helped to dismount his horse. Christine's natural ability with medical things amazed Rory. Mum had taught Christine herself, and though Christine had never attended a medical school, because there weren't any, she was a doctor—no doubt about it.

A guard helped Christine take the injured into the medical centre, past the main building and off the track that led to the newer accommodation blocks, and on to the stables and animal shelter area at the back of the compound. The main farmhouse was now a Chief Council meeting room and accommodation. Newer accommodation blocks sat beside the old barns converted into multipurpose areas. On this late afternoon, other members of the Militia were practicing hand-to-hand combat in the larger hall.

Sheds echoed with the *clack clunk* of a loom weaving cloth, while young girls sat outside in the sun spinning the yarn. Next to them, chatting happily as they squelched their bare feet in the sludge-wet used paper, two boys on paper-making duty held on to the edge of the wooden barrel as they prepared the pulp which they would pour into frames and dry in the sun.

Rory walked his horse beside Callum as they both headed toward the stables and smithy's forge. They passed an animal shelter, where a young lad mixed a pile of sheep dung and horse manure into the compost heaps, the definite scent of farmyard permeating the air.

Brendan approached Rory and Callum.

"Thanks." Brendan looked up at them both.

A pang of warmth shot through Rory at the sight of Brendan.

"No, I'm sorry for putting *you* in danger." Rory grabbed him and pressed him tight against himself. The young man's soft light-brown hair tickled his face.

"It's okay. You didn't know." Brendan's voice muffled into Rory's shirt. "Besides, you rescued me."

"Well, that's my job," Rory said. "Now Dad's not here."

The thud of running footsteps came toward them. Mandy headed for Callum. She was slim and beautiful, and her long wavy hair flew out behind her. Once beside Rory, Mandy embraced his twin, her pregnant belly protruding to show its six months' size.

Rory held back an ache now in the centre of his chest. He was happy for his brother, truly. But it still hurt. He might've had love with this tall, attractive young woman.

Rory disengaged his hug from Brendan and walked on, letting out a deep but quiet sigh. He'd thrown himself into his role in the Militia. Love didn't seem to work out for him. His parents had had a wonderful love, but he'd rarely seen anything like it anywhere else. No, that was a one-off. And maybe love wasn't all it was cracked up to be.

He continued walking his horse to the stables. Passing the mess hall, the aroma of chicken casserole hit Rory's nostrils and his stomach grumbled. Christine ran from behind Rory, passing him to approach Kendra, who walked her horse ahead of him. She wrapped her arms around Kendra in a tight embrace, their lips meeting briefly. The women grinned at each other, then Christine scurried back inside to the medical centre. Rory swallowed and kept walking.

Yeah, everyone had someone.

Except for him.

Sure, there were plenty of women in the Community. Nice women. But he didn't have a chemistry with anyone. And he wouldn't be with just *anyone*. His nostrils flared.

Stuff it.

Rory had had enough of wondering. He'd just forget about holding out any hope there would be love in his life. He was a soldier like his father. And sometimes, like his father, soldiers had a short life.

"What have you brought home, Rory?" George Stobbart, his mentor and friend, stepped next to him.

George's lined face wore a furrowed brow below grey hair, but his shoulders remained sturdy, reflecting a life of military service. First in the British Marines, then as the leader of the Community's Militia.

"I thought justice should rule the day," Rory answered. "Let the Chief Council deal with them. These bandits are a group of amateurs, desperates. Maybe they just need a chance."

"Hmm. There's a thought now," said George. "Well, here's another. I've just heard on the citizen band radio from the small Community in Loch Ewe. There is a submarine sitting by their pier and it seems to be in some difficulty. They want us to go help." George looked pointedly at Rory.

"You mean, you want *me* to go help," Rory asked.

George squinted as he eyed Rory over his glasses. "Yes, son. You're the only one I can trust. It is a submarine after all. Could be extremely dangerous."

"We found a dead man." Rory ran his tongue over his lower teeth. "Kendra thinks he died of radiation sickness. I need to speak to Christine when she's done with the prisoners. Connected do you think? Submarines are nuclear-powered, aren't they?"

"Some are," George tilted his head. "Was he military? Wearing a submariner's uniform? Where's the body?"

"Och, we left it there. Got distracted." Rory pointed to Brendan now joined by his twin, Murray.

Rory smiled at how different these twin brothers were. Brendan was outdoorsy, like himself. And Murray...well, Murray was a nerd. A brilliant nerd. The Time Machine could not have happened without his mathematical genius, but he'd never tell him that. Murray had been his co-conspirator in their efforts to protect Dad, and consequently Mum, in the past. He sighed; still not sure how successful it had been. They hadn't disrupted the future—the now present—but his father, Scott, had died in their successful attempt at saving his mother and his younger sister Kelly, from slavers. Rory released a long slow breath.

"You all right, son?" George's expression held concern.

"I'm fine." Rory shook himself out of his reverie. "Been a long day, 'tis all."

"So tomorrow you'll take a team and make your way to Loch Ewe?"

"Aye." Rory brightened. "Lovely weather for the beach."

Chapter Two

Scottish Government Bunker, Edinburgh

S iobhan strode along the long white LED-lit corridor, her high heels clicking on the polished concrete floor. Her computer was playing up again, so a break was in order. She didn't mind pen and paper, but it never ceased to amaze her how the IT guys kept the archaic machines functioning.

She stepped along the corridor, her clicking heels forming a beat. The beat brought a tune to mind, and she sang to herself—a tune from the Bunker archives of music stored digitally, as CDs had deteriorated years ago. Siobhan smiled as she sang, there would be live music tonight in the main hall, played by the musically talented among them. But there was nothing quite like the sound of the vinyl records she'd found in the archives—music from the 1960s was the best.

"I'm going up for a walk." Siobhan approached the uniformed guard who stood at the end of the corridor in front of the lift.

He was so pale, he needed to go *up top* more often.

"Sorry, Ms Kensington-Wallace." The guard barred the way to the lift. "No rides to the top today."

Siobhan stopped in front of him, eyebrows raised in query. "Who says?"

"Major McLellan, ma'am." The guard continued his stance in front of the lift.

Unusual. What's behind this?

"You are well aware of my rank and the privileges that go along with it. I need my regular fresh air and sunshine." Siobhan glared at the guard.

He didn't flinch.

"Very well, then," she said. "Can you tell me where Major McLellan is, please?"

"Possibly in the audio-visual room, ma'am," the guard replied.

Siobhan spun on her heel. She'd get to the bottom of this. The rabble *up top* had been quiet lately. Can't be due to them.

Click clack. Motown music floated through her mind again. The lyrics spoke about not being able to hurry love. Well, she'd been waiting for love—real love—and it definitely was *not* in any hurry.

Siobhan would find out why they'd banned going up to the surface. She'd wheedle it out of Antony. She was still good at that. Antony seemed to not be able to deny her information. Perhaps he felt guilty over their break-up, even though it was two years ago.

You'd think he would be over it by now.

He'd treated her like a trophy in the end. As though her good looks and brains, and the status she brought him, were her only importance. It had been the death knell.

Sure, she missed the sex.

Really missed the sex.

But she couldn't live with herself if she continued with that man. He was such a prat, and so biased. She continued beating her brisk steps down the corridor.

Siobhan stopped at the mirror at the top of the corridor where the offices were situated, and tightened her French twist, the usual style for her honey-blonde hair. Hmm. Lucky she'd inherited this hair tone—hid the grey. Siobhan allowed herself a slight smile of satisfaction. She *did* look good for forty-seven. She barely had any wrinkles. Living a sheltered life—literally—growing up underground, she'd avoided the aging effects of all year-round weather conditions.

Smoothing her skirt, she entered the audio-visual room where staff viewed and stored footage from the drones. Shelves and shelves of it.

The room was very familiar to her. Siobhan came here often, spending hours of her life watching the world *up top*. A teacher in her high school years had first shown her the room and how to use the equipment and ensured she had permission to go there whenever she wished. Mrs Smith had passed away, as had most of the original Brains Trust seconded by the Scottish Government and sent underground to this bunker when it became clear the world was not recovering from The Stock Market Crash over forty years ago. Her father had been one of them. Siobhan swallowed the lump in her throat. He had passed two years ago, but it still hurt.

In the audio-visual room Antony and a technician stared at a screen with their backs to her. Antony's medium height frame was, as usual, clothed in his Scottish Defence Force uniform. He wore his black hair short, also in keeping with uniform.

"Hi guys," she said.

The tech faced her and nodded a greeting. Antony turned from the computer screen; his brown eyes momentarily boring into hers.

"Hi Siobhan, you okay?" Antony asked, then returned to the screen, not allowing any time for her to answer.

Siobhan sighed as she followed his gaze to the screen. The visual from the drone showed a mountainous scene, then focused below on the grassy ground. It hovered over a human form.

"Is he dead?" She spoke over Antony's shoulder to the tech.

"Yes, but that's not unusual out there," Antony answered for the technician. He was good at it. "The ferals have a short life fending for themselves. They die of disease if they don't kill each other first." His cultured voice, loud in the small room, held his obvious disdain. "But this one is discoloured."

"*Discoloured*. What do you mean?" Siobhan stepped closer for a better view of the screen. "He's bald...?"

"No," Antony shook his head. "He's... injured."

"Burnt?" she asked.

Antony turned and glanced at her before walking to the door and closing it.

"Siobhan..." He chewed his lower lip as he walked back to her.

"What?" She raised her eyebrows, and her hand went to her hip. She *hated* it when he left her out. He'd better not be going to do that now.

Antony pursed his lips. "There has been some nuclear activity."

"Explain." Siobhan was curt, but she wanted the truth.

"Our cousins over the pond, as they say, have alerted us to a nuclear explosion on their turf."

A shiver made its way down Siobhan's spine. They had waited years for this, hoping and praying the nuclear warheads around the world would stay dormant and unused. One or two had been detonated in the past forty years, but none close, and none at home in the UK.

But damn it, it was only a matter of time. Siobhan, as head of Nuclear Surveillance for the UK government, monitored the nuclear warheads and nuclear reactors closely. Plus, as many foreign ones as she could obtain the data.

Oh, how she wished Dad was still here... her brilliant man.

Heat rose on the back of her neck. Antony wouldn't dare keep anything from Dad.

"And you have known this for *how* long?" She held back from yelling her question at Antony.

"We have detected a fallout cloud from a nuclear device detonated over the southern part of the United States, now dispersing and creeping its way northeast," Antony said. "Our meteorologists are tracking its present course and extrapolating to see if we are in the path."

"What has this dead man got to do with it?" Siobhan moved closer to the monitor to get a better view. "Where *is* this?"

The footage continued and now the drone hovered over another body lying face up in the long grass.

"The dead man has nothing to do with the cloud," Antony said into her ear before he turned to the technician. "How many are there?"

"In total about ten, sir. They start at Loch Ewe, and this last one appears to be somewhere near the mountain, Bhienn Fionn, in Achnasheen in the northern Highlands, sir."

"The man is Asian? Chinese?" Siobhan peered closer. "Am I correct?"

Antony nodded. "Think so. We suspect rogue state involvement."

The footage changed as the drone moved on. Siobhan's pulse raced at the view of this freshwater loch and the rugged hills surrounding it. The wind rippled across the loch, birds flew off the water and red deer drank at its edge. Its peace and calm filled Siobhan with a yearning to be there, to touch the cool water.

Maybe go for a swim. She screwed her mouth to the side... she never learned to swim. The footage sped up, blurring the idyllic view and disrupting her daydream.

"Here's something else I need to show you, sir." The technician fast-forwarded to a view of a forest.

The drone focused on a group of people coming out of the tree line. They all rode horses, both men and women carried weapons, and two men had bodies over their saddles in front of them. They looked up. One man grabbed the large gun slung over his shoulder. His mouth moved as he spoke and aimed at the drone. The young man's face was a scowl. The ground became smaller in the footage as the drone ascended and the man continued to aim the gun. The man's shoulder kicked slightly, and the screen blurred white.

"What! That rebel has destroyed government property." Antony shook his head in disgust. "It just shows how stupid they are. And the First Minister thinks we can negotiate with these anarchists and form an alliance when we surface?" Antony's political aspirations came to the fore—again. "How, I ask you?"

Siobhan didn't answer. Neither did the tech.

Having watched the drone footage for years, seeing the life of those *up top*, Siobhan had witnessed it all, including the devastation in the cities and the poor state of most people there.

The groups that lived in communities outside of the major cities though, had a simple and harmonious life. They'd gone back to basics and survived. They relearned old skills, didn't rely on technology and lived closer to the land. They depended on and supported one another. They even seemed happy. Sure, they were the original Doomsday Preppers, but they had survived, and their lives were fruitful and content. Yet they had to defend themselves. It wasn't all good out there.

Growing up, Siobhan had dared to question the truths her teachers espoused. They'd taught her and the other children of the Brains Trust, that those *up top* were barbarian, and they, the children of those especially chosen by the Government, were the *elite* who would put the world right when it was time to go *up top* again, permanently.

But surely not everyone up top *was bad?*

Siobhan had once spoken her thoughts to Antony when they were together, but he'd shouted her down. Now she dare not speak of her doubts to anyone.

She stood silent for a moment, refusing to answer Antony's question. Perhaps he meant it rhetorically. Sweat left a dampness on her palms.

"So, what about the burned man?" Siobhan asked. *Let's get back to the point.*

Siobhan crossed her arms over her chest, hiding her sweaty palms. "Are they radiation burns? Does it mean we've a nuclear incident here in Scotland? One of our reactors?"

"No," Antony said. "Rewind, please," he ordered the technician.

The image on the screen flew back to the footage prior to that showing when Siobhan arrived in the audio-visual room. A white pier jutted out into what looked like a bay and beside it docked a surfaced submarine.

"Where's this?" Siobhan looked past the submarine to the gently lapping waters and the hills surrounding it.

What a shame. Such a beautiful place.

"It's Loch Ewe," the tech said. "A deep-sea loch suitable for deep water anchorage. That's how the sub came in from the North Atlantic Ocean." The technician turned to face Siobhan as a broad smile crossed his face. "It was a secret base for the military during the Second World War. You can still see the remains of the turrets that housed the heavy munitions."

"We've got to check it out," Antony said, smothering the technician's excitement. "Make sure it's not got a nuke waiting to detonate, or its nuclear power source isn't leaking. Something has irradiated those submariners. Where's the nearest settlement?"

"There's a tiny community at Loch Ewe," the technician said, grabbing a folded Ordnance Survey map from the shelf above the screen. He opened it and peered closely. "But you would have to pass near the bigger, but more secluded, community at Invercharing. You may as well stop there as they know the area better than we do. Sir, if you don't mind me suggesting it, you may need their assistance."

Antony stared at the map, his expression tight, lips a thin line.

Siobhan shivered, but she *had* to ask it, despite Antony's sure recriminations.

"What's wrong with that, Antony? It sounds like a very good suggestion." Siobhan waited as silent moments passed. "Well?"

"Caitlin Murray-Campbell set up the Invercharing Community," Antony finally said. "Ms Murray-Campbell virtually started the Community Movement. She ran Invercharing with her husband, Scott Campbell, a legend of a man. She passed away about five or six years ago and *he* disappeared into nowhere. Now her children help run it. The oldest son is the spit of his father, or so they say."

"Well then, they'll be the best place to start." She held back the tremor in her voice. "Sounds like they'll be a good help."

"Help? You really think so?" Antony's sarcasm filled the small audio-vis room.

"Don't be so biased. You haven't even met them yet." Siobhan's hands came down to her sides, balling into fists. She drew deep and brought up courage to face another shouting down from Antony. "They are a resource we should tap into. After all, it affects them too." She narrowed her eyes at Antony. "I'm coming with you."

Antony stared her down, breathing hard. She'd backed off once before when revealing her beliefs on community people and their lifestyle.

But *not* now.

"I *am* the nuclear physicist and head of Nuclear Surveillance. I'll go to stores and organise the gear we'll need." Siobhan strode out of the audio-visual room before Antony had a chance to reply.

She wouldn't miss this opportunity of going *up top*.

Not for anything.

Chapter Three

Government Bunker

It was getting easier to bribe the guards at the lift. Bribe them into letting him *up top* in the first place, and now to keep silent about his regular forays.

The tall metallic doors loomed before him. He walked toward the lifts as soundlessly as he was able on the polished concrete floors in the silent Bunker. Most of its inhabitants were 'early to bed, early to rise'.

This Government Bunker still had plentiful supplies of luxury goods. People liked to feel special or surprise their loved ones. Having access to the stock kept deep in the stores, and even the archives, came in handy. It surprised him, sometimes, what people wanted. Jewellery and other valuables, small trinkets, old wines and scotch, perfume for both men and women. The corner of his mouth twisted in a smile.

Human nature, so predictable.

He slipped the small ball of very old, and possibly stale, marijuana resin into the upturned hand of the guard on the night shift in front of the lifts.

"Thank you, Major McLellan," the guard whispered.

The journey up was a quiet one. He'd read in the archives they used to play recorded music in lifts. Antony hummed to himself, returning to his thoughts.

In the Bunker, it was all altruistic. Everyone lived for the good of humankind. For the good of Scotland. But in the end, personal greed won.

Mostly.

Now he was all for Scotland. Pro the Scottish Government taking back its rightful position and ruling the people once more. He wanted to be part of it, for sure.

Power—another thing that made human nature predictable. There are those who have it thrust upon them and want it. Those who have it thrust upon them and don't want it. Those who work for it and get it. And those who would only get a look-in if they fought tooth and nail.

At present, he was the tooth-and-nail guy.

To get a *look-in* you had to impress. And impressing those who are the *watchers* in the Government Bunker—those who see the rising stars—wasn't an easy task. He'd tried. And, according to the *watchers*, he was second best to everyone else.

Not as gifted. Not as perceptive. Not a *people person*.

Well, do you want someone nice, or do you want someone who can do the job? What do they know anyway? They haven't governed for nearly four decades. Really governed. Those plebs out there, who don't know their arse from their elbow, wouldn't know what was good for them if it jumped up and bit their balls!

He had to do something grand. Be proved right. Prove another wrong.

Strange how you can sleep with the enemy and never suspect a thing. Well, he'd suspected it. As soon as Siobhan had outgrown her usefulness, he'd extricated himself from her. Broken off their relationship once she'd shown her hand. All the drone-footage-watching had turned her mind.

And she actually thought the Community plebs were the good guys?

Antony stifled a laugh, his shoulders quivering in silent amusement.

Then the corners of his mouth tightened in a snarl. It was good to express what he really felt, for once. He was the only one in this lift, and he'd ensured the footage from the little camera in the corner was on a loop.

A loop of a very empty lift going nowhere.

Chapter Four

Invercharing Community

*S*he lay face down on the crumpled bedclothes, her slender, naked back hid nothing of her female curves.

Rory kneels on the bed behind her and lays his body on top of hers, their bare skin touching. Her soft warmth contacts the entire length of his body, his firmness hard along her buttock.

She stirs and turns her head to the side.

Running his nose along her right shoulder and up into her fair hair, he inhales her scent.

What was it?

Flowers, he guesses. But what flowers?

He only knows the scent of thistle and heather.

They wouldn't make perfume out of those.

He pulls her hair away from the side of her face with his left hand, the gold band on his ring finger glints softly in the moonlight from the window.

She sighs.

He presses his lips to the side of her neck and traces her hairline toward the base of her skull.

He leans forward and grabs her earlobe gently between his teeth, avoiding the diamond stud earring she wears.

She wriggles beneath him and he gives a breathy laugh.

"What, again?" Her voice husky with sleep.

"Uh, huh." He presses his lips to her neck and tastes her fair complexion.

She opens her legs beneath him, and he thrusts himself in.

Rory woke, the sheet tight and damp around his manhood. He disengaged himself from his bed covers, walked to the bathroom, and washed.

He paced naked to the kitchen and opened the laminate cupboard door. From behind the preserves, he brought out the bottle of single malt whisky and poured a dram into the glass he kept on the bench. It was more than a dram, but he needed it.

That was no wet dream. It was real.

So real he could still smell her perfume, feel her smooth skin, sense her tightening around him.

He sculled the scotch in one hit, its warmth burning his throat and vaporising up into his nostrils. The lingering creaminess from the hint of sherry cask was comforting as the liquid's warmth filled his belly.

Rory slammed the glass on the tiled bench, sending the crack reverberating throughout the empty house. It was once the family home, but now only he lived here since Mum's death and Dad's permanent return to the past.

"Who was she?" His voice was loud in the room.

The quiet answered.

He'd never experienced it before. Not just the physical connection, nor the overwhelming, all-consuming sense of *her*...

Was it love?

Shaking his head, he poured another generous dram and drank, then walked to the bedroom. Maybe sleep would come.

***

"So, why am I not going?" Brendan led his saddled horse as he walked toward Rory.

"It may be dangerous." Rory glanced around the stables where the rest of his crew were mounting up.

"I'll stay out of trouble, I promise." Brendan now stood directly in front of Rory, his eager expression right in Rory's face.

Rory sighed and slowly shook his head. He recognised the emotion within himself—resignation.

"When we get to Loch Ewe, no *before* we get there," Rory said, "you will stay back somewhere safe."

His younger brother required the experience, and Rory wasn't sure of what he would find there, but he needed the manpower. He only had to keep him out of harm's way. Wherever *that* was.

The beaming smile from his wee brother brought a reluctant curve to his own lips.

Rory and his team trotted their horses through the misty rain. They set out toward the mountain Bhienn Fionn, wearing wet weather gear. The rain was so opposite to yesterday's sun. Mist shrouded the purple heather-covered mountains to either side, and water ran in rivulets along the ground beneath them. The cool wind blew the scent of horse and forest past his nostrils. They had a two-day journey ahead, with an overnight camp.

Rory had no idea if they would cross bandit country or not, but he'd made sure his crew came well-armed. Callum cantered his horse to catch up with him.

"Are we going over Bhienn Fionn?" Callum asked.

"No. I'm planning to avoid the well-known paths." Rory shook his head. "Might be safer that way. We'll make as much of a beeline as we can over the lower hills. The plan is to camp beside Loch Maree tonight, somewhere near Taagan."

Rory led them through the pass at Achnasheen, which passed beneath Bhienn Fionn. The grassy path took them across undulating heather and bracken fern-covered glens, wind-blown and treeless for miles. The rain came over with the gusts of wind and made for a patchy on-off rainy day.

By late afternoon, their path ran beside a brisk flowing grey-pebbled burn which wound its way to the remains of the old road for a short distance before making its way to Loch Maree.

Rory became increasingly aware of the triple buttresses of the mountain, Bhienn Eighe, to his left. Its massive presence glowered at them from its heights across the shore of the loch. Clouds of its own making topped its Cambrian quartzite, grey and intimidating. The white, grey and black colouring of the clouds, ever-roiling and changing within themselves, added to the menacing aura surrounding the mountain.

"Lord of the Rings," Callum spoke beside him.

"Aye. Mount Doom." Rory nodded, his mouth open, recalling their mother's choice of bedtime reading material. She'd believed in the classics. "Here's hoping our mission is nae as difficult."

Rory led his team across the small delta of Kinlochewe River as it emptied into Loch Maree and headed toward the forest on their right to make their camp in its shelter. So far, they sighted no bandits. Night time would tell.

They set up camp, lit a fire and over it they cooked bannock dough wrapped around a stick.

"I'll take first watch." Rory picked up his Glock, slung his rifle over his shoulder and pointed to the trees about fifteen metres away. "I'll come wake you in four hours," he said to his twin.

Callum nodded.

"Everyone else get some rest. With one ear open, aye?" Rory ordered as he walked out of their camp.

"Aye, boss." Kendra saluted, then grinned.

Rory's mouth tugged in a smile. Kendra meant it in a friendly way with no disrespect for him. His crew admired him, but at times Rory wondered why.

His mind settled on their current venture. This could be a dangerous mission. He shivered, and not from the cool night air. They travelled to an unseen danger. He recalled his mother speaking of radiation from atomic bombs dropped on Japan, which had caused cancer years later in the survivors. It was the Second World War, if he remembered correctly. A war in a world so different from now.

Had they ever dropped the later bombs of the nuclear kind anywhere else? Rory wondered. *Nukes,* Murray called them. The Community still listened intently to the CB radio chatter, but they only heard a little of what went on in the world out there. If only he knew more, and they had some protective gear like he'd seen in pictures in the Encyclopaedia Britannica in the Community's library.

What was he risking? What danger was he exposing his crew to? But if they didn't help, there may be a *nuke* out there, and *someone* had to deal with it. Unchecked, it could mean annihilation.

He had no other choice.

A crashing through the trees brought his walk to his night watch post to a halt. He stood stock-still. The odour of male red deer assailed his nostrils—like stale cat piss mixed with dead animal. They urinate on themselves to make their personal scent stronger.

Aye, a stag.

It stomped beside him.

Rory turned slowly. A fourteen-pointer stood not five metres from him among the trees. Red-brown fur covered rippling muscle. Hard as bone solid antler branches arose high above a noble head. Rory daren't move. It was rutting season, and those tines were sharp.

The old male honked and stomped again. That was two warnings he'd given in a matter of moments. Rory didn't move an inch. If he was lucky, the stag would sense he wouldn't harm him, if only Rory stood still. He prayed the others hadn't noticed and wouldn't startle the stag and cause him to charge.

There were more animal noises behind the stag. His harem of does. *That's* why he was so aggressive.

The large male animal honked once more. At the same time a raucous of noise erupted from the camp. A handgun fired, and horses shrieked. Rory flinched as his heart rocked in his chest. The stag raised his head and sniffed the air. Then, backtracking away from Rory, he turned and honked at his females behind him, causing a stampede of deer to crash through the forest away from the camp.

Rory sunk to the ground, releasing the breath he'd been holding. His hand trembled around his Glock as his pulse pounded in his ears. No matter how often he'd fought a human, in mock fights or real, it never scared him as much as facing the awesomeness of a protective, wild male animal.

Rory glanced through the forest to ensure the deer had left and turned to find the cause of the commotion in the camp. He raised his Glock. Callum paused, hands in the air on his way toward him.

"Don't shoot. It's me, brother. Saving you from a stag who wanted to chop your head off and mount it in his den." Callum's smile almost split his face.

Rory lowered his handgun and relaxed his shoulders as he took in the scene behind Callum. Xian and Kendra held the reins of spooked horses and Brendan still pointed his firearm heavenwards.

"I saw what was happening and thought a full-on noise assault would be best to scare him off," Callum said. "Couldn't have him impaling our leader. Didn't want to shoot him and risk hitting you. And I don't feel like butchering a stag and carryin' the meat around for days either. They're too tough anyways."

Rory stepped forward and hugged his twin. "Thanks, brother."

"Ahem." Kendra's feminine cough floated through the cooling air.

"And everyone else," Rory said. "Now settle those horses back down and get some rest. I'll look for another spot to keep watch."

***

Morning came, and Rory ordered his crew to pack up camp. They mounted their horses, and Rory led them along the east bank of Loch Maree. The rocky edge of the mountainside entering the loch interrupted the wide grassy flat on which they travelled. Rory guided his crew, jumping off his horse and picking his way through a rocky path to a level section farther up the hillside. They followed this for a way until the flatter shoreline returned. They mounted their horses once more and rode through a forest of bright purple thigh-high heather, bracken fern and moss-covered boulders shaded by silver birch and Scots pine until they came to grassy shore again.

"There's your island, Rory." Kendra pointed to their left, to the last of the three tree and rock covered islands in Loch Maree. "Eilean Ruairidh Mor."

"I ken." Rory turned to Kendra riding by his side. "My name means *red king,* you know?"

"I know," she replied.

"Dinnae you forget it."

Buzzards flew high in the sky on the opposite side of the loch. More argued on the shoreline next to where the road had once been, their raucous calls echoing over the loch toward them.

"Lots of birds over there on the other side," Kendra said. "What do you think, your majesty?"

"Buzzards. Maybe ravens too. Feedin' on something dead," Rory said, ignoring Kendra's comment on his rank. Rory got out the high-powered binoculars and held them to his eyes. "Och no." His mouth dried.

"What, Rory?" Callum rode closer.

"I think it's another body." Rory swallowed. "Hard to tell from here and ah... with the state it's in."

They rode on in silence for a while, past old roads and broken fences, through a windswept narrow valley following a river. Mountains hugged this valley, majestically green and dappled in light-cloud shade. Further along, rock faces edged their way, cracked and scarred by the weather. Here heather grew, grabbing a space in the cracks and holding tight. Before the small village of Poolewe, a slumped figure lay in their path. Rory went to dismount.

"No, Rory," Kendra said. "Remember it may be radioactive."

Kendra urged the others to pass by as far away from the body as possible. The horses trotted by and nickered their displeasure at the odour of dead human. It wasn't pleasant smelling for the humans either.

Not a scent easily forgotten.

Two dead bodies to add to the count. One for sure in the same condition as the man they found before they began their journey. What did it mean? How many more? And how could it affect him and his crew the nearer they got?

Too many unknowns.

"Oh, wow." Brendan's awestruck voice broke through Rory's thoughts.

The afternoon sun shone brightly in a clear blue sky over the water, reflecting off the brilliant deep-blue waters of the sea loch stretching before him, glimmering off its rippling surface. A bright green, grassed island, the Isle of Ewe, sat directly ahead. Behind it, smooth-topped mountains strung themselves in a row around the loch. Through the gap of two headlands at the end of the loch, spread the deeper blue of the ocean.

"We'll travel beside the road now, instead of beneath the mountains," Rory said. "Be prepared. We could find more dead men," he whispered to Kendra.

Rory led his crew beside the crumbled, pitted, churned-up bitumen. Years of weathering and lack of road maintenance had eroded its surface from smooth to crumbling gravel.

"These roads are now too dangerous to be usable," Rory said. "Too risky on the horses. Keep 'em away. Keep to the grass, okay?"

Rory manoeuvred his stallion, Boy, past a pile of churned asphalt and over a rutted stream running off the old road.

"Do you remember Mum sayin' roads were once smooth bitumen?" he asked Brendan riding beside him. "Roads carved their way through the countryside, over bridges and on long motorways covering the length of Britain and back."

"Wow. That's impossible," Brendan said.

"Aye, that's what I thought, until I returned to the past and saw it for ma'self. Even in the quiet Highlands, they maintained the roads. None o' any o' that now."

Near to Tournaig, with the smaller inlet called Loch Thurnaig to their left, there was another khaki-clad figure. The body lay on the soft grass beneath a mounded concrete structure. Rory led the approach. The body's arm moved, then it rolled slightly.

"He's still alive!" Rory yelled and kicked his horse on.

"No, Rory, he's radioactive!" Kendra's pleading shout came from behind him.

Rory pulled his horse up short of the man lying in the grass. The man contorted in agony and liquid ran down the side of his mouth. His red, peeling face sported no hair whatsoever. He held out red raw hands.

Xian came beside Rory, his horse joining with Boy in a snort of unease. The man on the ground held out his hands in a beseeching manner. Rory's heart tore. He lifted himself off his saddle.

"No, Rory!" Kendra shouted her warning from a few yards back, stopping him mid-dismount.

From the ground, the man spoke. Rory couldn't understand a word but could tell it was an Asian tongue. The man ceased speaking and closed his eyes. His breath was a gurgle in his throat, then it stopped.

"What did he say?" Rory twisted to Xian.

"I don't know. I don't speak Korean!" Xian's expression was one of exasperation.

"How do you know it's Korean then?" Rory asked.

"The badge on his uniform. It's the North Korean flag." Xian pointed with his chin.

"You are both too close," Kendra shouted. "Come back. And nobody goes near him," she said through gritted teeth. "Move!"

Rory trotted Boy well away from the dead man. Xian followed.

"We need to get to this submarine," Rory said. "According to the old map I checked, Drumchork isn't far away." Rory kicked his stallion to a canter and the others followed.

Not far along the road, there was an out-jutting of land. Rory led his crew to it and dismounted. In the near distance, sat the mottled-white pier at Drumchork making a long line out into the loch, its old timbers weathered and missing in places. Beside them on the sea loch, a pale blue boat motored up and slowed to a stop. The engine cut out, then a figure *ahoyed* them from the cabin.

"Rory Campbell?" A tall older man in faded jeans and a baggy jumper cupped his hands around his mouth.

"Aye," Rory answered.

"I'll meet ye, and you only mind, one mile up the road, aye?" The man raised thick eyebrows as he spoke.

"Okay." Rory turned to his team. "You heard him. Stay here."

"No, Rory. You're not going alone." Xian's eyes narrowed. "We don't know who he is."

"He kens who I am," Rory said. "He must be the man from the Loch Ewe Community."

"But he didn't introduce himself," Xian said in a low voice. "You're not going alone."

Rory paused. "Well, any closer and *no one* is safe. I'll take you up on your offer, but only you Xian. The rest of you go back aways and find a good camping place, away from the last body, mind."

Brendan started walking to his horse, and Kendra stood forward.

"I'll come with you," she said.

"No." Rory shook his head.

Kendra opened her mouth.

"No arguments." His tone was sharp.

She closed her mouth, looking stunned.

"Well, I'm coming, brother," Callum said.

"You definitely are *not*. You will be a father soon. Stay here." Rory exchanged a look with his brother; a private twin-look his brother would understand.

Callum's nostrils flared, then he pressed his lips tight, remounted and turned his horse to follow the others.

Further along the road, Rory and Xian found a small floating pier. The man had motored his small boat to it and waited for them.

"Hello and welcome. I'm Murdo MacDonald. Pleasure to meet you," he said.

He was a solidly built man in his sixties, if Rory guessed right. His greying wavy hair, which could have once been a light brown, sat above bushy greying eyebrows sheltering bright blue eyes. His tanned face was weather-beaten wrinkled. Rory shook his gnarled, sun-spotted hand; there was a faint fishy smell.

"Well, I'm Rory Campbell, but you know that already," Rory said. "This is Xian. We are from—"

"The Invercharing Community," Murdo interrupted. "And thank you for coming so promptly." Murdo beamed as he stared directly into Rory's face.

His handshake was firm and lingered. Rory flicked his gaze from the man's face to their clasped hands and back again. Murdo let go.

"Verra well then," Murdo said. "Let me take ye to my place and we'll see what's to be done."

Rory and Xian boarded the small motorboat. Murdo revved the inboard motor and steered the boat to the Isle of Ewe, which sat in the middle of the loch.

"This wee boat takes me to ma work and back," Murdo said. "I'm a fisherman and ma work boat's moored over there with the others."

Murdo pointed to a pier now coming into view nearer the righthand side of the outlet of the loch into The Minch. Along this pier sat an armada of fishing boats with men milling around or hauling nets, their early morning's catch on ice.

"The fishing has picked up greatly over the years since organised international fishing decreased after The Crash." Murdo's amicable chatter continued. "It's given the fish time to repopulate. There's a bounty of food out there the noo'."

Murdo steered his boat and made a sharp turn, heading for a cottage on the side of the island. In front of it was a small private pier where he docked the motorboat. Rory and Xian got out of the boat and followed him up a track to the small, whitewashed cottage with a grey slate roof.

Once inside the stone cottage, a stronger fish aroma greeted Rory's nostrils, and something else—coffee. Rory's mouth watered.

"Come in, sit doon." Murdo pointed to the only two chairs in the small one-roomed cottage.

An Aga solid fuel stove sat by the far wall radiating the heat which had bathed Rory's face on entering. A single bed sat against the back wall, and paintings in water colours lined the wall behind it. The largest was of a pretty woman with two boys standing in front of her. Another was a fishing boat, a young man with a hand full of nets stood in the foreground.

"Aye, that's my wife and boys." Murdo pointed to the paintings Rory stared at. "Morag has gone now, and my boys have grown and run the boat for me when I'm no' free." Murdo placed a cup for each of them on the small table.

"Coffee. Man, it's a rarity in our community," Xian said. "Thank you."

Rory took one cup and turned to look at the view. Directly in front of the window, were the faded white posts of the pier and the dark, almost black, submarine sitting high in the water, the top of it level with the pier. Rory swallowed the coffee, ignoring the slight scalding it gave his throat.

"During World War II this loch was a secret base." Murdo's gravelly voice lilted behind Rory. "Nice and deep for the big ships. They used to send convoys of supplies to the Russians via the Arctic. Even had a submarine net across the entrance to this loch, ken? Ye may have passed one of the old concrete gun turrets on your way here. It was way before my time, though. A *long* way before my time."

"It's dangerous," Rory said. It wasn't a question. Rory stared at the submarine, his back still to his host.

"Aye. The submariners coming from it show signs of radiation sickness," Murdo replied from behind him.

"A nuclear sub then?" Rory couldn't take his eyes off the submarine, now so close.

"No, it's a Russian 677 Lada with AIP. Diesel fuel cell."

Rory turned from the window and stared at Murdo.

"I *am* a mariner. I ken ma' vessels." Murdo indicated toward the window with his coffee cup and a nod of his head.

"Russian?" Xian broke the momentary silence.

"They don't look like Russians." Rory glanced sideways at Xian. "They are wearing North Korean uniforms, and we think it was Korean they spoke."

"You spoke to them?" Murdo's hoary brows raised in question.

"Yeah, one spoke to us before he died." Xian lowered his gaze into his almost empty coffee mug.

Rory turned once more to view the submarine just over the water. No one had exited in the brief time he'd watched.

"Well, I vaguely remember there was talk of Russia selling their out-dated subs to rogue states." Murdo scratched the stubble on his chin. "This one's definitely no' your nuclear-powered sub, just run o' the mill. Diesel fuel, like my boat."

"It's carrying a nuclear warhead?" Rory spun from the window.

"It's the only obvious explanation for the leak." The old man fixed his gaze on him.

The Aga creaked with its heat, and the wind blew the shabby curtains of the cottage.

Rory's heart missed a beat, then thumped faster.

"It's not safe then," Rory repeated the obvious.

"Well, it's probably no' safe here, but I wanted tae keep an eye on it. It's no' safe anywhere, to be honest." Murdo's shoulders lowered as he let out a slow breath.

Rory took a step toward Murdo. "We'll shut it down then," he said.

"How!" Xian stared up at him, mouth open, slowly shaking his head, his dark-brown gaze flicked from Rory to Murdo.

"It's no' a matter of shuttin' it doon." Murdo placed his cup on the table. "It's leaking and I dinnae ken how tae fix it." He pulled at the stretched collar of his baggy jumper.

"We don't even have the gear they wear." Rory visualised the pictures in the Encyclopaedia Britannica once more.

Where would we get the equipment from, anyway?

"We don't even know what to do if we did. We could accidentally set it off and wipe out Scotland!" Xian's mug slammed on the table.

"Aye, sobering thoughts." Murdo's voice was low and thoughtful. "Years ago, they knew. And if ye did nae know, ye could find out on the computer. They had a thing called *The Internet*. People had knowledge about everything right at their fingertips. Don't think much wisdom came with it, but the knowledge was there certainly. I suspect it's how we lost a lot of recorded information, well that sort of information, anyways. When the internet crashed and electricity became scarce and... well, all that's history now."

Rory turned back to the view of the submarine.

Knowledge from the past.

"If only we could turn back time and ken what they did." Murdo's voice lilted behind him in the sing-songy accent of an islander. "We'd ken how to proceed with oor wee problem."

Rory turned. Murdo was staring straight at him. An uncomfortable sensation on the back of Rory's neck accompanied the old man's look. Rory pushed it aside, as how to deal with the nuclear warhead was more important and pressing. Rory stood to his full height, trying to shake the feeling.

"We've got to get back to the Community," he said. "We have books, magazines and journals from before The Stock Market Crash. We'll find out what we can. How long do you think we have... until it blows up?"

Murdo frowned and shook his head. "Nae idea, lad. But dinnae stop to smell the flowers on yoor way home."

Rory made for the door, his coffee unfinished. Xian drained the dregs in his mug and followed him out. Rory turned to make sure Murdo was coming too, and there in the doorway, Murdo stood, his face creased even further with the smile he wore.

Chapter Five

Invercharing Community

The library was a large room partitioned off from the main school-room. Bookshelves lined three walls. Rory had come back from the north and gone straight there. Xian was helping him look in every and any book that could have a reference to nuclear warheads or nuclear power.

Papers lay strewn on top of the tables in the middle of the room and children, ranging in age from five to fifteen, stood at the doorway giggling.

"Could you please keep the children out of the library for a while, Mrs McKenzie?" Rory asked. "What I'm tryin' to do may take some time."

"Children, Mr Campbell has commandeered our library, so we'll find somewhere else to read. It's a lovely day outside so we may as well make the most of the sunshine." Mrs McKenzie gave him a rueful smile and ushered the children away.

Once the teacher and her pupils were out of earshot, Xian nudged Rory.

"She's got the hots for you, man," he said.

"*Wheesht.*" Rory dropped the last of their reference books on the table before him.

"What on earth is going on?" Angela now stood in the doorway.

Her long, red hair trailed over her navy-blue suit. Rory's heart sank. He wasn't in the mood for Angela. *Am I ever in the mood for Angela?*

He had tuned his hearing to the doorway since his return. Just in case she turned up.

His big sister—inevitable and unavoidable.

"I'm trying to find out as much as I can about *nuclear warheads,*" Rory whispered.

"Nuclear warheads?" Angela's voice rose.

"Angela, really?" Rory glared at her. "There are children around and I didn't want to alarm anyone."

"Are the rest of the Chief Council aware of what you're doing?" Angela's hand was on her hip, and she used her most officious tone. "*I* have heard nothing. When did you report back to us?"

Rory rolled his eyes. "I'm completing my information gathering *before* I report my findings to the Chief Council."

"Oh, of course." She seemed satisfied with his answer.

"Goodbye then. I'll call the Council when I'm ready." Rory stood, a sheaf of papers in hand, and ushered her out the door.

Rory turned to Xian.

"We need more information," Rory said. "Wonder what there is around the place outside o' this wee library. Mum kept everything she thought would be of value one day." He stood thinking for a moment, then raised an index finger. "Murray!"

"Your genius brother has a secret stash, you think?" Xian asked.

"Worth an ask." Rory tilted his head as he ran to the door, where he almost bowled Kendra over. "Oh, Kendra, could you please get ma' wee brother, Murray? Tell him it's urgent. I want all his textbooks, papers, scribbles, anything!"

Kendra pointed over her shoulder, opened her mouth to speak, but was interrupted.

"If you want all of that, you'll have to come to my room." Murray strolled behind Kendra. "But you'll have to tell me everything."

***

Murray sat at his desk. To his left was a pile of books, to his right a neat stack of freshly made paper. In the middle, arranged in his specific order was a ruler, a solar powered calculator, a short, stubby pencil, a slide-rule, and an eraser. Above his desk on the wall, a poster of Einstein in Andy Warhol style looked down on them. Murray's left elbow leaned on his desk as Rory stood in front of him, his debrief completed.

"A faulty nuclear warhead is leaking radiation into Loch Ewe, and we have to stop it and save Scotland from being nuked." Murray summarised Rory's information dump.

"Aye, and time is of the essence. What've you got for me?" he asked.

Rory sat on the end of Murray's bed. It squeaked. Xian joined him and it squeaked again.

Murray chewed his lower lip, then stood and walked past Rory and Xian to the other side of his bed. He reached under and dragged out a box with magazines piled to the top. Two spilled out onto the floor.

"Where d'you get these?" Rory reached over and pulled out car magazines, boating magazines, hunting and fishing magazines. "Och, why have I no' seen these?"

Murray ignored him as he emptied the top layer and rifled to the bottom.

"Mum gave me these years ago," Murray said. "I've only briefly looked at them. They're academic journals. Don't ask me where she got them from, but she said I would be the only one who would understand them, apart from the scientists. Oh, *they* might have more." Murray's brows lifted with this comment.

"Aye. But I did nae want too many people to know what or why I'm looking for what I'm looking for." Rory tilted his head.

"But we can trust Angus," Murray said. "And Martin, our cousin the *physicist,* will know more than *any* of us."

"Hmm. Maybe it's time to bring them in on it." Rory conceded. "But we'll read all o' this first."

"All of it?" Xian flicked through the magazine he held. "It looks complicated."

"They *are* academic journals." Rory squinted at the one he held. "Yeah, we'll need help."

"I remember Angus reading a journal once which had an article by a nuclear physicist of the late Twenty-teens." Murray played with his lower lip as he squatted in front of the box. "He wasn't aware I was reading it across the table from him. Not everyone can read upside down. I didn't know that. I thought everyone could." Murray looked up from the floor at Rory.

"We'll start with that one then," Rory said.

***

"And that's about it," Murray said. "But don't ask me how to disarm a faulty nuclear warhead."

Rory sat with Martin, Murray, and Angus, who were the main scientists involved with the Time Machine. George Stobbart and the other members of the Chief Council, the ruling body of the Community, sat around the tables in the book-lined library. The number of books the Invercharing Community had gathered always amazed Rory.

The laughter of teenagers, supposed to be doing their homework in the schoolroom, filtered through the closed door, while the vague scent of the communal evening meal wafted through the partially opened window. So did the crunch of footsteps on the path outside belonging to those who had worked all the summer's day in the fields and now headed home for their supper.

It had been a long evening, and mental fatigue numbed Rory's comprehension.

Or maybe, I'm not smart enough to understand it all.

But one thing *was* for sure. He took a breath to steady his pulse, for he had to tell them somehow.

"Even if we had the time, which we don't, to scour the land and gather every scrap of information that has survived the last forty years," Rory said, "we could never equip ourselves adequately to do it all, at all, or even safely."

The Chief Council sitting before Rory were grim-faced. Gasps and gulps had come from them as he relayed the information he had. Mentally Rory formed his next comment, endeavouring to shape his words so they would understand—and agree.

"I have a proposal I'd like to make." Rory eyeballed each one around the table in turn. "I will use the Time Machine to go back to before the Stock Market Crash and speak to this nuclear physicist himself." Rory held up the scientific journal belonging to Angus, to which Murray had referred. "And find out what we need to know in *our* specific situation."

Angus flicked his mop of thick, dark hair away from his eyes and gave a tight smile as he pushed his glasses back up his nose; a paperclip held the left arm of his spectacles onto the black frames. In his own quiet way, he seemed pleased he could help. He was many years older than Murray, but they were close friends. Their love of science and mathematics had brought them together. Good old Angus had covered for them when their youngest sister Kelly had made her secret, and unauthorised, journey to the past.

So far, Angus' journal had an article with the most up to date, for that time, information on nuclear warheads. Well, it was the most recent dated article *they* could find on the subject.

"We have a name and a place of employment. We should be able to find him," Rory said. He waited for cries of disagreement. None came, so he pressed his point. "We can make return journeys to the past. As I have done so, I am the best person for this mission."

Still no comments from the people before him.

"The beauty of time travel is I can go back and take as long as I need to gather information, and equipment even, and return in no time at all, literally. I can go and be back here immediately." Rory raised his eyebrows and nodded for emphasis as they still hadn't commented. "Which means I won't be wasting the precious time we don't have at this end."

Rory's pulse seemed loud in his ears. Or maybe it was just that the room was so quiet, devoid of comment. Angela's forehead creased in a scowl.

Oh no, here it comes.

"On your own, Rory? Surely you will need assistance." Angela sat taller, looking so much like she was enjoying the fact she was the only one with a question.

Well, at least it wasn't one of her usual objections.

"I've been to the past before, I know—" he began.

"Yes, we know *all* that. But you're not a scientist, are you?" Angela's piercing blue eyes bored into his, rubbing-in his inadequacies.

"No, I'm not but—" he began again.

"I'll go." Murray held up his hand. "I'll understand what the physicist is saying, what to ask him *and* I'll remember it."

That's right, the lad's got a photographic memory—when he wants to.

"But you're our wee brother." Angela found her objection at last.

"Angela, I'm twenty-one! I'm not a kid anymore," Murray said. "In *the good old days,* I could drink, vote and marry well and truly before now. Rory will need me. He can protect me. Be 'the Muscle'." Murray smiled.

Rory's guts niggled, but the lad was right. He'd need Murray's brains.

"You must do it without giving away where, I mean *when*, you're from." George Stobbart looked over his glasses at him.

"We'll keep it secret," Rory said. "Well, as much as we can. It's desperate though, I may need to divulge that information to find out what we need to know. I'll just have tae risk it. They'll never find the Time Machine, as it stays back here."

The Chief Council members made no objection, not even Angela. George nodded in silence. Relief surged through Rory like a wave of warm air dispelling the wind off Bhienn Fionn. Those present understood the gravity of their situation.

"We cannot expect to stay isolated in our safe, secure haven of a community for ever without the big-bad-world out there, or its issues, intruding on us," Rory said. "It would be naïve to think so."

"So, when are we going?" Murray asked.

"As soon as we can."

"No," Murray said. "I mean, *when* are we going?"

"Oh aye, when do you think?" Rory hadn't got as far as specifics in his plan.

"We should go when we know where this professor is and right before the stock market crashes," Murray replied.

"But you must step carefully, Rory," Martin said.

"I know," Rory answered, pushing down impatience. "I have been to the past before—"

"Yes, but then you went straight to Glencoe," Martin interrupted. "This time you must go further, into a city perhaps, where there's more people to interact with and more chances of affecting history. Stick to yourselves as much as possible, yeah? Keep out of anything, not just trouble."

"But what if you're caught in the chaos and can't get back?" Angela had a good point.

All eyes were on Murray.

"Why *right before*?" Rory asked Murray.

"We may need some historical happening to convince the man we aren't crazies." Murray raised his eyebrows.

Well done, Murray. You've been using those brains of yours.

"Where is he?" Rory looked at the scientific journal sitting on the table.

"Edinburgh," Murray replied. "He's in the employ of Welson Nuclear, at the time of the paper, that is. It was published 2018, but his research would've taken place before that. He could even have worked for the Government."

"So, it's a day to get from here to there, by car. We'll take some money and buy one. I'll drive." Rory looked pointedly at Murray. "A day or so to get the info—"

"That's if we find him straight away," Murray interrupted.

"The exact date?" Angus asked. "I'll need your help with the calcs, Murray, to set the Time Machine for both journeys."

The room was quiet for a bit while Rory's mind flew through his plan.

"A week before." Rory drew his eyebrows together.

"No, four days." Murray's eyes flicked as he spoke. "Two to find him," he glanced up at Rory, "two to convince him... and get home before the craziness starts. Which is around the twentieth of June 2018. So, we go the eighteenth. Be ready to get back from the twenty-second. It's imperative we get back to the Time Machine's pick-up point on time."

Rory nodded. It was all guesswork. It would have to do. Once again, as with his previous journey to the past, it was all risk. Only this time, he would go further away from the Time Machine's base.

"No one must know. Only us in this room." Rory glanced at them all.

These people were among the few who knew of the Time Machine's existence—and it needed to stay that way.

"Not the rest of the family." Rory stared at Angela. "Nor any of my crew." Rory looked at George. "It will be over quickly at this end, then we can get on with sorting the warhead." Rory gave a short, sharp nod. "Agreed then?"

"Agreed," those before him chorused.

"Come on, brother," Rory looked directly at Murray. "Let's prepare."

Chapter Six

To the Past

Rory stepped over the thick cables duct-taped to the earthen floor of the high-raftered barn that housed the Time Machine. He'd dressed plainly in jeans, T-shirt, jumper, and hiking boots. Comfortable shoes were always an essential item.

"No, no, no." George shook his head as he pointed out the long range rifle over Rory's shoulder, the handgun at his hip, then the hunting knife in its sheath hanging on his belt. "You can't carry weapons in that time unless you're a police officer or a member of the defence force. And you, son, are neither."

"You're joking." Rory tensed. No weapons? *I may as well be naked.* He swallowed as he removed the rifle from his shoulder.

"More." George's hand flicked forward.

"It's all I'm leavin'. I'll hide the rest." Rory took his hunting knife from his belt and tucked it into his right boot, then strapped its sheath to his calf.

"They have metal detectors everywhere," George said as Rory shoved his Glock in the waistband of his jeans at his back.

"I'll take the risk," he said. "We may need to defend ourselves. We're going back to when the world went crazy. I've been there before, remember? Nae body fussed about ma' weapons then."

"Rory lad, you were just in Glencoe," George said. "This time you're going to the big city. It's different."

"What about the Gung-Fu your friend has been teaching you?" Murray said as he sidled past him and headed for the machine's control panel. "Thought *you* were the weapon?"

"I can hold my own close-up. It's the ones who are too chicken and go you from far off that concern me." Rory looked back to George and tilted his head. "I'll no' be unarmed."

"Be careful." George shook his head slowly. "And if you drive, you'll need a licence."

"Och, Murray's got that covered." Rory indicated with his chin to Murray, who stepped closer.

Murray held a palm-size plastic card with a small identification photograph in one corner. He handed it to Rory who looked at a 2018 UK Drivers Licence. The photograph was of his father. Rory's gut clenched.

"You look enough like Dad for it to work." Murray half-smiled, his piercing blue-gaze locked on Rory.

"Where did ye get this?" George asked Murray as he looked closely at the licence. "Aye, you're the spit o' him."

"I found some documents in an old trunk of Mum's. Knew they would come in handy one day." Murray bit his lower lip.

"Who lives at Bridge of Orchy?" Rory asked.

"Dad used his Uncle Robert's address," Murray said. "He won't know if we lie low. And then we'll be back, or the world will be so crazy it won't matter that you, or Dad, don't actually live there."

Rory dragged his eyes away from the licence and looked at Murray.

"You okay, wee brother?" he asked. "You've not done this before. It's a bit disorientating."

Murray slipped his backpack on his shoulders, and he gave a brief nod. He'd shoved some cash, an old UK A-Z, and a spare pod into it.

"Where d'you get the jeans?" Murray glanced at Rory's legs.

"They were Dad's," Rory answered. "What he wore in the past."

The familiar ache in Rory's chest took over momentarily. Rory sniffed and inhaled Dad's lingering scent. If only the man himself was here.

"A bit different from your buckskins and loincloth." Murray unsuccessfully repressed a smile.

"Buckskins are more comfortable than this tough material any day," Rory said.

Rory emptied the rifle's ammunition from his own backpack and double checked he had a resin pod for the return. He was first to step into the old fibreglass shower cubicle which was the transporter for the Time Machine. *So simple,* he shook his head again at the thought.

Angus set the dials on the machine's control panel to the required date and then nodded to Rory. Rory stepped into the resin pod and began to close the clasps.

"See you there, brother," Rory said to Murray, then the world went blurry.

***

Rory awoke on a soft dirt floor. He heaved and lost the contents of his stomach, leaving an acid burn in his throat.

Odd. That didn't happen last time.

The pod lay in shreds beside him. Bright daylight angled into the barn from the east through the wide-open doors, bathing him in warmth. Fine particles of pale straw filled the air, wafting past his nose, threatening a sneeze. Close beside him there was a shimmer, so he scampered out of the way.

Murray appeared. Rory helped him out of his pod.

"You okay?" he asked.

Murray nodded. "A good summer that year? This year," he said, then blinked at the daylight filling the barn.

The grunt of a tractor engine filtered into the barn from a field out back. They walked the opposite way and exited via the large barn doors, then made their way around to the front of the house. His house in his future. It was cleaner and newer. Familiar, but not so. Parked out front, apart from a tractor, there was a newish sedan, a four-wheel-drive, and a rusted older model sedan.

"Can I help you, lads?"

Rory pivoted. A man dressed in overalls, wellingtons and a checked shirt, stood behind them.

"Aye, please," Rory said. "We were wondering if you knew the time of the next train from Achnasheen to Inverness?"

"Where have ye come frae?" The farmer squinted at them.

"Och, we've been hill-walking. Some braw Munros around here," Rory said.

People used to do that for fun, didn't they?

"At this time o' day?" the farmer asked. "Wee bit early to be making your way home."

"We stayed overnight on Bhienn Fionn, right up by the cairn, ye ken. On oor way hame tae Edinburgh the noo'." Rory laid his accent on thick. *It might help.*

The farmer's shoulders relaxed slightly as he eyed Rory and Murray's backpacks.

"Weel, the train from the Achnasheen station leaves at ten o'clock-ish," the farmer said. "But Contin is yoor nearest station as ye'll be going along oor road out o' this glen, aye?" The farmer blinked as he looked past Rory.

"Ten o'clock!" Rory couldn't keep the concern from his voice. Time limitations. He screwed up his mouth and glanced sideways at Murray.

"Do you have a car we could hire?" Murray asked.

The farmer's brows knotted. "Hire?"

"Could we buy a car from you, sir?" Rory asked.

The farmer twitched his head, his brows continuing their knot. "Ye lads in any trouble?"

"Och, no," Murray said. "I just underestimated our walking time and, well, we need to get to work, ye ken. In Edinburgh." He'd laid on a thick accent.

Quick thinking, brother.

A dampness of sweat formed on Rory's forehead. "How much for your wee sedan there?" Rory pointed to the rusty one.

"Och, weel." The farmer's eyes narrowed in thought. "How aboot six hundred pounds?"

Rory squinted. Perhaps it was a wee bit steep a price to pay for the old clapper. But the farmer was an honest, hard-working Highlander whose life would be turned up-side-down within days.

"Here's a thousand. Thank-ye for yoor trouble." Rory opened his backpack and handed the farmer the notes.

"And yoor licence, please," the farmer asked, then took a small rectangular metal object from his pocket, a mobile phone, most probably. He held it like he was about to use it for something. "I'll take a photo for the paperwork part of oor transaction, aye?" he said when Rory hesitated.

"Oh, aye." Rory showed him Dad's licence.

The farmer held the phone above the licence and a clicking sound came from it, then he grunted his satisfaction.

"Och, well. I'll check the oil and water for ye afore ye start." The farmer smiled and made his way to the garage behind the vehicles, mumbling something. It was in Gaelic, a comment about city folk possessing more money than sense.

"Don't flash the money around like that, Rory!" Murray whispered once the farmer was in the garage.

The ground began to vibrate, and a roar came over head. The sound pressed down on Rory, and he squatted beside the car, and reached for his Glock in the back of his jeans. Murray also squatted beside the car, his eyes wide. The air pressed overhead as the sound, an entity in itself, moved in the air above them. Rory looked at the bright sky.

Nothing.

"Wow!" Murray's face broke into a smile and his eyes shone as he stood and looked well into the distance, ahead of the sound. "Jet fighters. The Royal Air Force."

Rory stood to get a better view of the aeroplanes now almost out of view at the other end of the valley. The farmer returned, a scowl on his face.

"We have them come over every once in a while. Scares the life oot a ma coos. Here's your keys. I'll just check under the bonnet for ye."

***

Rory's gear changes were jerky at first but smoothed out the more he drove. His face had a constant glow of warmth.

"It's been a while," he said.

He drove the narrow winding road edged by moss-covered dry stone walls, interspersed with forest. The signs beside this road that read *walkers welcome* were bright-shiny and new looking compared to how Rory knew them, rusted, old and barely readable. They found the road to Inverness, leaving their familiar grassy, grey-stoned mountains behind them.

"You know if you get stopped by the police you need to show your licence." Murray faced the road ahead.

"So, we don't get stopped," Rory said under his breath.

"Better improve your driving then," Murray answered.

Rory squinted his eyes and repressed a growl.

It was early morning and the traffic on the bridge over the Moray Firth was thin. Traffic lights operated at the roundabout.

"Red means stop," Murray commented beside him.

"I know!" Now Rory's neck heated.

Rory glanced sideways at the road signs to Fort William and Glencoe. He would need to make one very long detour to find his way there and Dad may not be at the crofter's cottage yet. Rory's chest ached again.

No, I can't risk it.

He could *not* meet Dad now. It would change many things. His pulse raced, either from the traffic or his thoughts of diverting. It went against all his self-imposed restrictions on the use of the Time Machine for personal reasons.

Stick to the mission. Leave Dad in your past.

Rory gripped the steering wheel and drove on, the tension in his jaw muscles reached into his skull where a dull headache formed.

Rory followed the A9 to Perth, then the M90 to Edinburgh. They were through the heavily forested mountainous regions and closer to larger cities. His hands tightened on the wheel. Murray bringing the road map made it easier to avoid going into towns and villages and they could stay on the motorway. The roads were populated by vehicles of all sizes. A large vehicle, with wheels almost the height of the car, drove up beside them on the outer lane, catching Rory's peripheral vision as it passed. He held his breath.

"Och, that lorry is large!" He placed his foot on the brake pedal as they approached a roundabout.

"Give way to your right, Rory!" Murray yelled in his ear.

"D'you want to drive?" he asked.

After another long stretch on the motorway, the three great bridges that traverse the River Forth and lead into Edinburgh came into view.

"Wow. I've seen pictures of them, like on all those old calendars Mum never threw out." Murray's voice bounced off the passenger window, his eyes glued to the view. "But the real thing, wow. The engineering."

Rory focused on the traffic. Mum would be alive in this time, and a nurse in Edinburgh Royal Infirmary's Emergency Department.

No, we don't have time. And what would she make of two strange guys wanting to see her?

Stick to the mission.

They travelled over the Queensferry Crossing. Murray had been quiet for a bit, so Rory glanced sideways at him. Murray's mouth hung open, his gaze fixed on the red tubed, Meccano set-type structure to their far left. He would see the angles and geometry of the Forth Rail Bridge.

But to Rory, these three bridges were shockingly indefensible. It only required a troop of good militia to block one end of any of these bridges, and it would be theirs. Well, three troops. He'd take all three bridges at once. Explosives would be helpful too.

Rory's mind flew back to history lessons. According to the records, in the same year as The Stock Market Crash, a spate of terrorist attacks worldwide had severely crippled many major cities of the world.

What had been the fate of the Forth bridges? Newspapers were scarce and digital information no longer accessible. The bridges were a logical target. Rory glanced again at the elegant, white pillars and the straight, thick, steel cables as he drove past them on the newer road bridge, the Queensferry Crossing. He'd just been speculating. Maybe someone *had* done it—destroyed these intriguing structures.

"You know when they finished the rail bridge in 1890"—Murray's voice echoed off the window as he continued his gaze to the left— "it was the longest cantilever-spanned bridge in the world, at that time?"

"How do you know *all* this stuff?" Rory screwed up his mouth.

"I read," Murray said.

"Well, *I* read."

"Yeah." Murray turned to him. "But *The Art of War* by Sun Tsu won't help us much today, will it?"

Rory kept his eyes on the road. He wouldn't respond to his brother's sarcasm.

"So, once we get into Edinburgh," he said, "how do we find this scientist?"

"Telephone book." Murray's eyebrows lifted a fraction. "How many Kensington-Wallaces do you think there are?"

"And we can find a telephone book where?" Rory frowned.

"Anywhere. Everyone has one in their homes," Murray said.

Rory raised an eyebrow. *Sometimes this kid doesn't always think it through completely.*

"So, we approach just *anybody* and ask if we can look at their telephone book?" Rory asked. "I don't think everybody will be as helpful as the farmer back there."

"Post Office," Murray announced.

"Okay, and where do we find one of those?"

"Anywhere," Murray said. "I haven't applied *the-goodness-of-fit-test* to this variable, but my hypothesis is that they're a common occurrence in this time. We are almost in a suburb of Edinburgh now. Keep your eyes out."

"Do you always see everything in terms of statistical analysis?" Rory looked sideways at his brother, whose eyebrows had raised, and mouth dropped in response to his reply. "I learned maths as well," Rory said.

"Yeah, but probably only as it pertains to the strategies of war," Murray mumbled into the window.

A few streets later, Murray shouted, "There's one!" He pointed to a glassed red-fronted building in the middle of a row of other glass fronted shops. "Just park."

"Where?" Rory asked.

"In the gap." Murray pointed at a space between two cars. "I won't be long."

Rory drove into the parking space and onto the curb, then Murray got out.

"You'd better fix that parking," Murray said through the partially open window.

Rory glared at his brother as he walked into the post office.

This driving was exhausting. His eyes were gritty, and his brain was foggy from the concentrating. So much to see all at once. And the noise! Trucks were loud. Cars were noisy, and now in the city, loud music came from some of them. Sometimes, the *thump, thump* of drumbeats vibrated in the car as they sat next to those vehicles at traffic lights. He'd be glad when he could get back to the country.

People walked past and never looked his way. They were intent on their own lives. One woman passed pushing a pram. She wore a brightly coloured garment which wrapped around her. Another man vaped. Rory had seen it before. The cloud of mist following this passer-by brought back memories of another visit to the past. Rory tried to push those aside.

They came too frequently.

The one who vaped lies dead on the living room floor of the slaver's half-way house.

Four thuds sound along the corridor.

Four bullets.

His father yells for him.

He turns. A beautiful young woman dresses hastily and flees out the back door.

He runs in the direction of the room she left. A dead man obstructs the door.

His father lies collapsed against the bed.

"Rory, do ye have yoor mither?" His father grips his belly. A sheen of sweat covers his pale forehead.

"Alistair's got her," Rory says.

"Time to go, son."

His mind is numb. The cool evening darkens.

His mother, as a young woman about his age, walks out the back door of the crofter's cottage and sits next to him on the bench.

The light from the back-window glistens on her damp face and reveals bloodshot eyes.

"I'll take you to his body," he says and takes her hand in his.

The car door slammed shut.

"He mustn't live here anymore." Murray's face loomed close, peering at him. "Rory!"

Blinking, Rory left his vivid thoughts of his mother and focused on Murray in the seat next to him.

"You hear me?" Murray asked. "He's not in this year's phone book. Kensington-Wallace doesn't live in Edinburgh anymore."

Rory took in a breath, willing himself into the present.

This present.

"Aye," he finally said. "Where did he work? We'll go there and ask."

"Welson Nuclear Power. Its offices are at the nuclear power station near Torness." Murray grabbed the road map and searched. "Here it is. We need to head to Berwick."

"Okay, navigator, lead the way." Rory wound down the window to let in fresh air. "Think I need to eat soon too."

"Oh okay, I'll look for services on the way." Murray smiled as he perused the UK A-Z.

Glad one of us is enjoying himself.

***

They parked outside the offices of Welson Nuclear Power, a grey-brick, single storey building that sat apart from the power station. The building was the size of a small island in the middle of a bitumen-ocean, surrounded by flat fields. Soft waves rolled in along the beach that ran beside the coastline fence of the power station's eastern perimeter.

"No, you stay here. I'll go in." Murray rested his hand on Rory's forearm.

"Why can't I come?" Rory asked.

"I look like a student. You... look like what you are. Military. Messy military, but military. They'll get all defensive." Murray raised his eyebrows. "You stay here. I've got this," he said as he shut the car door.

Messy military?

Murray walked in through the doors of the building, which were glass from top to bottom, giving Rory a view of a guard in a navy-blue uniform standing at the doorway. Behind him, directly inside the clear-glass doors, was a reception desk where a young woman sat. She looked up at Murray, a tight smile on her lips, then she shook her head and frowned. Murray turned and left the building.

Rory had his hand on the car door handle as Murry walked out. Murray glared at Rory and gave a sharp shake of his head. Rory relaxed back into the seat.

"What?" Rory snapped as Murray sat in the passenger seat.

"They won't tell me anything." Murray slumped and pursed his lips.

"Did you say it was for your project at school?"

"Uni," Murray corrected. "I'm not a kid."

"I'm going in," Rory opened the car door.

"Not with weapons, Rory!" Murray hissed. "There's a security guard."

"Aye, I saw." Rory removed his hunting knife from its sheath strapped around his calf and his handgun from his belt and shoved them under his seat. "You coming with me?"

Rory stalked up to the door with Murray trailing behind like a puppy. Rory walked past the security guard and went straight to the desk.

"Hello," Rory said.

The young woman looked up from behind the glass up-stand at the front of her desk, separating her from everyone but giving her enough room to see anyone who entered. Her gaze ran from Rory's face all the way down his body to his feet. A curve arose on the left side of her lips, and she raised the corresponding finely plucked eyebrow in approval as her gaze scanned his body on its way up to his face, lingering on the tight fit of his shirt. The heat rose to Rory's cheeks at her perusal and intensified as she smiled fully.

"Hello, miss, my wee brother here needs to get in contact with Professor Kensington-Wallace." Rory swallowed as the woman ran her tongue over her bottom lip. "I know he used to work here, and we were wondering if you would kindly tell us where he is now." Rory forced his smile past his discomfort.

The young woman leaned forward in her seat, her upper arms pressed her breasts together, making her cleavage more pronounced in her low-cut neckline. Rory fought to keep his eyes above it.

"I'm sorry, but I can't. Privacy laws." Her top teeth scraped her bottom lip.

"But he worked here?" Rory asked.

"Can't even tell you that," she said.

"What? This is ridiculous." Rory's voice rose. "We need to contact him. How are we going tae do that?"

The security guard took a step closer. Rory sensed, rather than saw, the posture of the security guard tensing. Standing behind him, Murray tugged at his shirt.

The young woman mouthed 'google', then smiled.

Rory blinked.

"Thanks anyway." Murray spoke from behind him as the guard took another step forward. "We'll be on our way now."

"Thank you, miss, hope the rest of your day goes well." Rory tilted his head and walked out. The security guard's posture relaxed.

Once in the car, Rory faced Murray. "What's google?"

***

They searched for an internet café in the towns on the way back to Edinburgh and came across one in its outer suburbs.

"You can get coffee there too, aye?" Rory's mouth watered.

They walked into a shop with computers in booths along the wall. After paying a fee, Rory bought a coffee, then Murray sat at a computer and started clicking the keys.

"You understand all of this, don't you?" Rory sipped the cappuccino as he stood behind Murray. The froth stuck to his upper lip. He licked it away.

"Yep," Murray said absentmindedly.

Google in big letters was on the screen. Underneath it, Murray typed *Kensington-Wallace* into the elongated box and pressed a larger button on the keyboard. Immediately a picture and writing appeared. It was the same photograph as the one in the article.

"So, where is he now?" Rory asked.

"He's now a professor at Oxford University, England." Murray's tone held awe.

"So, we need to go there?" Rory's shoulders drooped.

It was a long way to drive.

In traffic.

"Don't get excited, Rory," Murray said. "We're not at war with England anymore." Murray had pressed more keys and different writing was now on the screen.

"Och, it's no' that. Just dinnae want to go *all* that way in the car, ken," Rory whispered to Murray's back. "It's hard work. I'm a wee bit tired from all o' this already. Och! Give me a horse any day!"

Murray stood, scooted the chair out from under him and started walking to the door.

"What, that's it?" Rory asked. "Do you no' want to write it down?"

"No. It's all here." Murray pointed to his head.

"What was all o' that about *privacy*?" Rory finished the coffee and followed him out.

"So, we'll go back to Edinburgh and park the car somewhere. *Long Term*, I think they call it," Murray said. "Then we'll catch a train to Oxford. The train station is right in the centre of town, and we can walk to wherever we need to go to find him."

***

"I really don't like leaving ma weapons in the car," Rory whispered under his breath.

"Ssh." Murray glared at him sideways as they walked to the ticket counter in Waverly Station, Edinburgh.

Murray spoke to the woman issuing tickets from behind the glass-fronted counter. "Two First-Class tickets to Oxford, please."

"You can use your credit card at any of the ticket machines," the woman said cheerily.

"Oh, that's okay," Murray replied as he gestured to Rory to get the cash out of the backpack. "I'm okay dealing with humans."

Rory glanced out through the automatic doors of the ticket office as Murray finished the transaction. Alert Scot Rail staff walked past, their not-so-casual glances taking in all would-be commuters.

"We've got to change at Birmingham," Murray said as he nudged Rory out of the ticket office. "We'll be at Oxford in five hours and forty-four minutes."

It would be late afternoon when they arrived, and it had been a long day. Rory's limbs were heavy, his whole body sluggish.

On this journey to the past, time travel is tiring.

Murray had bought first-class tickets.

"They're the best." Murray shrugged. "Why not?"

They walked along the concourse to the correct platform and made their way to the high-speed train. After boarding the train, they walked through the carriage to their seats. The cloth-covered double seats faced two more with a table between them. A young woman left as they sat, leaving the space to them. The train moved with a lurch and Rory gripped the armrests tight.

"Relax, let the train do it for you," Murray said sitting opposite him.

Rory turned to face the window as a wall of brick passed by. Then it cleared, and Murray whistled, raised his eyebrows, and lifted his chin, indicating the view. It was now the lower base-rock on which Edinburgh Castle was situated. Upward, the walls of the castle rose higher. If only Rory had time to go over it. It would surely be an inspiration for their outposts—on a smaller scale of course.

The train accelerated and house upon house flashed by. Miles of them. So many people and so many dwellings. The train flew past other bigger buildings. They could only be shopping centres and offices, and they were all intact. Then there were more roads and cars. Soon, green fields of crops replaced the buildings. The train was going *so* fast. Rory had never been at such a speed. Things were becoming a blur. The train rocked sideways, lulling his body. Relaxing his tired muscles...

He falls to the ground with a thud. He aches mid-torso. It's hard to breathe. He takes a gasp. The air returns to his lungs.

"Och, up ye get, son." Dad's gravelly voice says over him, and strong hands pick him up, sturdy arms encircle, and the scent of horse and pine surround him.

"Ye ken ye need to get straight back on that horse the noo'?" Dad's piercing blue eyes hold his.

Dad as a young man with his long, dark-blond hair tied back in a pony-tail.

He whistles, and the tall black horse walks over to them.

"He's wondering where ye got tae." Dad lifts him back up into the saddle and hands him the reins.

"You're not using Boy to teach him to ride, are you? That colt's barely broken in."

From the fence, Mum speaks with alarm in her tone.

Rory turns to her voice, the sound of his childhood. Mum stands next to the menage, her large, pregnant belly rests against the fence.

"You be careful he doesn't get injured." Her voice holds reprimand.

"Aye, lass. I'll be careful with the wee lad too." Dad chuckles.

The train jolted sharply, and Murray's face was in front of his.

"You okay?" Murray's brow creased.

Rory turned his gaze to the table between them, trying to regain his focus.

"Aye, I'm fine."

There was an elastic hair tie on the table. Rory picked it up and pulled his hair back, making it a small bun at the back of his head.

"A man-bun." Murray laughed. "They are fashionable at present." He tilted his head sideways at the young man in the seat across from them, whose hair was in a similar bun. "It's okay. You'll look like a student. Fit in... maybe." Murray's mouth twitched.

"Soft drinks, tea, coffee, crisps, sweets." A woman pushing a trolley came along the aisle.

"Want to try some early twenty-first century food?" Murray whispered as he got out some cash from his pocket. "Ahh, we'll have two packets of crisps, a Stamina Bar, an Energy Dose Bar, and two mineral waters, please." Murray handed over the money—the exact amount.

The woman placed the items on the table and moved on.

"Dose or Stamina?" Murray asked, opening a bag of crisps.

"Either," Rory said.

Murray took the Stamina Bar and left the Energy Dose Bar for him. Rory picked it up and read the wrapper.

"What's palm oil and glucose syru—" Rory began.

"Don't ask. Just eat." Murray chewed on the bite he'd taken. His eyes rolled, lids half-closed, and he groaned.

"You okay? You sound like you're having an—"

"Just eat!"

Rory ripped open the wrapper and took a bite. A sweetness filled his mouth in totality, a vague bitterness of chocolate became an after taste. He took another, and another. His head began to buzz, and now he was *not* tired. It was similar to the effects of coffee but like his eyes would pop and his ears rang.

"They sell this drug just anywhere?" he asked.

"Ssh!" Murray's eyes closed as he munched on the last of his bar.

"People eat this stuff all the time?" Rory asked.

He read more of the packaging. *Three hundred and ten calories and seventeen-point-eight grams of fat.* He blinked. He wasn't up on food values, but he suspected it was a lot of calories and fat for such a small amount of food.

Rory leaned back in his seat. Others were eating the bars too. People here were bigger than people in the Community. Not taller, but larger. The young man with the man-bun had thick arms, but they didn't appear muscled. The middle-aged lady next to him was a round shape, and another woman walked down the aisle with legs the size of tree trunks. Now he thought about it, it had niggled at him all day. People in this time were fatter, and the majority didn't look strong and healthy.

Rory put the unfinished chocolate bar on the table and picked up the bottle of water. Its label read *Highland Water*. He unscrewed the cap and took a sip to find fresh cool liquid with the distinctly mineral taste found in water from the mountains. He noticed another, smaller label with a price on it.

"Och! You did nae have to pay for the water?"

"Yep," Murray answered.

"Water?" Rory's voice trailed away. "When Scotland's full o' it?"

Chapter Seven

Oxford, England, 2018

They changed trains at Birmingham and arrived at Oxford in the late afternoon. Rory and Murray walked out of the station and down the steps.

"The Physics Faculty," Rory said, gazing around at the buildings immediately in front of him.

People surrounded them in a rush, eager to get home for their evening meal, he guessed.

"Yes. The physics building is nineteen minutes away past the Ashmolean Museum, according to Google Maps." Murray pointed to his head.

"Och. The roads are intact bitumen." Rory blinked, recalling his mother's descriptions of the past.

"Concrete footpath!" Murray pointed to the ground.

They walked along the street past honey-coloured stone buildings, and people rode by on bicycles and cars drove close.

"What's that smell?" Murray asked, sniffing the air as a car passed.

"Burned petrol," Rory answered. "Something I have nae come across in a long time."

Their route took them by the Ashmolean Museum.

"Looks like something out of a history book on ancient Grecian architecture." Murray paused in front of it.

Rory grabbed him by the arm and tugged.

"We don't have time, brother," he whispered.

Many people walked by Rory, bumping his arms now and then. A red double-decker bus passed them every ten minutes.

"Tourists seeing the sights." Murray informed him.

In the front of sandstone buildings, older style, ornate and imposing, groups or individuals stood and smiled, holding a long pole in front of them that held a mobile phone.

"What are they doing?" Rory nudged Murray, who shrugged.

The crowd pressed in on Rory. People walked by with head's down, intent on their destination, or stopped and stared into shop windows, or laughed with companions. Rory blinked, ears twitching. It was almost sensory overload. He always watched and listened for anything suspicious. Anything he could interpret as an offensive action. His arm muscles tensed. If only he had a weapon. His knife at least. But people seemed relaxed and self-absorbed. No one appeared overtly aggressive. None had the tell-tale signs of darting glances or the jumpy movements of someone with sinister intent.

No one had a weapon, that he could tell. No bulges in jackets or the back of trousers. There may have been knives tucked in boots, or was he looking unnecessarily?

Up ahead, a young black woman in a neat black dress played a violin. Its high-pitched melody went before her, and people stood in a circle around the open violin case. They watched, their heads inclined, listening. The music swam around Rory as they approached the outer edge of the circle, by-passing the listeners.

A young lad bumped into an older man standing at the edge of the crowd. The lad's hand slipped something square and brown out of the top inner pocket of the man's jacket. Rory blinked. *A pickpocket.*

Rory stiffened. No, he'd have to keep out of it.

Most people were the same age as him and Murray. Students. Passers-by spoke to each other in many different languages. Rory only spoke English and the Gaelic, but the languages floating past him were probably French, German, Spanish and Italian. There were strange English accents too. He recognised a North American accent from his Canadian brother-in-law, Alistair, but a group of students spoke it differently again to anything he'd ever heard.

"Australian, I think," Murray said when Rory gave him a questioning glance as the group of speakers passed by them.

The building that housed the Physics department was newer than most. No honey-coloured stone, just grey, lots of windows and geometric shapes. They walked into the front door and found the noticeboards.

"What now?" Rory asked.

In front of him were physics posters—*another* language all together.

"How were you going to find him here?" he asked.

Murray looked at a noticeboard that had timetables on it.

"Oh, it's Summer School." Murray turned as a group of students walked past them. "Hey guys..." He strode off with the group and was soon deep in conversation with them.

Rory pressed his lips together as warmth for his brother centred in his chest. Murray seemed so at home here. He looked like a student. He would love this. Excel at it. In another time he would have been here, in his element. A momentary heaviness came over Rory.

Murray walked back, his expression alight.

"He's not teaching Summer School this year, but they think he's at home," Murray said. he was the most animated Rory had ever seen him. "They didn't know where, but he lives here in Oxford."

Rory made to go but Murray hadn't moved. Murray stared at the poster on the wall next to the noticeboard, covered in mathematical symbols.

"What is it?" Rory moved next to him.

"Oh, an equation." Murray breathed through his mouth.

"Come, let's go," Rory said. "Telephone book again?"

Murray didn't move. Rory got hold of his arm and tugged gently. Murray resisted.

"They've dedicated this whole building to teaching and making new discoveries in physics," Murray said, his voice husky. "And there's a building like it solely dedicated to mathematics."

Murray turned to face him; his eyes were watery.

"Oh, no you don't, brother," Rory said in a quiet voice. "I need you. The future needs you."

Rory tugged Murray's arm again, but his feet remained in place.

"Murray." Rory's voice was firmer now. "In a few weeks these hallowed halls will not be as they are now."

"But think of what I could learn in those few weeks!" Murray's face contorted.

"I'm sorry," Rory said. "But you can't. Your brains are required for a higher purpose. Greater things where there is a greater need... Brother... Murray...We must go." Rory had never pleaded before, but he had no qualms about doing so now.

Murray finally moved. "Google. White Pages." Murray's voice was flat as he walked ahead of Rory, shoulders slumped.

"Aren't all pages white?" Rory asked.

***

They walked along Buckingham Street until they got to the third of the red-brick three-storey dwellings.

"You sure this is it?" Rory asked.

Murray nodded beside him. He'd said little since they left the Physics building. The evening light was still with them, the long day of the summer solstice only days away. Rory turned to Murray.

"I've still no idea what we'll say to him." Rory lifted an eyebrow at Murray.

"We'll start by pretending we're students." Murray turned to face him.

"Wing it?" Rory asked.

"Yep. Wing it," Murray said.

They climbed the few steps and Murray knocked on the blue door. A man's voice spoke behind the door while quick, lighter footsteps moved away from it. The door opened and a man of medium build with greying hair and glasses looked at them both in turn.

"Hello, Professor Kensington-Wallace. My name is Murray Campbell, and this is my brother, Rory." Murray extended his hand.

The professor hesitated then reached out and shook it, then took Rory's hand. His eyes squinted a fraction.

"My brother missed out on Summer School, but Murray had some questions he wanted to ask you personally," Rory said. "We've come all the way from Scotland, and I was hoping you'd let him. Ask you the questions, that is."

Rory turned on his best smile and manners, willing the man to invite them inside.

The professor glanced to his right. Behind him, a small child peeked around the corner of the door frame. A faint scent of food, steak and gravy, wafted into Rory's nostrils. His hunger hit him with a vengeance, gnawing at his insides but he'd have to ignore it.

"I apologise," Rory continued. "We haven't arranged to meet with you. We won't take too much of your time. You see, it's what my wee brother here wants to speak with you about. He has a theory on time travel."

"Many do." The professor didn't move.

"May we please come in?" Murray asked in a very polite tone. "We really need to speak with you."

The professor gave a brief nod and stood back, allowing them entrance. "Please take a seat in the front room."

Murray looked at Rory.

A look which said to *let him do the talking*.

The small room had a two-seater couch and a leather chesterfield, in which the professor sat. A musty smell emanated from the bookshelves that lined each wall of the room. Rory sat next to Murray on the couch. It was lumpy and caused Rory to lean into his brother. He held himself back and knocked his arm against the books sitting sideways on the shelves behind him—the overflow—causing them to fall. A girlish giggle erupted from the hallway.

"Play with your toys, sweetheart. There's a good girl," the professor said.

Rory turned to pick up the books and saw a small girl with long honey-blonde hair and sapphire-blue eyes staring at him from the doorway.

Rory smiled. "Hello," he said, his Scottish accent shouting itself in that one word.

So far, the room had been full of well-spoken English. The little girl, about five years old, giggled once more and ran to another room.

"What's your theory?" The professor grinned and rubbed his hands together.

On you go, lad.

"Well, basically, it isn't as impossible as everyone thinks," Murray said.

The professor nodded.

"Do you believe one day it *will* happen?" Murray asked.

Rory held his breath, not too certain of the angle Murray was taking.

"We have Newton's thoughts on time, which sparked speculation on travelling through it. Einstein and his wormholes. And there's Gödel... but wouldn't it be *marvellous*?" The professor was breathless, and his eyes lit up as he spoke. "Being a nuclear physicist, I haven't performed any research on the subject. My research concerned warheads and before my post here at Oxford I worked in nuclear power."

"We read your paper," Rory commented.

Murray turned and glared. Rory shut his mouth tight.

"But *my own* thoughts on the matter," the professor continued. "Well, it *may be*, but our equipment isn't sophisticated enough at present."

"What if I told you it's so much simpler than it seems and once the world loses its technology, we find out how uncomplicated it is, and we do it?" Murray asked.

The professor opened his mouth to speak, looked from Murray to Rory then back to Murray. "What are you saying?" he asked.

"We have travelled back in time," Murray said. "From this future where time travel is achieved... simply."

Silence engulfed the room. The professor's eyes flicked rapidly from Murray to Rory and back again—several times.

"Please, sir," Rory had to speak. "Dinnae think we are mad, or *at* it. It's true, and we need your help. In a matter of days, the world will have an economic crisis from which it will never recover. You would say the world will go backward into violence, anarchy, and poverty. We come from that future, and we need your advice about a nuc—"

"Enough!" The professor shot out of his chair and pointed to the door. "Please leave now!" His command was curt.

"But—" Murray began.

"No, Murray," Rory interrupted him. "We've disturbed Professor Kensington-Wallace enough." To the professor he said, "We're going, but please listen to the news. It *will* happen."

Rory grabbed Murray by the arm and let himself and his brother out. Kensington-Wallace slammed the door behind them.

"But—?" Murray began.

"Keep walking, Murray," Rory growled. "Don't ruin it. Give the man time."

Rory marched Murray down the street.

"But you know it's already started?" Murray said.

"How would I ken that?"

"The news running beside the White Pages. The US market started its slide yesterday, and today UK and Europe have followed suit. Asian markets were beginning when we were in the Internet Café."

"And you didn't think to tell me?" Rory asked.

"I thought you were reading it. Oh, I forgot, you got caught up with your *cappuccino.*" Murray waggled his head from side to side as he spoke. "Again."

"He'll think I've made it up because of *that*. We mustn't be as early as we planned," Rory said. "We'll be right in the middle of it by the time we manage to convince him."

"We're going back to the professor?" Murray asked.

"Of course. Give him a day to think about it," Rory said. "Especially now *it's* happening. Well, it may be to our advantage. Anyway, we aren't going back to our time until we get what we need from him."

He'd spoken gruffly to his wee brother. Perhaps he'd been too harsh. But this was too important to spare Murray's feelings.

Chapter Eight

All the way back to the shopping centre, Murray didn't say a word to Rory. Rory bought fish and chips for dinner.

"Must get some ocean fish off the old man at Ewe. This is delicious," Rory said around a mouthful of hot battered cod.

"The guy from the Loch Ewe Community?" Murray asked, then shoved salted chips into his mouth, one after the other.

"Said there was plenty o' fish now." Rory rolled his head to the side, indicating the future. "Then."

"So, where are we sleeping?" Murray asked.

"There's a wee forest near to town. We'll camp there."

"You know we can get into trouble for that?" Murray said. "They call it vagrancy."

"They'll no' catch us." Rory shook with his mouth open, for emphasis, and to cool the fish in his mouth.

"So, tomorrow we're just doing nothing?" Murray asked.

"The professor will need the day to mull it over, see what's happening around the world and come to believe us." Rory popped a chip in his mouth. "We can keep an eye on the news."

"Well, I might sightsee Oxford." Murray glanced sideways at him.

"You keep your head doon." Rory spoke low, commanding.

"Uh, huh." Murray nodded.

They walked through the town, through Christ Church Meadow and by the River Thames. It was calm here; the traffic noise was distant, and copse of ash and birch trees edged the green meadows. The fresh comforting scent of forest wafted into his face, soothing him with its familiarity.

People walked their dogs in the cool evening and picked up their dog's faeces in plastic bags. *Huh?* There were a variety of dogs; small white fluffy ones with ear-piercing high-pitched barks, ones with faces that looked as if their snouts were punched in at birth, and the larger breeds he was more familiar with. Dad had said that early on after The Stock Market Crash, packs of larger dogs would kill the smaller breeds of dog when they lost their masters. These dogs of larger breeds then began their roaming in packs. His parents had recounted being attacked a couple of times. The Community trained and bred larger dogs, the community members' pets, to be guard dogs. 'An early warning system', his father would say.

Once in the Kidneys Nature Park, Rory found a copse away from the track and nearer the river where they could spend the night.

***

The next morning, a rhythmic splash on the water nearby woke Rory. A canoe-type boat, with four girls holding an oar each, passed by on the river below him. Each pulled on their oar at the command of a smaller girl who sat in the very front of this boat.

"We'd better move, Murray," Rory said, sitting up and stretching. "Oxford is awake."

At the nearest café, and Rory ordered two English breakfasts. The waitress served plates piled high with bacon, fried eggs, beans in a red sauce and fried mushed potato, which looked like a greasy biscuit.

"That's baked beans and they're hash browns," Murray explained as Rory poked at the items. Murray ate his with noises of appreciation.

"You're enjoyin' this food, aren't you?" Rory asked.

"Aye," Murray said between mouthfuls.

The large screen on the wall was a constant noise accompanying the chatter of the patrons in the café. Rory focused on the words moving along the bottom.

Run on banks. Three of the Big Five fold.

"What are the Big Five?" Rory placed his knife and fork beside his plate, his meal only half eaten.

"Oh," Murray swallowed his mouthful. "That's the banks folding," he said into Rory's ear. "The violence in London will probably start today."

Rory glanced around at the patrons in the café. A few were concerned; others barely lifted their heads from their breakfasts and conversations.

So, it had begun.

"Hopefully by the end of the day our man will be ready to listen," Rory said.

They finished their meal and wandered into the street.

"One question. How do you ken so much about the twenty-first century?" Rory asked. "I mean this part of it, not ours."

"Research." Murray pressed the walk button on the traffic lights.

"But we left immediately," Rory said. "When did you have time to research it?"

"Before you went the last time," Murray replied. "I looked up life before The Stock Market Crash. There wasn't a lot. Well, there were magazines and books. Newspapers would've been helpful too but, according to Mr Stobbart, they used most of those for lighting fires until people realised they could be a valuable source of history, and in fact, were history themselves."

The pedestrian lights changed from a red man standing to a green man walking. Murray stepped off the curb and walked onto the road. Rory trod beside him as they crossed the street.

"But the information, like what was good to eat, came from Aunty Bec and Uncle Brendan. He likes chocolate bars." Murray looked up at Rory with a broad grin, and the corners of Rory's own mouth tugged as a smile emerged.

"We need to find the gear they wear and buy some. You know, the radiation protection suits? We'll google it, won't we?" Rory wiggled his eyebrows. "Hey, I'm getting to know the language."

"Rory, they won't sell those suits to just anybody. Even if you could order them from the internet, it would take days to deliver, and you need an address."

"Well, we could find out where they make it and go get some." Rory opened his eyes wide and stuck his chin out, hoping Murray would get the hint.

"Rory, we can't steal them," Murray said. "It's not that simple. Security. The police and so on."

Rory's heart sank. What made him say that, anyway? He wasn't a Desperate Measures kind of person. Normally, he'd never consider taking anything that wasn't his.

Why else had they come then? They needed information *and* equipment.

"We could try," Rory persisted.

"We don't have a car down here." Murray stood still, a look of disbelief on his face. "And if the police pursued us, we'd have to make a quick escape, on foot and public transport. *And* we'd still have to speak to the professor. It wouldn't work, Rory."

"We'd get caught." Rory put his hands to his face and rubbed. It was getting complicated. He *had* to have a plan. "When we get back to Edinburgh, we'll head for the nuclear power plant. They'll have some," he added.

Rory passed the day walking through the many green parklands of Oxford. He felt refreshed and finally the tiredness, which had hung around him since travelling back in time, was receding. In the late afternoon, he walked back to the café where they'd had breakfast. He ate a cold pork pie and watched the news. There was now rioting in most of the large cities. He stared out at the street. People walked by in their usual hurry. Oxford was still peaceful, but how long would it last?

Murray walked past the window with a group of students, the same physics summer school students they'd met yesterday. Rory paid for his food and hurried outside to follow them. Murray held his own in an intense conversation with a student.

When they reached the corner, Murray said farewell and turned around to face Rory.

"Had a good day?" he asked Murray.

"Uh, huh." Murray beamed as he walked beside him.

"What have you been doing?" Rory asked.

"I sat in on one of their summer school lectures," Murray said. "During questions afterward, they held a discussion on time travel."

"Oh, no." Rory stopped walking. "What've you said?"

"I'm not stupid. I kept it all theoretical. No mention of being a time traveller myself," Murray whispered.

Rory recommended walking and they crossed the street then headed for the professor's home.

Murray rummaged in his backpack and brought out a wad of paper held together with big fat staples. "Got you something." He handed Rory the handmade book.

"What's this?" Rory's brow tightened in a frown.

The book was heavy. He flicked through the pages. The print was small and tightly packed on most pages, interspersed with diagrams of gauges and control panels.

"During the lunch break—you get an hour," Murray said, "a student let me into the library computers with his password and I googled."

Rory blinked. "*Googled...* what *is* this?"

"How to drive a submarine." Murray's smile was very much a smirk. "Some light reading for you."

The street was quiet as they passed houses with several bicycles in their small front yards. They approached the professor's door, and Murray reached up to knock. Before his knuckles landed on the door, it opened, and the professor stood there.

"Come in," the professor ordered.

Rory exchanged a brief glance with Murray before they walked inside.

"Please tell me how you knew." The professor ushered them into the same musty-scented, book-filled room as yesterday.

"We *are* from the future," Murray said. "The kind of future that develops after the events caused by the activity on the stock market that's occurring right now. But it isn't why we are here—"

The professor held up his hands. "So, the world is to descend into chaos, and yesterday you tried to tell me there's *another* problem? Wait. What year are you from?"

"2061," Rory answered. "And there's an unstable nuclear warhead on a North Korean submarine in the North Western Scottish Highlands, which may blow, but we want to try to disarm it. How do we do that?"

"We are sure it's leaking radiation," Murray added. "Rory saw submariners suffering from radiation sickness."

The professor blinked a few times. "What equipment do you have? Are there cars?" he asked. "Is there fuel? Do you have electricity? Who's manning the nuclear power stations? Who's in pow—"

"Wait!" Rory raised his hand. "We have little modern technology. There's no oil being refined; electricity, well, any power, is in only a few hands. Those who have power have *the power*, so to speak. Vehicles are rare. We haven't heard from the government for years, except to spy on us with drones..."

"Who is 'us'?" Professor Kensington-Wallace asked.

"Those of us who live in self-sufficient communities and want to live peacefully," Rory answered. "Others, who are not so friendly and live outside of community-life and its values, make it difficult for those of us who do—let me put it that way."

Rory's summary would have to be enough. They *had* to get on with the solution to their nuclear problem.

"Daddy, what's wrong?" The little girl's voice came through the door beside Rory.

She held a doll in her arms and ran over to her father and placed her head in his lap.

"It's okay sweetheart, these men are friends," the professor said. "We have lots to talk about. Why don't you play with your dolls?'

She shook her head and frowned. She twiddled with the corner of her dress and scowled at Rory and Murray in turn. The centre of Rory's chest softened. He'd seen enough children scared. Please, not this one too.

"What's your dolly's name?" Rory reached out and touched the doll's dress. "She's pretty. Almost as pretty as you, lass." His thick Scottish accent lilted once more.

"Amy." She rocked her doll and the corners of her mouth curled, brightening her face.

"Go play with your dolls, Siobhan. There's a good girl." Her father ushered her out. "My wife was Scottish, hence my daughter's Gaelic name."

Within moments the lass was back, dragging a doll's house into the room. She placed it to the side of her father and began opening it to show the miniature furniture it contained. She played quietly for a while, content to be in the same room as them.

"North Korean, you say?" the professor asked. His daughter's antics hardly disturbed him.

"It's an old Russian cast off. Not nuclear," Rory said.

"You've seen it?" The professor's eyes widened.

"The sub. We're assuming the radiation leak is a warhead," Rory said. "Well, that's what the man from the Loch Ewe Community thinks. He's a seafaring fisherman and seems to know what he's talking about."

"You will need to detonate the warhead," the professor said. "You probably don't have the means or the time to seal the leak."

"Detonate it!" Rory spoke in unison with Murray.

"Yes. I'm referring to a safe detonation. Drive it out to sea first, well away from any land, and set a timer. Loch Ewe is a sea loch." Kensington-Wallace shook his head slightly. "Nuclear warheads usually detonate on impact, but you can switch it to a timer. If it's your usual nuclear device."

"What do you mean by 'usual'?" Murray asked.

"It depends on who made it. If it was a country that is part of NATO you should have no difficulty, but if a rogue state assembled it, say India or

Pakistan, well then..." The professor twisted his mouth to the side. "I can't really say."

Apart from the little girl playing with the tiny furniture and making soft comments to herself, the room was quiet for a time. Rory clenched and unclenched his fists. Murray jiggled his right leg making the whole couch shake.

Rory took a deep breath.

"Do you like my house?" Siobhan stood in front of Rory, holding two miniature dolls, a man and a woman, just the right size for the house. "I'll show you where they go. Come." She hooked her arm through his and pulled back.

Rory leaned forward and knelt on the floor in front of the tiny house. Behind him, the professor asked Murray more questions on their life in the future.

"You see this is the kitchen, and she's making the daddy his dinner." Siobhan explained her demonstration of the doll's activities in the small house. "The children are in their rooms doing their homework. They must finish it all first. Then, and only then, can they go play on their computers." She was beside him and tilted her head to the side, expecting an answer.

"Oh, aye." Was all he could think of to show his interest.

Rory *was* interested, as he'd never seen such a thing before, nor had a little girl explain it to him.

His response seemed enough, as she continued. "So, they are having roast beef with Yorkshire Puddings for dinner. I love roast beef. Do you like Yorkshire Puddings... what's your name?"

"Rory," he said. "It's the Gaelic, like your name. It's spelled diff—"

"Yes, I know," she said. "I spell mine like this, S-io-bh-an. But you say Shivonne. My teachers get stuck when they read my name and I have to explain it to them *every* time." She spoke like it was a chore. "How do you spell your name? Wait!"

She ran out of the room and soon skipped her way back in with a notebook and a pencil in her hand.

"So, here's my name." She put the notebook on the floor in front of Rory and wrote her name using the pencil in her left hand.

Then she swapped hands. "Spell Rory for me, please." She waited, pencil poised in her right hand.

"R-u-a-i-r-i-d-h." He spoke slowly as she wrote the Gaelic spelling of his name. Her writing was perfect in both hands.

"Ambidextrous," he said.

"Yes, that's correct. Are you a genius too?" Her dark-blue eyes looked intently at him. They were mesmerising.

"Och, no. I leave that for my wee brother there. Murray's the mathematician."

Rory spoke his comment into the quiet. The professor had paused his conversation with Murray and was listening to Rory and Siobhan's.

He turned back to Murray. "You did the calculations for the time travel?"

Murray nodded.

Rory listened to the conversation as he watched the little girl play with the doll's house.

"When I grow up, I'm going to be a scientist *and* a mummy. I want lots of babies. I like babies. Do you?" she asked.

"Oh, um, aye," Rory answered.

He hadn't thought of the impending birth of his niece or nephew for a while, at least not since they'd arrived in the past. It would've been his parent's first grandchild. And if things had gone differently, it would have been *his* child.

His throat thickened. This wee lass would probably never see her dream of a house and children. She might be one of the lucky ones who survived the coming violence and grew to adulthood. History books, written by the intellectuals and historians in the community system, had told him many children of this time didn't make it. If the violence didn't get them, then the ensuing food shortages and disease with scarce medical supplies would.

Had. He blinked. This aspect of the past had never touched him so closely.

Poor wee lass.

Rory continued to respond to her questions and keep a smile on his face, despite the thoughts of her future.

Siobhan chatted away happily for a while and Rory caught snippets of the conversation behind him.

"...protective gear," Murray said.

"Aye." Rory twisted to the professor from where he sat cross-legged on the floor in front of the doll's house. "We need some and we dinnae have time to buy—or procure it by other means. Can you help us?"

The professor crossed his arms over his chest and his shoulders rose with a deep breath.

"It *is* exceptional circumstances." He seemed to speak to himself. "I'll see what I can do."

Kensington-Wallace left the room, and in the kitchen had a one-sided conversation with someone. Rory looked over at Murray, raised an eyebrow and lifted his shoulders in a querying shrug.

"He's speaking on his mobile phone," Murray said.

The professor's voice drifted out to them, his tone a mixture of asking and ordering. Then a loud bell-like noise began right beside Rory. He jumped and reached behind into the back of his jeans for his handgun—which wasn't there.

Siobhan started at his movements, then looked at him.

"It's the land-line, silly," she said.

"The what?" Rory removed his hand from behind him as his cheeks warmed. His Glock was in the car parked at the railway station in Edinburgh.

"The telephone," Murray explained as the ringing continued.

"How do you stop it?" Rory asked. It appeared alive, and it was *so* demanding.

"You answer it, silly." Siobhan took the phone off its rest and pressed it to her cheek. "Hello," she said into it.

A faint voice came from it.

"Um, I'll get Daddy. Please hold." Siobhan put her hand over the section she spoke into and yelled, "Daddy, a man's wanting you to get ready for the badger-set."

In the kitchen, the professor ended his phone call. He hurried back into the room and took the phone from Siobhan. His face was pale, and his brows drew together.

"Excuse me, please," he said then strode back to the kitchen with the phone.

"Your father's a nature lover?" Rory smiled at the smart and talented wee lass in front of him.

"No." She shook her head.

Murray gasped and sat straighter on the couch, his eyes wide.

"What?" Rory frowned.

Murray shook his head as the professor returned.

"I'm sorry, but I must end our little time together here. Siobhan, come here, sweetheart." He held out his hands to her, and she obediently walked into her father's arms. He turned her around to face Murray and Rory. "Siobhan. This is very important. I want you to do something for me, darling girl."

"Yes, Daddy."

"Look at these men," the professor said.

She glanced at Murray and then fixed her deep-blue gaze on Rory.

"I want you to never forget them. Promise me?" the professor asked.

"Yes, Daddy." She nodded her head as her eyes remained locked with Rory's.

The professor released his daughter from their hug then led Rory and Murray to the door.

"I have to go... somewhere now," he said. "I'll email the office at Torness. I've just spoken to the manager, and he'll give you two suits. I said you'd be there tomorrow." He looked both of them in the eye. "Good luck."

Siobhan was by his side as Professor Kensington-Wallace saw them out the front door.

"Bye-bye." The little girl waved vigorously as they walked along the street.

Chapter Nine

Edinburgh 2061

His footsteps echoed in the dark night, his shoes disturbing the puddled road beneath his feet. Misty rain covered the street like a fog, darkening the buildings, dampening his hair, and leaving a fine sheen to cool his face as he slipped through the narrow street. He'd have to dry himself before they saw him below ground. How would he explain wet hair *and* a wet coat in a place where the rain never reached?

Night-time strolls in the up-ground compound of the Government Bunker were dissuaded. Frowned upon. He'd had his fill of that—enough for a lifetime. Well, he'd now ensure he stood out from the crowd in a good way. He'd be proven right and little Ms Perfect-Double-Barrell-Surname wrong.

The disgusting rabble were keen and eager. Too keen and eager. But they'd do the job, he was sure.

His requests were nothing they weren't used to.

Ahead, footsteps and voices came his way in a hurry. His pulse thumped in his ears as sweat covered his palms.

Had they sold him out? Sent someone to kill him?

He slipped into a narrow space in between two buildings. His feet scrunched in the litter, and the scent of human excrement wafted into his nostrils. The wind blew more loose litter and leaves along the street like a tumbleweed in one of those old Westerns they screened in the Bunker. The surrounding buildings would've once been shops. They'd boarded the windows and covered the wood with graffiti. Voices came from the other side of the boards. People must live in there. What sort of accommodation was that? They'd live in hovels and think it was okay, this lot.

The group of men walked nearer, seemingly disinterested in him. Or he'd been lucky. Or they didn't want him. They passed by, the acrid aroma of human bodies to whom personal hygiene was an unfamiliar notion, wafted into his hiding place.

Did they never wash?

He blew out his breath and went back into the rain. He had to return to Arthur's Seat without the rabble noticing him further. His clean, neat, tailored trousers were a dead giveaway; he hadn't had time to change. It was all *go* in the Bunker and he'd had to let his contacts know. His patriotic, Scotland-loving contacts who still lived with the dream of an Independent Scotland. The government, keeping close to themselves, had never informed the plebs of how things stood since The Crash.

Keep them ignorant. Keep them under control.

Now his own plans were all set. He would be on his way. Not only to sort out the nuke, but on his way to being part of the New Scottish Government.

And if it worked out—if the plebs played their part well—he'd even be a hero. At the least, it would show those Community reprobates to be the barbarians they were, and ensure they have nothing to do with the future rule of Scotland.

Chapter Ten

Scottish Government Underground Bunker, Edinburgh 2061

S iobhan stowed the last of her casual clothes into her duffle bag. Beatles' music came from her record player. John Lennon sang a slow ballad as his nasal tones filled her room. No skirts or nice cardigans for this trip. Practical and warm—they were going to the Highlands, after all. She recalled from her reading—and a vague memory of a family holiday—that it could be cold. *And* she would wear decent shoes—no heels.

Siobhan left her packing and made her way along the corridor to the lift for the next level. There was no *click-clack* this time from the serviceable boots she'd borrowed from Stores. She hummed to herself despite the lack of beat her footsteps usually provided. The music put her in a calm mood. She'd had heart flutters on and off all morning.

Don't look too eager to go up top.

The long LED-lit corridor led to the section of the Government Bunker that held her office. Louise sat at her desk in her adjoining office, she looked up and smiled as Siobhan walked by. In her office, Siobhan took the USB sticks out of her computer and placed them in her bag, ensuring she had everything she could possibly need with her on this trip.

"Louise"—Siobhan poked her head into her assistant's office— "please monitor the reports of the fallout cloud. Get communications to send me an update if it looks like it's heading our way."

The most recent communiqué from the US Government's sources mid country, reported it was possible that the cloud would only travel as far north as Italy. It was smaller than previous ones. They were comparing it to the cloud of radiation emitted from the Chernobyl reactor mishap of the 1980s. Britain had survived that, hadn't it?

"Yes, Ms Kensington-Wallace." Louise looked up and smiled again, her dimples puckering. "You go. I'll be fine. You've taught me everything you know, Siobhan. Time to trust me."

Her eyes opened wide, then she giggled, the gesture easing the tension in Siobhan's shoulders.

Yes, Louise would be fine.

Siobhan had been preparing her for years in all things nuclear. Louise was her designated replacement. Everyone had one. It was protocol. Every position in the bunker—political, security and defence, Brains Trust, quartermaster, anything—had the appropriate and highly qualified personnel ready to instantly take over the role.

"Ms Kensington-Wallace, the First Minister is waiting for you." The secretary stood at the door to Siobhan's office.

Siobhan took the long way around to the First Minister's office via the garages. Men loaded equipment into the armoured vehicles, as well as radiation suits, Geiger Counters, computers, food, ammunition, and tents. A soldier secured a 30 mm automatic chain cannon to the back of a jeep, and a tank was getting a last-minute overhaul.

Tanks! What did Antony think we would be up against?

That was enough! She strode the rest of the way to the First Minister's office then knocked on the door, smoothing her shirt and army camouflage patterned cargo pants with her other hand. Antony opened the door and Siobhan walked into the room.

The First Minister of Scotland sat behind her desk wearing a military suit, her dark hair shone in the LED lighting. Bethany Watts was similar age to Siobhan and also a child of the Brains Trust, and the first of the *elite generation* to be elected to the office.

Scotland had recently voted for a new First Minister. Well, not all of Scotland, Siobhan reminded herself. Only those originally called to, and living in, the Government Bunker underneath Arthur's Seat in Edinburgh. The rest of the United Kingdom and Scotland were on a level playing field financially since The Stock Market Crash. England's financial backup had ceased to exist, and Scotland could disallow access to her invaluable resources of North Sea oil and abundant fresh water. Not to mention the many wind power sources dotted throughout the Scottish countryside. Not long after going underground, the people of the Scottish Government

Bunker had decided devolution was the appropriate line to take, and a totally Independent Scottish Parliament began its rule.

It's all I've ever known.

Standing before the new First Minister, Siobhan pressed her lips together to stifle a laugh. It was still so incredulous that Antony had encouraged Siobhan to put *herself* up for election. She had no wish to govern and was more interested in practical concerns, such as keeping the nuclear reactors ticking away safely and all warheads dormant.

Antony had pushed her to it out of his own ambition. *He* was the one who wanted the office, as many did. In fact, the desire for position motivated most of the machinations of the *elite generation*.

It was quite tiresome at times. And one had to watch one's step in case someone else's foot was inadvertently underneath it. It would be nice to have a break from it. Siobhan glanced at Antony standing beside her in his camouflage Defence Force uniform. His mouth twitched.

Antony was manoeuvring now. She was convinced his main motivation for volunteering to go on this mission was to earn *Brownie points,* as they say.

"I know you understand the gravity of this situation, Miss Kensington-Wallace. The Government appreciates the bravery involved in co-leading this mission." Bethany Watts pursed her lips and looked at both of them in turn. "We haven't had direct contact with the outside world for many years. We hope and pray you will have a safe journey and the people of the Invercharing Community are friendly."

"We have prepared for any reception, First Minister," Antony replied.

Siobhan turned her head to give her opinion, but stopped herself, her hands trembled as she clasped them in front of her.

"Do you wish to say something, Siobhan?" The First Minister's focus was now on her.

Did she? She sure did. And this time, she actually would.

"First Minister, I have just checked the preparations for our expedition, and I think we go a little heavy-handed."

To say the least!

"Oh, why is that?" The First Minister tilted her head.

Beside Siobhan, Antony stiffened.

"Do we really need tanks?" she asked. "These people who live in communities don't seem to be aggressive and they don't have any heavy weaponry."

Antony answered for the First Minister. "We must prepare ourselves, Siobhan. We don't fully know what we're up against. We will deal with the very strong possibility of a nuclear weapon. What if there are other hostiles out there?" Antony's shoulders made their slight shuffle they always did when he was on the defence.

"Yes, but the people of the Invercharing Community may think we are coming to attack, not ask for assistance." Siobhan took a deep breath. "And what do you mean by *other hostiles*? People who live in community are only interested in survival, not mutiny."

"You don't know that, Siobhan," Antony said. "They have lived out there for years with their own form of governance. They are reluctant to comply with anyone's wishes but their own." Antony's voice filled the small office. Lowering it, he continued. "They are like the hippy communes of the sixties and seventies of the last century, but with *armies*." He turned back to the First Minister. "They could even have plans to resist the Government's influence. They're rebels, and this community would be the worst. It's run by the son of Caitlin Murray-Campbell!"

Siobhan's pulse raced. Antony was painting an inaccurate picture of the community lifestyle. The First Minister's eyes had widened further with each of his outlandish and unfounded statements.

"First Minister"—with her pulse thudding in her temples, Siobhan interrupted before Antony could do any more damage— "I'm sure we'll find a truer picture once we have actually met the people who live there. This is a chance to work with them and see what they are like. What their wishes are regarding government."

"*You are sure*," Antony's eyebrows raised, coinciding with his pitch. "Siobhan, just because you have watched the drones for years doesn't mean you know what goes on in those peoples' minds."

"And *you* do?" she asked.

That silenced him.

"Let's focus on the mission to make safe this nuclear problem," Bethany said, regaining control of the conversation. "It can be a fact-finding mission regarding community life."

Bethany stared directly at Siobhan, then her gaze turned to Antony.

"Get a feel for these people, but please do not use any force or be aggressive in any way, Major McLellan."

"Yes, ma'am," he said.

"So, the tanks?" Siobhan asked.

The First Minister pressed her lips together and looked from Siobhan to Antony. "Just take one."

***

Back in her room, Siobhan finished her packing, sat on her bed, and sighed. Directly opposite on her dressing table sat the photo of her father with her as a child.

Daddy, I'm going up top.

Her heart fluttered again.

Siobhan recalled the day they came here to the Government Bunker. She was so young at the time, but every detail was etched in her memory. Daddy had been tense, and they had packed in haste after the phone call, then left Oxford at once. That whole day had been strange. The two men from the previous evening, who Daddy had thrown out, had returned, but he had let them in and called them friends.

He had told her to never forget them. Good old Daddy.

"Well, I haven't," she said to the photo.

Especially not the older brother with the dark-red hair tied up in a bun. He was so nice to her, and his Scottish accent had reminded her of Mummy. He'd smelled of wild things. The scents she'd recalled from a holiday in the Highlands—when people used to holiday.

She was going back there now, to the Highlands. There would be danger to get through on the way, but this community seemed particularly friendly. Except for the young man who shot the drone. He looked a little like the man she had to remember. Were they related?

Maybe all Highlanders are related.

"Ms Kensington-Wallace?" the soldier at her door interrupted her thoughts. "It's time."

Chapter Eleven

Back to the Future

Rory and Murray caught the 8.01 p.m. train to Edinburgh. This would take them twelve hours and six minutes. *Not* the high-speed train.

They'd got a two-seater facing two once more, and slept on the train with Rory's legs stretched out underneath Murray's. In front of Rory, the rising sun's beams lit the side of Murray's face as the countryside flashed past the window. Murray's head drooped, and drool trickled down his chin from the corner of his mouth. Rory had been awake for a while, mulling over many things. They would get the car, get the suits, avoid the riots—hopefully, then make their way back to Invercharing. And wait for a shimmer.

Well, it's what he'd done last time.

They'd gone over and over their plan on the way to Oxford railway station. Rory had more questions to ask Murray, but there were people around and the air was getting a tense edge to it with all that was happening with the fallout from The Crash. Now, in the almost empty train carriage, Rory had his chance to ask something that had niggled at him for most of the night.

Rory kicked Murray's foot. Murray snorted but didn't wake. He kicked again. Murray jumped with a start, unfolded his arms, and grabbed the backpack sitting on his lap. Murray's eyes were bloodshot, and he wiped the saliva away from his chin.

"What?" Murray's voice was hoarse.

"Tell me," Rory said. "What's the *badger-set* all about."

Murray shrugged.

"Come on, I know you ken." Rory tilted his head.

Murray laid his head back on the headrest and closed his eyes.

"Psst!" Rory kicked again. "You're awake enough to tell me. So, tell me."
Murray's eyes opened, but his mouth was a thin line.

"I shouldn't say," he said after a pause.

"Come on. After you tell me, you can kill me." *Like that'll be possible,* Rory smiled at the thought. "It's secret code for something, isn't it?" Rory asked.

"I don't know. I'm only guessing." Murray raised his shoulders.

"What are you guessing?" Rory whispered. "Give me your theory."

The train continued its gentle rocking and Rory continued his stare at his brother.

"Oh, okay," Murray said. "Not sure mind, but I *think* it was the government."

Rory nodded, encouraging him to continue. *Boy, it's like drawing teeth.*

"So, they have, like, a list of people they want to save if it's TEOTW," Murray finally added.

Rory wracked his brains for the possible words that went with the initials.

Oh, the end of the world. "Got it," he said.

"At last!" Murray shook his head. "Well, there is a high probability *the professor* would be on it."

"So, when the Gov... *they* went underground..." Rory said. "He's been there all that time?"

"He may have passed away by then," Murry said. "By now. Oh, you know what I mean. He's middle-aged now, and that's forty years ago."

Rory sat back in his seat. "Which Government?"

"Huh?" Murray grunted.

"UK," Rory asked. "Or did England and Scotland do their separate thing back then?"

"Well, he's English," Murray said.

"But his major work was in Edinburgh, was it no'?" Rory reminded him. "And his wife was Scots, and so would be his wee lassie."

Murray shrugged. Rory, dissatisfied with the lack of information, opened the handmade manual on driving submarines and began to read.

***

The train pulled into Waverly station as Rory nudged Murray awake. They stepped off the train and walked to the multi-story carpark. Once in the car, Rory checked under his seat. His weapons were still there. He started the engine and drove as Murray navigated them out of Edinburgh through early morning traffic. The journey to Torness Power Station took forty-five minutes through the Lothian countryside. Hedgerows edged the road and flat fields lay either side of them, skirted to their left by a rolling coastline. Farmers busy bringing in their harvests blocked the road occasionally with mobile farm equipment, so different from the horse-drawn methods they used in the Community.

Once at the power station's office, they parked the car, got out and walked in through the glass doors, passing the security guard on their way to the desk.

"Oh, hello. I have something for you." The young woman at the reception, wearing a blouse buttoned up except for the top two, leaned under the desk and brought out two large plastic bags and passed them over to Rory. "My boss told me to give you these."

"Thank you, miss," Rory said to the receptionist, then lifted his eyebrows at the security guard while he and Murray walked out of the building.

"These won't fit in our backpacks, but we can shove them in the pods with us. It will be tight. We'll hug them," Rory said as he rummaged in the bag he held.

"I think I've got yours." Murray held the bag open in front of him.

"They're both the same size. What makes you say that?" he asked.

"I'm sure the odds are against *Sarah's* phone number being meant for me."

***

The drive back to Invercharing was long and slow. The traffic travelling the other way was even heavier than on their journey down—car after car, and bus after bus.

"Must be the tourists heading home after sniffing trouble," Rory commented.

When they arrived at Invercharing, the farmer was driving his tractor in his fields, bringing in hay as if there was nothing wrong in the world. They snuck past him and waited for the shimmering, which would indicate the activation of the Time Machine.

It didn't take long.

"You go first, I'll keep watch." Rory helped Murray into his pod with the bulky suit, and the book on how to drive a submarine tucked into his jacket, as there was no room for the backpack. "Leave it here."

"It's full of cash!"

"Does nae matter," Rory replied. "The farmer will need it."

Once Murray disappeared, Rory prepared. He had even less room in the pod than Murray, and he tossed the other backpack against the wall beside Murray's.

The world went blurry, and then it went blank.

He stands at the Community's gate, his submachine gun in his hand. Ready.

The waves of headiness from his return from the past still echo within him. The dogs' barks are frantic.

Large solid-looking vehicles approach—army camouflage coloured. Five of them head straight for the Compound's gates.

A tank follows.

Each vehicle bears the Scottish Saltire—bright blue with a white diagonal cross.

The flags flap in the wind as the heavily armoured vehicles approach. He stands with legs apart and braces himself for what is to come.

"Rory?" Christine's voice accompanied the shaking of his shoulder. "He's coming around."

Rory opened his eyes. He lay on a trolley in the medical centre. A churning feeling bubbled in his mid-section. George, Murray, and his Aunt Bec were there, all wearing frowns.

"You okay, Rory?" Murray's face came into view, his forehead a crease of furrows. "He's been spacing-out while we were there, too."

"I'm okay." Rory's voice sounded firm to his ears, belying the shaking in his gut. Those around him stood back and their expressions relaxed a fraction. "What happened?" He pushed the nausea away with a deep breath.

"You were unconscious when you came through." Christine tightened the BP cuff around his arm. "All normal." The ripping sound of the cuff coming undone accompanied the release of pressure on his arm.

"Okay. I'm normal. The doctor says so. You can all go now. Thank you."
Rory raised his eyebrows and Murray left. "Really Christine, thank you."

Rory watched Christine and George exit the room. Only Aunty Bec remained. He'd grown up in the medical care of this *courtesy* aunt, an old family friend. But more importantly to him at this moment, she knew him, and she was a truly honest woman.

"Please, don't go," he whispered.

Aunty Bec stopped mid-stride and returned to him. She took his hand in hers; arthritis deformed her aged hands. Her deep-brown eyes searched his. The rims of her pupils were a circle of white, while her mostly grey hair stood wildly around her face. Aunty Bec was the only one he could talk to now.

She glanced at the door as it closed.

"What's wrong, son?" she asked.

Rory took in a deep, shaky breath. Should he tell her?

Should I tell anyone?

She'd take it the best.

"I think I'm going mad," he said.

"No, Rory." Aunty Bec's smile was gentle as she shook her head. Her fingers were cool on his hand, but her stare pierced his soul. "You're the sanest man I know. And the bravest. So like your father." She let out a sigh. "You're the only one game enough to travel through the unknown—twice."

His heart warmed at the compliment and the obvious love behind it.

"I keep seeing things," he said.

"You think they are hallucinations?" she asked.

"Aunty, they are *so* real, it's like I'm there, doing it."

Rory's mind briefly returned to his dream the other night. The dream that wasn't a dream. He swallowed.

"I... it's like I'm reliving things from the past." He looked at his hand, covered now by both of hers. "Like Dad's death." He swallowed. "Even things from my childhood. Like how I felt them when I was a child. I saw Dad young. He was great... I miss him!" Rory's shoulders shook, and his throat tightened.

No, he wasn't going to cry. He took in a steadying breath.

"I see things that haven't happened, but maybe they will," he said.

"You mean visions?" Aunty Bec tilted her head, her eyes still locked onto his face, searching. She opened her mouth to speak, but then paused.

Go on, say it. Please tell me I'm not mad. Or get it over and done with, and tell me I am.

"Rory, you've gone back in time and returned to the present—twice. As far as we know, no one else has ever done it."

Rory blinked.

"Who knows what effect it's had on you," she said.

"Madness!"

"No, son." Aunty Bec hesitated once more. "I'm not speaking as a doctor or a scientist now. I'm speaking with my intuition." She gave a gentle nod. "It's possible your journey through time has given you the ability to *see* time. The past... and even the future. Time, perhaps, has become fractured for you, in a sense."

He had no thoughts at first... just blank. Then...

"Nothing I have seen that wasn't the past, has come true." A thought hit him like a shock wave. "But what if it does?"

He jumped off the trolley and released his hands from her grip.

"Rory, where are you going?" she called.

"I need to speak to George. We're about to be attacked."

Chapter Twelve

Invercharing Community

Rory stood at the gate. He'd hastily put on his SAPI vest and held his light machine gun in front of him. Behind him stood his crew. George had mobilised the other Militia who were placing themselves strategically around the compound and at certain shielded points outside it.

If he was right about his vision, it could only be the Government coming with such heavily armoured vehicles. There were men with private armies, but none so well equipped around here, and *none* with tanks. And if it was the Government, and they discovered the existence of the Time Machine, it would be the *last* the Invercharing Community ever saw of it.

"George!" he called over the one man he could trust with this issue.

"Yes?" George held a submachine gun.

"I need you to round up the Chief Council," he whispered hoarsely into George's ear. "And my family. Order them to no' say a word about the Time Machine, on pain of death if you have to!"

George blinked. "Okay, Rory. Consider it done."

He disappeared into the main building.

Rory hated taking a good soldier from the front but, as the Time Machine was secret knowledge, he could only use a man privy to it to do the job. He hated giving George, his senior, an order.

Rory and the Militia stared at their valley and the empty road in front of them. The quiet high mountains were sentinels beside them. A damp sweat built up on Rory's forehead as his heart gradually increased its rate.

I'm being stupid.

The dogs tied at the gate stood with ears pricked, then barked their early warning, and a cry from the tower beside the gate chased away any feelings of stupidity.

"There's five armoured vehicles and a tank, Mr Campbell," the watchman on the tower shouted down to him.

Rory gripped his submachine gun to his thudding chest. His faithful crew surrounded him—armed and ready.

"Nobody fires anything without my signal. Got it?" he yelled so all could hear then waited until all had answered.

Rory faced the vehicles approaching along the rough road toward the Community Compound. The Saltire fluttered from each one.

Rory tightened his jaw and his grip on his machine gun.

Stay calm, Rory. Determine their intent before you aim at anything. Your people are watching for your cue.

He let out a breath. The vehicles slowed and made their way to the gate; the heavy machine gun on the back of the jeep was unmanned. The tank stayed back.

The door of the lead vehicle opened, and Rory stood taller as a woman emerged. A man's voice from inside the vehicle spoke loudly to her, the words a mumble to Rory's ears.

She turned back in and said clearly, "I'll explain."

The door closed, and a tall, slim woman dressed in trousers with honey-blonde hair pulled back tight, approached the gate. She was unarmed. As she got closer, her features became clearer—deep-blue eyes and a fair complexion. Rory's heart seemed to skip a beat.

She walked to the gate and stopped.

"Hello. My name is Siobhan Kensington-Wallace, and we are from the Scottish Government. We need your assistance." She smiled.

Rory remained silent, battling with his breathing, and trying to settle it and his pulse at the same time.

The woman was beautiful, spoke with a very well-educated English accent with just a hint of Scots, and, he guessed, she was in her forties.

Och, no. It could nae be. But it is.

"Hello," he said, trying to sound steady. "I'm Ruairidh Campbell. Second-in-command of the Invercharing Community's Militia." In a subconscious way, he registered that he'd said his name in the Gaelic. "What can I do for you?"

If only he could say, *do you remember me?* But it would involve explaining the Time Machine and revealing its existence to the government. That wasn't going to happen.

Not by him.

"May we come inside?" Siobhan asked. "We have a mutual problem, I think."

Rory nodded, and his feet began to move again. He signalled to the men at the gate to open it.

So, the Government was here to help, not attack? Well, they'll help, if they must, but he would make sure it was on the Community's terms.

When the gate opened, he stepped through to her.

Up close she was even more beautiful—*if that was at all possible.*

"You must promise me you won't use those weapons on us." He looked at her face.

Aye, sapphire-blue eyes.

"And you, Mr Campbell, must promise the same." The gruff order came from the man who now exited the vehicle. "Call off your soldiers."

He wore army camouflage and looked military. He strode toward Rory with brown eyes that bored into his. Hate lived behind them. The centre of Rory's chest constricted. His arms tensed.

"We'll not use ours if you do the same." Rory clenched his jaw, his cheek muscles tightened.

So, he had promised. This man had better do the same *and* keep his word.

Siobhan turned to the military man.

"Mr Campbell has kindly obliged. Now return the gesture, Antony," she ordered the man.

Antony gestured, and the Government soldiers visibly relaxed. Especially the soldier who had made his way to the back of the jeep housing the heavy machine gun.

The military man's glare remained on Rory.

Siobhan's gaze flicked to him. "Introduce yourself, Antony."

"I am Major Antony McLellan of the Scottish Defence Force." McLellan gave a slight nod.

"Rory Campbell." Rory was curt, but he was beginning to not like this man already. "What do you want?" he asked.

"May we come inside and talk?" Siobhan picked up the conversation. "We both have a problem. Well, Scotland has a problem, and we need your—"

"A faulty nuclear warhead on a North Korean sub leaking radiation into Loch Ewe," Rory said, enjoying the shocked look on Major McLellan's face and the expression of admiration on Siobhan's.

"Well, then." Siobhan glanced at McLellan. "Let's pool our knowledge and resources and see how we can fix this." She smiled at Rory.

He stood aside and indicated they were to enter the compound through the small side gate.

"What about our equipment?" McLellan demanded.

Rory glared briefly at him, then shouted to the guard, "Open up, please."

The guards drew aside the two large wrought-iron gates, and the vehicles drove in, the doors of the heavily armoured vehicles opened, and Government men and women piled out.

"Where shall we set up our equipment?" McLellan stared at Rory. "Do you have electricity? Our computers need power."

Siobhan turned to McLellan, a duffle bag in her hand. "The windmills aren't for decoration, Antony."

Rory looked closer at Siobhan. She had well and truly grown. She was smug and bossy and a wee bit arrogant.

What happened to the sweet wee lass?

"We'll make space to set you up in the main hall." Rory turned and bumped into Murray.

"Did you say computers?" Murray brushed past him and went to the men unloading equipment from the vehicles.

Murray watched as they brought box after box out of the vehicles, then trailed behind the men carrying them into the hall.

Rory followed into the hall, which the government people were making into a control centre. The men dragged tables and chairs, positioning them as they wished. Murray's mouth gaped as they brought out laptops and opened them. Rory's mouth curved; his brother was now in his element.

"It's done. They've all promised," George whispered into Rory's ear from behind him. Rory gave an imperceptible nod, avoiding attracting their guests' attention.

One of the Government's technicians beckoned Murray. He was a young man with black hair, brown eyes, and medium-brown skin. He showed Murray the computer and began explaining things to him, often with a surprised expression as Murray rapidly understood and revealed his own knowledge. Maybe it would make up for Murray having to leave the university behind.

Rory sensed someone beside him once more.

"Mr Campbell. We are ready to meet with your leaders and discuss our plan of action." Siobhan stood beside him, hands on hips, her manner authoritative, like she was used to giving orders.

"Verra well, I will summon the Chief Council." He strode away. He wasn't into being bossed around.

At the door to the main hall, Rory spoke to Xian. "Please get all the members of the Chief Council to come here. Miss hyphen-hyphen wants to speak to them." He flicked his chin in Siobhan's direction.

The corner of Xian's mouth tweaked, he raised an eyebrow, and left without a word.

Rory turned back to survey the proceedings.

Within ten minutes Angela entered the main hall, which was now full of Government personnel in military uniform. Technicians sat at tables with computers set up. Others had opened metal trunks and pulled out paperwork. On a larger table, a technical assistant opened an Ordnance Survey map and placed a silver compass on it.

Angela would be happy to see the Government. Anything to do with bureaucracy and politics got her going. She was the youngest member of the Community's Chief Council, and she revelled in it. She'd been ambitious from the outset.

Rory blew air out between his teeth. He would have to keep an eye on her.

Angela's gaze ran over the Government personnel and every piece of equipment they'd brought. The rest of the Chief Council entered the makeshift control centre and introduced themselves to Major McLellan and Siobhan. Angela's hand shook McLellan's for a prolonged period; she gazed at him until she blinked and let go.

Take it easy, sister. No need to look so eager.

"Would you all like to come around this table where we have spread out the map?" Siobhan asked the members of the Chief Council.

They obediently arranged themselves around the table. Rory stood at the end of the oblong table and looked across at Siobhan and McLellan. McLellan shuffled next to George and darted glances at the members of the Chief Council who stood near him. He bristled when Dr Farquhar accidentally brushed his shoulder as he moved to take a place next to George.

Siobhan looked around, ensuring they had everyone's attention, and glanced Rory's way.

"Thank you for your welcome. I know we can work together on this. It's of vital importance to the safety of Scotland." She paused, like she was steeling herself for what she had to say. "We are well aware you know this part of our country better than any of us, and we would like some of your people to accompany us as we journey north to deal with this nuclear threat."

Siobhan scanned the group and she seemed to be gauging people's reactions. She then opened her mouth to speak but McLellan interrupted her.

"How do you know it's a leaking nuclear warhead?" McLellan directed his question and his stare to Rory.

"Yes, I was getting to that question." Siobhan looked daggers at McLellan.

"We've been there." Rory pressed his lips around a smirk that threatened at the corners of his mouth.

Every one of the Government personnel looked at him.

"What do you think we do?" Rory said. "We don't sit in our underground bunkers keeping ourselves safe while the world goes to hell around us." Rory couldn't keep the edge off his voice. "We *know* what's going on and we do something about it, even with our limited resources."

After watching years of the Government's inaction, even wondering if the Government was a myth, he now found it hard to quell the feelings of betrayal. He took a breath.

Count to ten, Rory. Don't let your red-haired temper show.

An uncomfortable silence descended around the table. Someone coughed.

"Well, we are here now, and we will help," Siobhan said, sending a placating look in Rory's direction. "We have the resources, we need your knowledge of the Highlands and, now it seems, your intimate knowledge of this submarine and its warheads."

"How *do* you know about it?" McLellan's question was almost accusing. Siobhan glared at McLellan then looked back at Rory.

"You've not been in it, have you? Not unprotected?" Genuine concern tinged Siobhan's voice.

"We may be isolated Highlanders, but we aren't ignorant," Rory said. "No, we haven't been in it without Personal Protective Equipment. We've been near and assessed it." Rory concentrated hard on sounding amicable and informed, not the *angry* he wanted to *yell* at them.

"May I ask you, Mr Campbell, how did you hear about it and what makes you sure it's a non-nuclear submarine." Siobhan's deep-blue eyes fixed on his.

"A mariner at Loch Ewe alerted us to its presence," Rory replied. "He says the sub isn't nuclear powered."

"A mariner?" McLellan's question barely hid his derision.

"A fisherman," Rory clarified.

"What!" McLellan again.

"He knows his stuff. I trust him." Rory spoke through gritted teeth and mentally recommenced his count to ten.

"We're very willing to help you." George entered the conversation.

Rory relaxed his clenched jaw. "Yes. What were your plans?" Rory directed his question at Siobhan, determined to ignore any noises coming from McLellan.

"We are going there to assess and—" McLellan had opened his mouth again.

"How?" Rory ignored his previous determination to ignore McLellan.

His gaze remained on Siobhan, who hadn't got the chance to answer his question.

"We'll drive our vehicles and equipment to Loch Ewe accompanied by yourselves," McLellan answered.

McLellan *was* as stupid as he looked.

Rory's laugh was soft at first. He shook his head. George pressed his lips together attempting to suppress a grin, and Rory's crew standing behind him shuffled their feet and stifled laughs.

"You'll not go in your vehicles unless you *want* to be attacked," Rory said with a tilt to his head.

Siobhan's gaze flicked to McLellan then back to Rory. "What do you suggest, Mr Campbell?"

"I ken they're armoured vehicles, but truly, it's no' a good idea announcing your presence to the world," Rory said. "Everybody's going tae want to find oot what's going on, the Government bein' rare and all. Armoured vehicles will no' make any difference when it comes to determined bandits.

Also, forty years of weather and nae road maintenance doesn't make for a smooth ride. How much petrol do you actually have? It's a wonder ye have nae had trouble getting here."

Siobhan looked at the map on the table and McLellan shifted on his feet. Rory's eyebrows lifted.

"People did notice us, but we avoided any confrontation." Siobhan raised her head once more.

"People haven't followed you here, have they?" Angela's officious tones rang across the table.

Good question, sister. Never thought of the fact they may endanger us, did they?

"We have outrun any pursuers," McLellan spoke again.

"You had *pursuers*?" Rory straightened and crooked a finger at one of the Militia who immediately stepped toward him.

"We outran them, Mr Campbell." Siobhan sounded defensive.

"Aye well, we'll see about that." Rory gave the Militia member orders to send out scouts to their perimeters to check. The man left without a word. "We need to do this together, but you will do it on *our* terms. You're in our world now." Rory stood taller and took in a calming breath. "You will load the essential gear you require on our horses and determine who is vital personnel. We will all ride together to Loch Ewe and sort this. Minimal numbers on your part. Useful numbers on ours. You'll need our protection. Forget about your vehicles, they won't make it the way we need to go."

Rory glanced in McLellan's direction. McLellan had opened his mouth but shut it again.

"Decide what you're taking," Rory said. "It's too late to set out now. We leave at first light tomorrow."

"Very well then, Mr Campbell," Siobhan said, then placed a firm, restraining hand on McLellan's arm.

***

The cooks brought in an evening meal of lamb stew and vegetables, which those in the meeting hall ate while standing due to computers and maps covering the tables. Rory took a mouthful of the stew, enjoying the tender lamb. They wouldn't eat this well while on this mission.

He sensed someone beside him. A hand tapped his right shoulder and he turned to find Angus' green eyes peering into his.

"I think the Community needs to send a scientific representative and I'm volunteering." Angus bit his lip, and a slight crease ran vertically between his black eyebrows.

Rory spooned another mouthful of the lamb stew and looked at Angus. It was probably a good idea. And it would be an excuse to deny Murray the privilege. He picked meat from in between his teeth with his tongue and slowly nodded.

"Granted," he said.

"Thanks." Angus' eyebrows shot up as a smile emerged.

"But I have some reading for you," Rory added. "A *how-to-drive-a-sub* manual."

"Certainly. Where is it? I'll start now." Angus looked eager.

"Did I hear right? Angus is going?" Murray was directly behind Angus. "What about me?"

"They will nae be taking the computers, so they'll be here. You don't want to miss the computers, do you?" Rory asked.

"They'll be taking one," Angus said. "They need one to set the timer on the nuke."

"You're stayin' here." Rory bore his stare into Murray. "And give Angus the wee book you made, okay?"

"Okay." Murray stepped over to the nearest computer and started conversing with the man sitting there.

"Where are the important people sleeping tonight?" Kendra spoke into Rory's left ear.

He took another mouthful of stew, chewed and swallowed, determined to finish his meal. He hadn't considered accommodations.

"I guess Her Royal Highness and Major Importance can sleep in the spare rooms in my place," Rory said. "I'll need to—"

"Make the beds. Done." Kendra's left cheek dimpled.

How does she do it?

"So, who of us is going?" She pursed her lips and tilted her head.

He knew that look.

"I don't want anybody who has someone to—"

"I'm going, Rory Campbell," Kendra interrupted. "Christine is okay with it. She knows you need me." Her voice was low and her words steady. There'd be no dissuading her.

Rory shook his head in resignation and spooned in another mouthful.

"So, George, Xian, me, Brendan?" she asked.

Rory swallowed his mouthful. "Not George. He'll stay here in case of trouble. The Tsar and Tsarina may have brought the revolution to our gates. Have we heard from the scouts yet?"

Kendra's cheek dimpled once more.

"What?" he asked.

Kendra leaned in close "I saw the way you looked at her," she whispered. "Can't hide it from me."

"Who?" He blinked. "No." He shook his head.

Kendra's dimpled smile accompanied a slight nod.

"You can show them to the rooms when you're ready." Rory put the final spoonful of stew in his mouth, finishing the conversation.

Chapter Thirteen

A young woman with a long black plait approached Siobhan.

"Ms Kensington-Wallace, I have your rooms ready when you are."

Siobhan placed her empty bowl on the table beside her. The young woman was friendly enough, if not a little fierce looking. She wore soft leather trousers, and a finely woven wool shirt. She had a long knife hanging from the belt around her waist, a tactical knife army personnel would use. A quiver of arrows hung beside it and a bow was over her shoulder. Tattoos of a Celtic design, if Siobhan wasn't mistaken, covered her arm.

"You and Major McLellan will be staying in Rory's accommodation tonight. Please follow me." The young woman pivoted and strode toward the door.

Siobhan picked up her duffle bag and followed.

"Umm... Antony. This young lady is taking me to our rooms," Siobhan said as she passed Antony.

"I'll follow later." Antony barely glanced up from the map he studied with the older man named George.

He was the same military type as Antony. At least they had found something, or should she say, someone, in common. Their reception hadn't been as friendly as she'd hoped but going in with a tank wouldn't cause their hosts to receive them with open arms!

Siobhan walked behind the young woman who had a straight back and tanned, muscled arms. Hmm. She must spend a lot of time outdoors. She seemed to be close to the young man, Mr Campbell, whose name was Rory. The same name as the man her father made her promise to remember. This Rory could be related to him—a son or grandson.

The corridor from the hall led to a house, which had three bedrooms to the right as Siobhan entered, and a bathroom followed by a kitchen on the left. The walls were dirty, the couch in the living room had permanent dents where people had sat and was devoid of scatter cushions. A pile of old books sat beside the arm of the couch and others were strewn on the coffee table and the floor in front of it. The whole place required a fresh coat of paint and perhaps a new floor covering. Siobhan sensed it hadn't had a woman's touch for many years. Freshly washed dishes drained in the sink.

"May I have a shower before I retire?" she asked.

"I can't see why not." The woman pointed to the first bedroom. "You can have that one, Ms Kensington-Wallace."

"Oh, please call me Siobhan." She placed her duffle bag on the bed next to the towels.

"I'm Kendra," the woman said. "I'm a member of Rory's crew and I'll be coming with you tomorrow. Goodnight." Her plait swung out behind her as she turned and walked through the door.

"Goodnight," Siobhan said to the closing door.

Siobhan shrugged, then got her things out of her duffle bag and headed for the bathroom where there was a shower cubicle with loose tiles and missing grout.

What a day it had been. More like it, and worse, were on their way. Siobhan needed a shower to start fresh and clean before their journey north on horses and camping.

She stripped, stepped into the cubicle and turned on both taps, adjusting the temperature. The water was warm and soothing as it ran down her back. Siobhan glanced down at herself as she washed, satisfied that years of going to the Bunker's gymnasium had paid off. She didn't appear a weakling when compared to the Militia woman, Kendra.

Siobhan tingled with excitement, and there was a chill in her spine at the same time. They would be outside in the mountains. She grinned while washing her hair.

Sunshine, blue water, green hills.

Wait. *Maybe* not sunshine. The sun didn't always shine in Scotland.

Most of her trips *up top* were not sunny walks around the small compound surrounded by high concrete walls. She'd have to stop herself from making things seem better than they actually were.

She was on a mission to make safe an unstable nuke, of all things. If it *was* the real problem. Mr Campbell, Rory, believed the fisherman. It's all they had to go on. Siobhan had prepared for anything and detonators with timers were among the things she'd brought.

She stepped out of the shower. "What every girl should pack, huh?" she said to the steamed-up mirror.

Siobhan dried herself and then rummaged in her toilet bag.

"Perfume? Why not?"

She gave herself a *scoosh* of scent. She'd be camping for the next who-knows-how-long? There would be no chance to wash. She'd have to cover up her unwashed-body smell with *something*. She wondered briefly if the women in the Community had perfume. Kendra certainly didn't wear any.

Siobhan put on her pyjamas and dressing gown then walked to the bedroom as the front door opened and banged closed. She placed her toiletries on her bed and waited to hear who it was. There was a sniff and then a deep voice groaned.

"Och, no," a male voice said.

"Um, hello is that you, Mr Campbell?" She pulled her silk dressing gown around her and tied it tight, then stepped out of the bedroom alerting her host to her presence and intending to tell him Antony was on his way.

Rory Campbell stood outside the bathroom door leaning against the wall with his head resting on his arm. He'd removed his armour-plated vest and now his tight T-shirt moulded around the very firm musculature of his torso. Tattoos of a similar design to Kendra's covered the exposed section of his right arm. Tight jeans surrounded muscled thighs. A large knife and a handgun in a holster hung from his belt. He turned. His eyes were open wide, and his pale face was surrounded by curls of russet-ginger hair, and a few days' growth stubbled his chin. He took his arm away from the wall and stood taller, his chest rose and fell as he blinked a few times.

His throat worked like he was swallowing. "Ms Kensington-Wallace," he said.

"Please, call me Siobhan. Um, Antony will be here soon. Thank you for a nice place to sleep tonight. I guess we won't have a bed for the next few days."

Why did she feel so uncomfortable? The man didn't stop staring at her. He'd regained his composure and didn't look so pale anymore, but his gaze was becoming disconcerting.

Siobhan cast her eyes around the room to be anywhere but under his stare.

"Is this your mother?" She picked up the only photograph in the room. It was in a tarnished silver frame and covered in dust.

"Aye." His voice was hoarse. He coughed to clear it.

"She's beautiful," she said. "Do you have any photos of your father?"

He shook his head.

"I've heard you are the spitting image of him."

He didn't reply.

He had a lot to say at the meeting. Why was this man suddenly mute?

"Was his name Rory, also?" she asked.

"No. He was Scott Campbell." Rory Campbell stood straighter, his voice now clearer.

"Oh. Did he ever go to Oxford?" she asked. "Before the Stock Market Crash?"

"Not as far as I ken." This Mr Campbell blinked a few times.

"What was your grandfather's name?" she asked.

A knock at the door finally took his gaze off her. Mr Campbell opened the door and Antony stood in the doorway.

"Oh, I've found the right place," Antony said gruffly and brushed past Mr Campbell, who barely moved out of his way.

Mr Campbell's lips became a thin line and his eyes narrowed.

So, he either didn't trust Antony, or he didn't like him. Siobhan would need to find out. They *had* to get along for this to work.

"I'll be wishing you both goodnight," Mr Campbell said, his tone gruff. "We leave at dawn, and at this time of year, that's four am. Be ready." He went into his bedroom and shut the door behind him.

Antony stared at the closed door.

"Something's bothering the boy," he whispered, then glanced around the room. An expression of disgust crossed his face as he noted its simple furnishings, posters from calendars stuck to the walls and bland floor coverings.

"Goodnight, Antony. Early morning apparently." Siobhan shut the door behind her. She wasn't in the mood for his belittling everything about the place.

***

Gruff male voices on the other side of the door awakened Siobhan. Mr Campbell was not to be seen as she left her bedroom. Antony was sitting on the old couch.

"The boy says he'll be waiting for us in that excuse for a hall and they'll serve some sort of breakfast there as well," Antony said.

"Antony, do be a bit more charitable." Siobhan grabbed her toiletries and headed for the bathroom.

"He thinks he's king around here," Antony replied.

"Well, maybe he *is*." Siobhan shut the door behind her.

After she finished in the bathroom, she walked back to her room and shoved her toiletries into her duffle bag and then headed out the door.

"He strikes me as a 'My way or the highway' kind of guy." Antony followed her.

Siobhan didn't answer, only rolled her eyes.

"George, now he's a great guy, well he says Rory is his father-all-over." Antony commented behind her.

They entered the hall where three of the Community's women served a breakfast of porridge and scrambled eggs. The aroma of freshly baked bread greeted her nostrils and her stomach grumbled.

Mr Campbell was in deep discussion with another man who looked identical to him. *Twins?* Mr Campbell tied back his long hair, but his brother wore his cropped short. Both were armed. Mr Campbell had a rifle slung over his shoulder and his twin had a holstered handgun strapped to each thigh. This man held a pregnant woman to his side. Mr Campbell broke off conversation and walked outside as his twin embraced the woman.

"So, Sundeep and I have pared down to essentials, Ms Kensington-Wallace." Sanjay held a black computer bag in each hand. "We've allowed for no power source. I've packed two fully charged spare batteries." He grinned.

It sounded odd, her good friend calling her Ms Kensington-Wallace, but they were on official duty now and they would adhere to formalities.

"Very well." She turned her attention back to her task of preparing to leave. "You and Sundeep have everything I specified, though?"

"Yes, ma'am," Sanjay said.

Antony approached her. "We're taking only two armed men! They have the *boy*—"

He glanced at her expression, stopping his line of attack. "Rory and his crew. Let's get this equipment on the horses. This will be fun. I used to ride as a child. You ever ride, Siobhan?"

"No," she replied. Oh, she hadn't considered that. Horses need to be *ridden*.

Siobhan followed Antony outside to where they loaded horses with gear. Silver-coloured nuclear protective-gear and respirators hung in bags from the harnesses of the two pack mules. Detonators and timers, and the other small items of required equipment, were on the mules along with the camping gear, although they'd pared it down. Tents, sleeping bags and food. No camp stretchers?

Wow, we're going to rough it.

The saddled horses waited beside the building. There was one for her. A younger lad, with a look of Campbell about him, held the reins of horses and smiled as they approached.

"We've chosen our most placid animals," he said. "We thought you may not be familiar with horse riding." The young man's friendly smile continued. He looked similar to the one who hovered around the computers, but this one was sturdier. *Another* set of twins?

"Mount up." The deep voice behind her belonged to Rory Campbell.

Siobhan turned. He was sitting on a tall dark horse, a stallion, which nickered and pranced briefly before he pulled its reins and spoke softly to it. The language wasn't English.

"Can I help you, Ms Kensington-Wallace?" the young man holding the reins asked.

"Oh, please. My name's Siobhan. What's yours?"

"I'm Brendan," he replied. "Hold the pommel with your left hand and put your left foot in my hands." Brendan knitted his fingers together and held them at knee height. She put her foot on his hands, then he hoisted her up until she could swing her right leg over the animal and sit. "Now put your feet in the stirrups and hold the reins."

Siobhan did so and grimaced, her palms moist and slippery around the leather reins.

"You know the basics, yeah?" he asked. "Kick to go. Pull on the reins to stop. Tug left or right whichever way you want to go. Got it?"

"Umm, yes." She gripped the reins tight and pulled back. The horse let out a breathy nicker and stepped to the side. The ground was further down than she expected. Her legs trembled against the side of the horse. "You're coming, aren't you? You'll keep me right?"

"Och, no. Rory will nae let me." Brendan's gaze dropped to his feet.

Antony, Sanjay and Sundeep had already mounted and looked more comfortable than she felt.

"Come on now, Siobhan, don't let the side down." Antony sent a warning glance her way.

The group filed out. The Chinese man led the way and the Community's contingent split in two. Some in front and some behind the Government group. The Government Communications Officer, Geoff, who was of medium height and rather plain, but knew his job, was managing the horse well too.

Why am I finding it so difficult?

They followed the gravel road, which made its way between the two hills behind the Community's compound. Siobhan's only view was the small section of it between her horse's ears. It nickered and its ears flicked back often, as though it was trying to hear her. She was a little way behind Sundeep, so she kicked, and the horse trotted. It took all her balance to stay in the saddle. She pulled the reins, and it stopped dead. So, she kicked it again, much softer this time, and it walked. Sanjay turned and smiled encouragingly at her. Antony kept his eyes forward.

Thanks for the support, guys.

"You need to let the horse know *you* are the boss." Rory Campbell came beside her. "Hold the reins a little shorter. That's it. And give her a wee gentle kick now and then to let her know you haven't forgotten her, and that she can't do whatever she wants. Like eat any blade of grass that looks nice."

"Thank you, Mr Campbell."

"Rory," he said.

"Rory. So, this is a mare then?"

"Aye. One of our most placid animals." Rory's mouth curved up on one side.

Was he quietly amused or genuinely helpful?

Now slightly more confident with the guidance she'd received, she relaxed a little into the saddle. Siobhan glanced sideways at him. Rory rode a horse as if his mother had given birth to him while riding one herself. He looked like he was part of his big black animal, like a centaur. Maybe that's how the myth arose.

Rory looked around constantly.

Siobhan had been so intent on riding and not falling off, she hadn't yet looked at the surroundings. To their right was an enormous mountain covered in green grass with grey rocks protruding from it here and there. No heather on this one. She'd expected purple heather, but it may not have flowered yet. She followed Rory's gaze to the top. It was quite a way up and she was glad they wouldn't be walking it. It appeared they were to travel along its base.

"That's Bhienn Fionn, a Munro, isn't it? Glad we are not climbing it," she said, trying to make conversation.

"Aye." Rory gave a distracted reply then turned his horse and trotted back to his crew behind them.

Siobhan glanced over her shoulder. Rory conversed with his twin. The older man, George, had stayed back at the compound, in case there were any unwanted arrivals. Like the rag-tag group they had outrun on their way here. George oversaw the Militia, but Rory was their *leader*. His crew, as he called them, always deferred to him and obeyed every command he uttered. They appeared to be genuinely fond of him. Admired him, even.

Kendra was there too. She was often by Rory's side. Siobhan recalled that on the previous evening, Rory had been in close conversation with her. She had whispered something in his ear, and he had looked uncomfortable, even blushed. They could be together, as he was a very attractive man. It was surprising no young woman had kissed him goodbye, like the woman who had kissed his twin brother.

Passing the base of the mountains, they were now in an open area where the wind howled across a green glen which opened out into an undulating area of grass and low growing heather. An elongated loch ran beneath the opposite mountain and an old road, now in chunks and more than half washed away, drove down the middle of the valley they headed through. A pebbled covered burn snaked beside it weaving its trail of grey through the whole valley.

The highland wind blew loose strands of Siobhan's hair into her eyes, brushing her face like an unseen hand. It whispered to her of these highlands, and she floated for a while. Perhaps it wished her well, or warned her.

Her horse had strayed away from the others, further into the grassy flat and near a clump of brown bracken fern and heather not in flower. A sudden fluttering of wings to her left accompanied a medium-sized brown bird flying away from her direction. Then another followed quickly. They emitted a rapid clicking sound as they flew low over the ground. The horse reared, and Siobhan landed heavily as the mare galloped off.

"Umph." Siobhan lay dazed for only a moment then sat up.

Callum, Rory's twin, rode fast to catch the horse. Hoofbeats came behind her then footsteps landed nearby. She turned. Rory stood over her, an amused expression on his face.

"Are you okay?" His lips pressed together, as though he was squashing a smile.

"I'm *fine,*" she said.

Rory held out his hand, and when she took it, he pulled her to a standing position. He was a tall man, and her eyes viewed his shirt at the level of two open top buttons where russet chest hair peeped out.

"Thank you." She swallowed.

His brother returned with her horse.

"Callum has brought your horse back for you, and you ken what you have to do now?"

"What?" Siobhan shook her head slightly.

"Get back on." He raised his eyebrows.

Get back on. Was he daring her?

Of course I'll get back on.

She took the reins from Callum and positioned herself for a *knee up,* as Brendan had called it. Rory grabbed her knee, and, with little warning, she was right at the height to throw her other leg over and sit in the saddle. The mare pranced, but soon settled.

"You okay, aye?" Rory asked.

"Yes. Thank you."

Rory remounted and walked his horse back to the group, which had paused for her. Staring. Siobhan turned her horse and followed, her face warming. Once she was back in line, they continued their journey.

"You ken that was a wee grouse and his mate you disturbed there?" Rory remained walking his horse beside her. "It's best you dinnae leave the trail, aye?" His Scottish burr sounded thicker.

"It wasn't my intention. It's just... so lovely out here." She let the awe stay in her tone.

Rory smiled. "That it is."

He kicked his horse forward to the front group and spoke with the Chinese man, Xian, for a while.

Siobhan recalled the equestrian events from the old films of the Olympic Games that had been part of history classes at school in the Government Bunker. Comparing Rory to those riders, he sat a horse well. For that matter, every rider from the Community did.

Up top, it was the age of the horse once more. And she didn't know how to ride. Just her luck. It wasn't coming naturally, as it seemed to for the men in her group.

Her horse began to gallop of its own accord. Siobhan held on with her legs, but it was no use. She shook as she desperately tried to cling to the saddle, her hands losing their grip with the jolting motion of the horse. Ahead was a section of the narrow burn.

Oh, no. This horse is going to jump it!

Siobhan lifted her feet out of the stirrups and brought her right leg over, letting herself fall into soft heather. The horse galloped on.

She hadn't landed so hard this time and stood up quickly. Xian rode past at a gallop and Rory's horse snorted as he pulled it to a halt in front of her.

"What are you doing to that animal?" His tone was a mixture of reproach and disbelief.

"Nothing!" Siobhan said. "She just took off! Really!"

"Really?" he asked.

"Yes. I'm as bewildered as you are." Siobhan put her hands on her hips.

Rory remained on his horse and shook his head silently. Callum, pulled his horse up beside him and spoke to him in a fluid, breathy language. Siobhan could only guess it was Gaelic. They'd had lessons in Gaelic in the Bunker in her early years, as the survival of the Gaelic tongue was a priority for some, but she soon found her forte in the sciences and devoted her energy in those fields. She recognised little of what Rory and Callum spoke.

Rory nodded. He hadn't taken his eyes off her.

"I have a solution," he said in English.

He jumped off his horse then walked his tall, black horse closer and held out his hand to her.

"What?" Siobhan stood straighter, her shoulders tensing.

"I'll give you a knee up." Rory's hand held steady.

"I'm not riding your horse!"

"That's correct." He wriggled his fingers, indicating he still wanted her hand.

She put her hand in his and he held it to his horse's neck. Rory's hand was warm on top of hers and the soft shiny coat on the horse's neck rubbed soothingly against her fingers. The horse nickered, and the sound vibrated under her hand.

"Let him see you." Rory nudged her closer to the horse's head. The black animal turned and eyed her. Then Rory put his hands together for a knee up.

Siobhan grabbed the pommel of the saddle, it was at a greater height than the one on the mare. Rory boosted her up, and she sat astride the saddle then put her feet in the stirrups.

"You can take your feet out of those," he said.

She took them out and frowned. Leather creaked as he placed his foot in the stirrup and his hand grabbed the pommel in front of her. A further creak indicated the tension on the saddle as Rory lifted himself behind her. His firm legs were the full length behind hers and his solid body warm against her back.

"Now, nae more falling off. You'll be holding us up too much if you continue on that horse. Sit quietly now. I'm driving." He spoke into her ear from behind and his left hand holding the reins brushed against her thigh as it rested on his.

Siobhan's heart stuttered. She wasn't sure if it was from the horse riding or from the nearness of the young man behind her—the young man who smelled of horse and heather. It had been a while since she had been so close to a man.

Keep it professional, Siobhan. Besides, he's Community.

They continued and, not having to concern herself with riding—her own horse now tied to one of the pack mules—Siobhan surveyed their surroundings. The burn began to meander its way through the glen. Brown water flowed rapidly over grey stones, its murmur constantly beside them. The wind blew across their grassy path and sent the fragrance of the Highlands into her face—pine, faint heather, freshness, and far-off rain.

The sun warmed her cheek, and the motion of the horse's gait caused her to bump gently into the man behind her. His body was firm and fit. He had a vitality she had never seen in the men with whom she'd grown up. Glancing at the calloused hand holding the reins she saw strength, matching his character gradually revealing itself.

"I meant what I said about your mother," Siobhan said. "She was a stunningly beautiful woman."

"Aye, that she was," Rory replied. "And clever, and a great leader, more importantly."

"So, your father..." she let her question linger.

"Aye?" There was an edge to his voice.

"His name was Scott?" she asked.

"Aye," he said.

"May I ask what happened to him?"

Rory's torso tensed against her back. After a moment his chest rose behind her, staccato, as he took in a halting breath.

"My father, Scott Campbell, died." His voice was husky and held a deep sadness.

"Oh, how thoughtless of me. I'm sorry," she said. "You miss him."

The soft clop of the black horse's hooves on the grass-covered moor was the only reply. His hand fiddled with the reins.

"And your grandfather's name was...?" she pressed.

Behind her, his breath dragged through his nostrils. Was this an out-of-bounds subject? Or had she been too insensitive in her efforts to find the man her father had told to remember?

Her own now deceased father.

"Ma faither's faither was Robert Campbell. Why?" The edge continued.

"Oh, only wondering," she lied.

Siobhan, just tell him!

"When I was a girl—"

"Och! Would you look at that." Rory's arm came beside her, pointing to the edge of the far forest.

A small group of deer came out from a clump of tall green pine that skirted the widening glen. They grazed as they made their way to where the meandering burn became a delta of sorts, flowing its way into a loch far ahead of them. A large stag emerged from the forest behind the herd of does. Muscles rippled under his russet coat and his many pointed antlers stood tall on a proud head. He sniffed the air and turned in their direction.

"He's caught our scent." Rory's voice was in her ear, his warm breath brushing the hair on her neck. Shivers began a decent down her spine.

Stop it Siobhan. The lad's young enough to be your son.

The party of travellers didn't halt in their stride, confident the stag would turn the other way. The male deer raised his head, tilting his antlers over his back, and let out a loud, long bark-like cry, which echoed across the moor. His harem scattered in front of him. He honked once more, and they returned to the forest. He nudged the slower does in the rear with his sharp antlers. The last doe flinched after a nudge from the stag.

"Oh, the bully," Siobhan said. "That looked like it hurt!"

Rory chuckled. "He has tae keep his women in line."

Siobhan could not stop herself from turning her head with raised eyebrows at his comment. His stubbled chin, glowing a soft ginger in the late morning sun, was at her eye level, and a dimpled cheek below blue smiling eyes came into view.

"That's a very male chauvinistic comment, Mr Campbell," she said.

"Possibly, but he's protecting them from us. He kens we like tae eat them." He raised one eyebrow.

Wow, this man was handsome. His auburn-haired masculinity reminded her of the stag. He was untamed, a man-of-nature, and part of this country as much as the creature. She spun back to face the front again, suppressing any further thoughts she might have regarding him.

She had a job to do. She had to concentrate. How on earth could she contemplate a liaison with a man from a Community?

But he was *so* much like the man her father had made her promise to remember. And she *had* remembered him. The kind, handsome Scotsman who had played dolls with her. As a teenager she had dreamed of him. *Him* being the man she would one day marry. Silly teenage girl stuff. Her father had never told her *why* she had to remember him.

In her young girl fantasies, the heroic figure featured, like the knights in shining armour of which she'd read. But now it was *so* embarrassing. Siobhan's face heated at her thoughts. She'd had love. Well, a relationship with Antony, *if* that was love. He'd used her for position and if she was honest, she'd used him for companionship and sex. The male population in the Bunker *was* a limited pool. She scratched the back of her neck and shuffled in her place in front of Rory.

"You uncomfortable, Ms Kensington-Wallace?" Rory asked.

"No, I'm fine," she answered. "Why do you ride a stallion? I thought they were vicious. And please call me Siobhan."

She had to change her mental subject.

"He's a stud in our breeding program," Rory said. "Horses are important to us. But when he's not performing that particular duty, he's mine. He needs to stay fit to service the mares." Humour tinged his voice.

So much for changing the subject.

Chapter Fourteen

Invercharing Community

"And the program does the rest." Stan rubbed his palms on his thighs and sat back from the computer.

"Now *that's* smart." Murray's heart continued its pounding. *This is all so awesome.*

"I take a bit longer to do it with a slide-rule," he said.

Stan's glasses slid down his nose a fraction. "You know how to do calculations with a slide-rule?"

Murray nodded, wondering what the big deal was. "Why? Can't you?"

Martin stood behind them as Stan ran through programs with Murray, commenting often on how he had used computers in the past when he studied postgraduate physics at Edinburgh University and computers were an everyday item.

Government camouflaged-coloured people who stayed behind occupied the control centre. People lounged while others looked outside at the surrounding mountains. They had unexpected time on their hands now Major McLellan wouldn't allow them to go any further on the mission to the submarine. McLellan ordered only the select few essential personnel to go with Rory and his crew. Community Militia members mingled among those who remained, their brown buckskins and dirty-green coloured shirts almost as camouflage-looking as the Government's uniform. Murray bet the odds would be in favour of the Militia standing out less in a forest than the Government guys any day, but for once he wouldn't calculate them.

Stan's mouth had remained open as Ceilidh, passing behind them carrying the dirty dishes from their luncheon, joined the conversation.

"Our Murray is somewhat of a mathematical genius," she said. She squinted over their shoulders at the screen. "He's helped Martin and the others over the years with his calculations and theories."

A flash of cold ran along Murray's spine and he turned behind to his sister. Martin stiffened and glared at Ceilidh. Ceilidh blinked and trotted off to the kitchen.

"What were the calculations for?" Stan asked.

"We have maths games with the children during school time. Got to make it interesting." Murray spoke the first thing that came into his head. *Well, I'm not lying.* "Could you have a look at my dinosaur while you're here?" he asked Stan. "I've been trying to get more RAM, but I don't have the tech I need."

That was close.

"You're quite the bright spark, aren't you, young man?" Another military-looking man stepped next to Martin. Every Government person looked military, but this tall man with a closely cropped haircut, almost completely shaved, involved himself with the technical equipment. "Bet you'd love to come back to the Government Bunker and have a look at what we've got," he said to Murray.

The man's badge read *William MacIntosh. Technical Support.*

Murray couldn't prevent his eyes widening and his jaw dropping at Mr MacIntosh's comment. He shut his mouth.

"I'd love to." Murray's pulse thumped in his ears. "But I don't know if it's allowed. I'd have to ask my brother, Rory."

"Oh, he'd be okay with it, surely," MacIntosh said. "An opportunity like this?"

"Um, I'll have to ask," Murray said.

No. I'll have to beg.

Mr MacIntosh shrugged and pursed his lips.

"And you already know this room, Lieutenant Wilson." Angela's fawning tone came loudly from the doorway.

Murray turned. Angela wore one of her suits she'd had made especially for her. Angela had tied up her long, red hair, much like Ms Siobhan Kensington-Wallace's. Not Angela's usual style. Walking beside her, in neat combat uniform, was another non-deployed member of the Government team. He nodded approvingly and wore an interested smile.

Hmm, the Guided Tour.

"Well, that's the inside facilities. I'll change out of these heels and show you how we are self-sufficient." Angela said as the tour continued out the door.

Murray glanced at Martin, who raised his eyebrows. Murray rolled his eyes. It would surprise no one that his eldest sister ingratiated herself with the Government, as everyone in the Community was aware of her ambitious nature.

Murray passed his afternoon with the tech guys. Oh, how he'd love to know what *they* knew, and have the equipment they had.

"You've got this!" Murray jumped at William MacIntosh's loud voice over his shoulder.

Murray had just completed the finishing additions to a program with little assistance from Stan. A firm hand patted his right shoulder.

"You'd better ask that brother of yours," MacIntosh said. "And he'd better give permission."

Murray let out a silent sigh. He didn't hold out much hope.

In the yard outside, the dogs were barking a somebody-is-coming bark. The lookout shouted from the tower and the Militia in the control-room grabbed their guns and ran outside to the front forecourt. More shouts came from outside, plus the faint sound of horses' hooves galloping toward the compound.

Then the *pop* of gunfire came through the open doors. The air outside rang with cracking gunfire. Government people grabbed their handguns and small machine guns and filed out.

Murray left the desk and ran to the doorway. Outside, Mr Stobbart yelled commands to the men and women of the Militia, who readied their weapons and ran to their positions. The Government soldiers were obeying his orders as well.

On the road leading to the compound, a group of about twenty armed men on horses galloped to the front gate. These untidy men wore dirty clothes, had scruffy hair and beards. Their horses looked in poor condition and their weapons were rifles and handguns. Many had swords strapped across their backs and knives glinted on their belts.

They didn't slow, and now aimed their weapons and let fire. The rapid fire banged around the compound. Bullets pinged off metal posts and thudded into brick and timber walls.

Wow, these guys were serious.

The crack of gunfire echoed everywhere, ringing in Murray's ears.

Government personnel ran to their armoured vehicles. It would shield them from bullets and allow closer aim. A soldier sprinted to the back of the jeep that carried the larger machine gun and loaded a chain of bullets. One attacker at the front of the group let out a yelp and fell to the ground, blood spurting from his neck. His horse whinnied and ran. The fallen man's companions began an angry cry and aimed more purposefully. Now bullets thudded and skidded off the armoured vehicles.

The soldier fired the larger machine gun attached to the back of the armoured jeep. A succession of loud *thunk, thunks, thunks* accompanied the jolting of the soldier manning the large gun. Horses screamed as one fell, landing on its rider who yelled for help, his leg stuck under his horse at an awkward angle. One of the attackers jumped from his horse and dragged this guy out from beneath his dead animal. The machine gun's rapid fire didn't drown out the injured man's ear-piercing scream. The attacker threw him over the saddle of his own horse. The man's cries continued. The rider remounted, kicked his horse to a gallop and retreated down the road the way he came. The rest of the bandit group continued their firing on the armoured vehicles, ducking back and forth, attempting to remain moving targets, Murray guessed.

A whoosh of air whizzed past Murray's ear followed by a ping through the ceiling.

Wow, that must've been a bullet.

He retreated from the doorway, no longer interested in watching all that went on. Loud, rapid gunfire filled the compound forecourt. Screams from horses and cries of pain from men floated through the door.

"We're gonna need Christine and Aunty Bec," Murray shouted over his shoulder to Martin and ran for the door to the main building.

Murray sprinted through the internal corridor to the medical centre. Inside, Christine was laying out equipment, IV lines and medications. Ceilidh was helping her.

"They're shooting at us. Seriously shooting!" Murray yelled at Christine as another volley of rapid gunfire sounded from the front of the compound.

"Who are *they*?" Christine opened a cupboard and took out cloth wrapped trays. "Are our people hurt? Is that a machine gun? Is it ours or theirs?"

Over the trays, her pale blue eyes seemed grey as she darted her questions at him, impatient for an answer.

"The Government guys are shooting their machine cannon at the bandits," Murray answered.

A high window shattered and sprayed fine glass shards around him. He ducked. Ceilidh let out a yelp and covered her head with an empty tray.

"Keep low, Murray!" Christine had ducked as well, but now the glass had settled, she stood and continued her preparations for the wounded.

How could she be so calm!

"I suppose we should be thankful they haven't started using their tank!" Christine shouted from the cupboard of supplies.

She handed gauze and bandages to Ceilidh who placed them on a bench.

"Where's Angela?" she asked.

Murray shrugged. "She was giving a government guy a guided tour."

"Go find her!" Christine ordered.

Murray ran out of the medical centre, keeping low. Last he heard, Angela was going to show the government guy the farm, but that seemed like hours ago. Murray ran to Angela's room at the back of the accommodation block. Here the gunfire was distant. He approached Angela's room.

"Gotta go!" The government man, who'd been receiving the guided tour, bumped into Murray as he barged out of Angela's room. He buttoned his shirt as he brushed past Murray. The man's neat uniform was not as neat as the last time Murray saw him.

"Where's the action?" he yelled.

"Out front." Murray said, facing Angela's open door.

Angela sat on her bed wrapped in a sheet. Only a sheet. Her long red hair fell over her shoulders as she pulled the sheet over her breasts. Murray blinked.

"What do you want? What's going on?" Her voice was terse. Husky.

"Ah, we're being attacked, but the Government soldiers are machine-gunning them down. I think." Murray looked away, his face heating. "Um... Christine wants you."

"Oh, go away!" she yelled.

"Okay. I'll be in the medical centre." Relief welled through him. His embarrassment was becoming unbearable. He'd rather be back in the gunfire than stay with her any longer.

Chapter Fifteen

Camping

The gait of the horse was a gentle rocking, relaxing in its own way. A high grey mountain loomed into her view as Siobhan opened her eyes.

"Was the morning start too early for you, Siobhan?" Rory's deep voice held a hint of amusement. He spoke *so* close to her ear.

"Oh sorry, the motion of the horse must have lulled me to sleep." Siobhan leaned forward... away from his warm chest.

In front of them rose a massive grey mountain of mainly rock. Dark grey cloud covered the top half. The cloud seemed to move constantly with a life of its own. The mountain's imposing presence glared at her, reinforcing her growing feelings of insignificance compared to the expanse of the world around her. Her travels through the Scottish Highlands had made her feel small and inconsequential. It was such a contrast to the Bunker.

Well, maybe in the big scheme of things, she *was* of little consequence.

Unused to these thoughts, Siobhan's discomfort grew. Her teachers and mentors had told her from a young age that the future of Scotland rested with the children of the Bunker. But in the past day, she had realised there were others capable of being part of the restoration. That she and her kind were not the only ones to make things right. The people of the community assisting them now had already begun the restoration.

Siobhan took in a deep breath of the cool mountain air; it chilled her throat. It was refreshing and such a change from processed, conditioned air, that the large units in the bunker dehumidified constantly to prevent damp taking hold deep underground.

"You okay, Siobhan?" Rory's voice rumbled in his chest as she leaned against him—again.

Siobhan remained silent and sat straighter, breaking the contact with him.

"Awesome, isn't it?" Rory pointed briefly at the mountain ahead of them.

Siobhan nodded but made no comment. She had no words.

"We'll make camp opposite it in the forest there. Not far now," he said. "You may be a wee bit saddle-sore tomorrow. Having not ridden much, or ever, before."

"Saddle-sore?"

"You'll ken what I mean tomorrow." There was a smile in his voice. "Hold on."

Rory kicked the horse to a canter, and they made their way across to Xian. Siobhan bounced with the rhythm of the horse's gait and grabbed Rory's thighs to steady herself.

"We'll make camp at the same place as last time," Rory said as he reined his horse to a halt beside Xian.

Xian nodded his reply. He looked at her, and then raised an eyebrow at Rory, who turned the horse away and didn't respond.

The campsite was among tall pine trees. They were Scots pines, from the look of the orange-brown coloured bark. Rory jumped off behind her. Siobhan brought her leg over the horse; her thighs were stiff and her dismount slow. She eased herself to the ground, grabbing the saddle to steady herself while her legs wobbled beneath her.

"Whoa. Take a minute to get your land-legs, lass." Rory held her upper arm, warm and strong... and too inviting.

She took a breath and clipped her reply. "I'm fine, thank you."

Rory raised his eyebrows and removed his hand. He walked away and began giving orders regarding the setting up of camp beside the pebbled shore of the large loch.

The constant rhythm of the waves reaching shore, combined with the whistle of the wind through the trees as it came off the water, was both comforting and cooling after the day's ride. Once they'd erected the tents, Kendra lit a fire in the cleared area they had prepared in the centre of the tent circle. Rory's crew tethered the horses in a line behind the tents. Rory delegated members of his team to stand watch.

Rory took the first watch. His broad shoulders sagged as he walked to the perimeter of their camp, back the way they had come. Strands of his hair came out of its leather tie and blew in the strengthening wind. He wasn't wearing jeans today, instead the same soft suede-type trousers as the others. They moulded to his form.

Droplets of rain splattered on Siobhan's head. She had smelled it earlier and had seen the cloud near the three-humped monolith, which now faced them as they camped opposite it on the shore of Loch Maree. The wind hissed through the pines and wafted their tangy scent into her face. The rain patted on the pine-needle covered ground. She was getting wet, but she didn't care. It was freeing.

Liberating.

Siobhan always ran back down when it rained *up top* in the small, well-guarded, concrete up-ground enclosure of the Bunker. Now she only had a tent to run to, but she wasn't in a hurry to run anywhere. She stood there, face turned toward the grey sky, cool dampening her eyelashes, dribbling into her mouth. Stray strands of hair stuck to the side of her face. A trickle of cold made its way down her back and one had started its cool, sensuous journey on her décolletage.

"Ms Kensington-Wallace?" The voice was deep, like Rory's. She opened her eyes. Callum stood near her.

"Yes?"

"We have wet weather gear, and a dinner is almost ready," he said.

"Thank you." She followed him to the fire and took the plate of scrambled eggs, a chunk of bread and a mug of tea he held out for her.

Kendra walked over with a raincoat and gave it to Siobhan. She placed her food on the large log, which had become a seat by the fire, and shrugged into the coat. It was oiled animal skin, stiff but waterproof. Kendra then walked away with a plate of food toward Rory who stood on watch.

Yes, there was something between those two.

Siobhan *hmphed* quietly, all peace and sense of freedom the rain brought now disappearing. Why did *it* bother her so much? Rory was a young man who needed a young woman. What on earth was she even thinking? Yes, he was gorgeous, and yes it had been *very* nice leaning against his wonderful body all day. *But really, Siobhan!* She shook her head. She was sounding like a teenager.

"Is your meal okay, Ms Kensington-Wallace?" Xian asked.

"Oh, it's delicious. Thank you. Fresh eggs. Wonderful!" She took another mouthful to prove it.

Siobhan walked stiffly to the tent designated for her. The smoke of the campfire permeated the air with its charcoal mixed-with-pine scent, and followed her to her tent. She took off her coat, set out her bedroll, and lay on it for a while and listened to the gentle patter of the rain on canvas. It brought to mind rainy days of her childhood, when she would stay inside and have to entertain herself. She would sit at the window, elbows on the sill, watching the street get dark with wet, and people splashing through puddles on their bicycles. It must have been Oxford. She didn't remember much of her early childhood in Edinburgh when her mother was still alive. She'd not heard rain on a roof for a very long time, and never on a tent roof.

Siobhan rummaged in her duffle bag for her toiletries and then brushed her hair, tidying it back into a French roll. The day's wind had blown her hair wildly around her face. She must look like a crazy woman. She'd nothing to wet her face washer with so she scooshed her perfume. Siobhan smoothed her shirt and cargo pants as she emerged from her tent.

The rain had ceased, and Rory sat on the log beside the fire. Antony and the others from her government group sat opposite him. Angus, the Community's scientist, had his nose in a thick booklet and barely raised his head. She walked over to join them. Her legs felt heavy, and she was sore around where she sat.

Ahh, saddle-sore. It had started already.

Rory briefly glanced at her as she sat next to him. His eyes had dark circles beneath them, and he sat slightly slumped.

"You're tired, Rory?" Siobhan spoke softly.

"Aye." He tilted his head to the side. "A lot has happened these past few days. It's involved a great deal of travelling."

"Where have you been?" Antony asked. The man just could *not* keep out of it.

"To Loch Ewe and back... and other places." Rory sipped his tea, having made his latter comment under his breath.

The portable CB radio near the tents emitted a loud voice with a call sign. Geoff, from Communications, spoke briefly into it, then hurried over to the fire and spoke to Antony.

"It's the Invercharing Community. They were attacked today." Geoff held the mic, and the portable shortwave radio sat in its bag slung over his shoulder.

"When?" Rory stood, his tired posture gone, his slump replaced by tense muscles and an instant alertness.

"Late this afternoon," Geoff said. "Bandits on horseback—"

"Give me that!" Rory snatched the CB handle from Geoff. "This is Rory Campbell. Who am I speaking to? Over."

It's George. Dinnae worry, Rory. All's okay now. The Government Defence boys shot their large calibre machine gun and scared them off. Over.

"Anyone injured? Over," Rory asked.

They lost three. We have some wounded. Nothing Christine couldn't handle. A few bullet holes around the compound though. Nothing you need to come back for. Over.

"You sure?" Rory asked. "I could send some of us back. Over."

"Who got injured?" Kendra and Callum had moved closer at George's comments.

Rory blinked as his mouth twitched in slight annoyance.

"Were Christine or Mandy injured? Over."

No, they're fine. Your mission is way more important. You keep your crew there. Just be aware there are especially bad people out there. Over.

"Aye. Keep safe then, George. Over and out."

Kendra and Callum both stood back, tense shoulders easing and tight foreheads relaxing.

Rory handed the CB back and sat heavily on the log.

"Our local bandits are nae usually so bold," he said. "They must be the ones you thought you'd outrun." He bore his stare into Antony's face.

Antony's mouth became a thin line and he remained silent.

"Well?" Rory's voice rose as his back straightened. His fists curled into a clench in his lap.

"Our guns scared them off. They probably won't come back." Siobhan spoke beside him.

Rory turned his glare onto her, his eyes narrow and jaw muscles tense. Cold ran along her spine. His expression was sharp. She had glimpsed Rory the protector.

Angry Rory.

Please may he never direct it at me in its fullness.

Rory's Adam's apple bobbed, and his face relaxed slightly.

"Double the watch!" Rory said loudly, still holding her gaze.

Siobhan flinched at his sudden volume. Callum left his side and spoke to those who would take turns at lookout.

"We're miles from the Community," she said in a soft voice. "The bandits don't know where we are."

"It's views such as that, which make people dead." Rory stood and walked away.

Siobhan looked across the fire at Antony. Under a scowl, his gaze never left Rory's back.

***

The dark of night came so late this time of the year. Siobhan stared up at the sky while she sat alone by the fire. The members of her team had left the campfire to tend to duties or retired for the night, but she couldn't force herself to move. Her body had the dullness of fatigue, but there was more to her immobility. Stars peeked through the diminishing cloud now the rain had passed. Deep, deep-blue sky dotted with twinkling diamond stars and planets so clearly visible Siobhan reached out to touch them.

"Your arms are nae long enough," Rory said. His tone was much more amicable than only an hour ago.

His footsteps padded from behind, then he sat on the log next to her. She pulled her arm down from pointing at the stars. Rory's thigh rested against hers, firm muscle with his warmth seeping through her cargo pants.

"Forgive me for before, Rory. I wasn't being flippant. I'm just... well, not as experienced as you," she said.

He flicked an eyebrow and pursed his lips tight. "Well. You're in the-big-bad-world now."

Siobhan returned her gaze to the magnet of the night sky. Bright stars twinkled, glowing, and prominent. Clusters of them spread across the heavens. She stared, surprised at her own reaction. It was hard to speak. She had seen maps of the night sky and once or twice briefly glimpsed the stars *up top*, but as it was night time, the most dangerous period, the bunker's guards had ordered her back down again. Now she was out in it. The Milky Way was thick with stars and... *milky*. It made sense.

What her mind could never fathom was the distances involved as reported by the textbooks. Rory shuffled on the log beside her, his thigh nudged hers. She blinked.

"Have you never seen the stars before?" Rory asked, his breath brushing her ear and his tone one of amazement.

"Yes, I have but never like this. It's all so...so..."

"Mind-blowingly awesome?"

"You could put it that way," she said.

The wind sighed through the trees while the fire sparked as it burned through the wood. A smoky-pine scent permeated the air. Neither spoke, and as the others settled in their tents for the night, they both focused on the starry host above them.

"There is an intelligence behind all of this, with an intention," Rory said. "Despite our chaos, there is purpose. There must be." He spoke softly, the warrior showing an intellect, and something else. A faith?

The fire crackled, and its warmth continued to bathe Siobhan's face.

"I've missed out on so much," she said. "I've been safe but... until I saw all this." She waved her hand expansively, then pointed to the sky. "I hadn't realised how sheltered the bunker is." She turned her face to his. "You've always lived here. You were born out here. You're *so* lucky."

"You were lucky too, Siobhan," Rory said. "Your father was a great man, and he kept you safe down in the bunker. You probably would nae have survived the post-crash world if he had nae."

"How do you know my father was a great man?" she asked.

"Och, I read about him, and we have one of his papers." Rory looked down at his feet.

"You spoke like you knew him, though," she said.

Rory didn't answer. The firelight lit his face with an orange glow, the ginger flecks in his long stubble stood out as he returned his gaze to the heavens. Then he pointed low to the horizon over the loch.

"See that cluster of stars?" he asked. "That's Pleiades. The seven daughters of the Greek gods. They sail, according to mythology. Verra appropriate as we're going to the sea."

He'd done it again. Changed the subject. What *was* he avoiding? Some subjects were definitely on his *not-to-be-spoken-about* list. Siobhan's stomach churned, but she had to do it.

She took a deep breath.

"When I was a little girl, two men came to visit us right as the stock market was crashing and before we went underground." She spoke quickly, in case he tried to interrupt again. "My father made me promise to remember them—and I did."

Rory started to speak, so she placed her fingers on his mouth. His lips were soft and warm, and his moustache tickled her fingertips. His shoulders froze with an intake of breath.

"One of them looked very much like you, Rory. And his name was Ruairidh." She made sure she pronounced it the Gaelic way.

Rory's warm breath from his nostrils blew past her hand. His gaze was intense, and he seemed to decide on something. He took her hand in his, removing it from his mouth, and his eyes never leaving hers. She couldn't pull her hand from his, mesmerised by the reflected firelight flickering in his eyes.

"Come with me," he finally said.

Rory stood and pulled her beside him, then turned and rushed into the forest dragging her behind. She had to run to keep up with his long strides. Her temples thudded as he brushed her past the lower branches of pine, their footsteps soft on the pine needle covered ground.

What is he doing?

The man she'd known for only a little over a day was a man she was certain she could trust. There was something so familiar about him. And she wanted to know *why* that was. She let him lead her, determined to find out why he was so intense.

Rory stopped once they were far away from their camp, its fire now a small glowing dot many metres away. He turned to her, his face a dull shine in the reflected starlight dappling through the pines. His Adam's apple bobbed in the shadowed light.

"Siobhan." He swallowed again. "I know you. I am the man who played with you when you were a little girl."

She could feel her eyes widen. Her mouth opened, but nothing came out.

"You showed me your dolls' house," he said. "You're ambidextrous, and you wrote my name in the Gaelic."

"But you..." Siobhan had found her voice, of a sort. "You can't be. It was forty years ago. He'd be in his sixties now." She shook her head. "You're his grandson."

"No, I'm not." Rory held both her hands in his and pressed them to his chest. His heart thumped through it. "It was me. Murray and I needed to find out how to fix this nuclear warhead before it goes off."

"How did you...?" she began but her voice trailed off into nothing.

He raised his eyebrows. "Join the dots, Siobhan. You told me you're a genius, remember?"

"You... time travelled? No." She shook her head again.

Rory's nod was barely perceptible at first, then he nodded fully.

So, she was right! It *was* him. The man from her childhood stood with her, here and now. Her mind buzzed with the notion.

No, her whole body did.

"You used a time machine, or is there a wormhole nearby? Or even a portal?" she asked. "How did you do it?"

"I cannae tell, Siobhan. Stop asking, for I will nae reveal it."

The edges of his angular features softened in the starlight. His hair was loosely pulled back. It had been in a man-bun that day she'd first met him, but its irrepressible russet curls remained ever obvious. He'd had moments of gruffness with her this time, now that she was an adult. It was the circumstances though, surely. For the kind man who'd taken time to listen to a child, was still there. She saw *him*, that same man, as he now held her hand and explained.

"But you have to keep it secret. Siobhan, I'm trusting you with a great deal, lass. Please dinnae say a word, especially not to your pal, Antony. Please," he said in a firm voice, but a hint of pleading edged it.

Rory had risked a lot in telling her.

Oh, so much.

"Promise me," he demanded when she hadn't answered.

"I promise." She had easily voiced it, but she would keep her promise.

"When did you go back?" she asked. "I mean, how long ago from now?"

"Yesterday."

She gasped. "That's why you look exactly the same as I remember! And why you're so tired. You *have* done a fair bit of travelling in the past few days!" A small laugh escaped her mouth.

Rory's gaze lowered to her lips, and in the dim light his own lips parted, and his face slowly descended to hers. Painfully aware of his closeness, and the escalation of her pulse rate, Siobhan stood stock still, willing his lips to meet hers.

A crack of gunfire to the far left of the campsite stopped his momentum to her mouth. He whipped his head in the shot's direction. She jolted at the sound, and snapped her lips closed as he dropped her hands.

She eased away from Rory. He had raised his handgun, ready to aim.

"Keep low. Follow me," he ordered her.

Siobhan followed meekly behind him, but there were no further gun-shots.

That would have been nice, Siobhan thought. A kiss from a man such as Rory. The same one she'd dreamed of for years, but always thinking it an impossibility to ever meet in real life the man who had come to their old house in Oxford.

Very nice, but wrong.

What was she thinking? Was he really going to kiss her? She was old enough to be his mother, for goodness' sake. Why would he do that? She was imagining things. Wishful—but stupid—thinking. She was caught up in her girlish memories and not in her current reality.

Get a handle on it, Siobhan.

They made it back to the camp and he turned to her.

"You okay?" he asked.

Siobhan nodded, then he left her and ran over to Kendra, who had been on watch and was the one who had fired the shot. They spoke for a while, heads close together. The other members of his crew wandered back to the fire.

Antony came from the forest, eyes on the ground before him. He walked with a small torch lighting his way. He didn't look toward the fire where Siobhan and others now gathered but went straight to his tent.

Rory turned to those who had joined her at the fire, which was now glowing embers.

"It's okay everyone. False alarm. Go back to bed," he said.

He left his crew, after giving Xian orders for his watch, and walked back to the fire. Others had returned to their tents. Rory looked at Siobhan.

"You best get some sleep yourself, Siobhan. Goodnight." Rory turned and followed Xian.

Chapter Sixteen

---

*H*e is enclosed.

The suit is stiff, and the fit is snug.

The helmet is the worst. It's as though he rebreathes his own exhaled air.

The respirator mask, tight around his mouth and nose, doesn't help these feelings of asphyxia.

He turns to his companion. Angus wears a silver radiation protection suit as well, his green eyes peer out through the clear polycarbonate visor.

Angus nods then they walk along the narrow corridor lined with pipes; a red glow colours everything in the same hue.

They enter a room. No, it's not a room. It's a continuation of the corridor, only wider in this section. There are dials and knobs and small lights indicating something.

He doesn't know what though, as the writing is Korean.

How do I know it's Korean?

"Okay, Great One, get up. Time for exercise." Xian stood in front of Rory's tent with his arms crossed.

Rory rolled over and half sat in his bedroll.

Och no, he'd had another vision.

He blinked, got up without a word then followed Xian to a small clearing where he stood opposite his friend. They both began the exercises, with arms and legs moving in controlled flowing patterns, punches and kicks, blocks and holds. Rory was still stiff from sleep but loosening up gradually. Xian moved with grace, his punches strong and legs supple and more flexible than his own.

One exercise involved a wide stance followed by a high kick, then returning the leg to the ground. Rory was awkward, his torso stiffer and kick not as high as Xian's. In a swift movement, Xian leant over and pushed him on the left shoulder. Rory staggered back, desperately correcting his balance, attempting to not fall. Xian lifted himself off the ground and lightly kicked Rory's chest. Rory completed his decent, landing on his bottom.

Rory jumped to a standing position, his face hot in the cool morning. Mist hugged their campsite and hung close to the mountainside, swirling through the trees, and mingling with the smoke from their campfire. With luck, he was far enough away from the camp for the mist to hide him. He stood with his hands on his hips and tilted his head to one side as laughter erupted from the on-lookers by the fire.

Thanks, Xian. Why was Xian deliberately embarrassing him?

Xian approached him, the set of his shoulders and the flow of his movement told Rory Xian hadn't finished with him. Rory tensed, focused on keeping his feet fixed to the ground this time.

"Your *chi* is in your throat, white-man," Xian said, as he pushed Rory in the chest. Rory stepped backward to regain his balance.

Rory shook his head. "I'm too tired for this, Bruce."

"You too tired to not die?" Xian's deep-brown, intelligent eyes locked with his. He stepped closer, his voice a whisper. "Humility is a noble trait in a leader, Rory."

Humility or humiliation?

It was hard to tell the difference in the present situation.

Xian shook his head slightly, then placed a hand over a closed fist in front of himself and bowed to Rory.

Rory returned the bow then walked to the log by the fire. A breakfast of porridge was cooking in a pot over the flames, its almost-charred aroma hit his nostrils and smoke stung his eyes.

"Well, it seems you aren't infallible after all, Mr Campbell." Antony's voice rose above the fresh bout of chuckles that had erupted on Rory's return.

"Never said I was. Just human, like you." Rory picked up a mug of tea and sat next to Siobhan.

"Why did you call Xian Bruce? Is it his anglicised name?" Siobhan asked Rory.

She glared over at Antony sitting on the opposite log. Antony's chuckles quietened.

"Och, no. It's the name of a brilliant Gung-Fu artist. Bruce Lee," Rory said. "He made some movies. You may have seen them."

Siobhan shook her head. "What is *chi*?" she asked.

"It is centre of balance." Xian sat on the other side of Rory. "And like most big white men, his is too high."

"Maybe you should stick to our way of fighting, Mr Campbell." Antony raised his mug of tea and took a sip.

Rory ignored him. He didn't need the *sassenach's* ridicule.

"What was that last night?" Antony asked. "One of your people seeing things?"

What the cheek? This man is pushin' it.

"No. One of my people just being cautious." Rory gritted his teeth. He'd have to work with this guy today, so he'd have to suck it in, as they say. But what he actually wanted to do was—

"How much further is it to Loch Ewe, Rory?" Siobhan asked, looking directly at his face. Her right eyebrow cocked.

Was there a slight warning in her expression?

He didn't answer her, distracted by those sapphire eyes.

Man, this woman was beautiful. And he'd stupidly nearly kissed her last night. What was he thinking? Thank heavens for Kendra's jumpiness. He'd no time for any o' that, despite the vision... and her perfume. They had this nuke to neutralise.

But no, Kendra had not been jumpy. She'd seen something, she assured him. And he believed her. The intruders had disappeared with the gunshot. Not wanting to alarm people, he'd sent everyone to bed, except Xian and Callum, and stayed up most of the night with Kendra in case the unwelcomed visitors returned.

"It will take us most of the day," he replied to Siobhan. "We'll leave as soon as we've breakfasted and packed up."

It was hard to take his eyes away from Siobhan. He had to trust her with the knowledge he'd given her last night. Time would tell if his impulsiveness was a mistake or no'.

Breakfast finished, then they packed up camp in a surprisingly short time. Everyone helped except Angus who had read his way through three quarters of the *how-to-drive-a-sub* manual already. Rory helped Callum and Sanjay load the technical equipment onto the mules. A horse whinnied in the woods of the steep brae beside them. The clank of cooking utensils being loaded onto packhorses, the banter between Geoff and Xian, and the general orders being issued by himself and Callum ceased abruptly.

"All our horses are here, right?" Sanjay's dark-brown eyes showed a lot of white.

Rory nodded and put a finger to his lips. Antony looked far into the mist in the direction of the mountain top behind them. Rory followed his gaze to the foggy mountain side, which was a thick green and white monochrome. Horses' whinnies as the animals crashed through the forest increased in volume.

Those with weapons held them ready.

Siobhan crept beside him. "What if they're just horses running wild? Or if they have riders, they're friendly?" she whispered.

Rory tilted his head. "I doubt it," he whispered back. "I won't give away our location on the chance they are."

They stood motionless, weapons at the ready, as the crack of horses through the undergrowth receded. Then there was silence for a few minutes.

"I think we can say it's safe to move now." Antony holstered his handgun.

"Aye," Rory was reluctant, but the urgency of the day ahead compelled him to move on. "Everyone keep alert, okay?"

They mounted their horses. Once again Rory helped Siobhan into his horse's saddle and then sat behind her, they couldn't afford to lose time. She flinched as she sat, and he smiled to himself.

The company started the day's journey, making their way by the eastern side of Loch Maree. The loch was grey and dully reflected a sky of the same hue. Its cold waters attracted the water vapour which hung over it in the breezeless morning. The steep-sided mountain to their right retained its misty coat. Anything could hide in it—and follow them.

Rory directed his hearing to the right, and he kept attentive to his horse's ears. The stallion would notice and react to danger. With the deep waters of the loch to their immediate left, they were sitting ducks if attacked.

They came to the rocky section, which sloped steeply to the shoreline, and dismounted and walked the animals. They picked their way higher up and around this section of the mountainside. Siobhan walked awkwardly, but stretching her legs would help. They came upon a flat, green shoreline and they remounted once more.

Siobhan shuffled in her seat every now and then. Rory daren't speak to her today. He had to stay focussed, no matter what crazy feelings were going on inside him. Loch Ewe and radiation leaking from a submarine, which may or may not be abandoned, were ahead of them. If his most recent vision was correct, he and Angus would be the ones to sort it. Although that made little sense.

Then again, it did.

Somehow, he was certain he'd have to be the one to take the risks.

His stallion, Boy, flicked his head, and with ears back, gave a throaty nicker and began to rear. Rory put his arm around Siobhan's waist, holding her tight as a crack sounded on the mountainside nearby. A whizz brushed past his ear.

"Everyone, take cover!" Rory pushed Siobhan off the horse and jumped down beside her. Her startled expression met him as he crouched low next to her. "Go and flatten yourself in the dip on the shoreline and dinnae move!"

She ran to the loch's edge without questioning him. Rory grabbed his submachine gun from where it hung on his saddle and let his jittery horse go. The air filled with gunfire. Loud cries and whoops of men bore down the ben toward them.

The thud of galloping hooves came along behind him. Rory turned. A man wearing dirty leathers, lifted a sword high and galloped his horse toward Rory. Rory dropped and flattened his body to the ground. Breath coming fast, pulse racing. The hooves of the horse passed. Air whooshed right above him. A stinging sensation began on the righthand side of his head. A tuft of hair with skin attached floated to the ground in front of him.

Rory cocked his submachine gun and aimed at the back of the man who'd clipped him. The man lifted his sword high and commenced a decent on Callum. A flash of alarm coursed through Rory's being. He fired. The man jolted in the saddle and fell at Callum's feet, the sword landing impotent beside him.

To Callum's left, Kendra fired arrows into the mist. Riderless horses joined their own in flight. Men groaned in the fog. Xian ran to an injured man who pulled an arrow from his shoulder. With his uninjured arm, the wounded assailant raised a handgun. Rory yelled to Xian. With an effortless flick of his foot, Xian kicked the weapon out of the man's hand then descended onto his throat with a knuckle punch. The man held his neck, gasping for air. Turning deepening shades of blue, the man's stridor-like breaths diminished as he soon fell silent.

With a cry to his companions, a rider waved his arm in a circle at shoulder height, then the group of assailants followed him back into the mist. Horses crashed through bracken-fern, their thunderous passage receding up the cloud-covered ben beside them.

"Inventory. Who's injured?" Rory snapped as he surveyed the damage.

The members of his crew were standing. Xian walked back from the hillside, leaving the body of the man he'd killed. Kendra collected arrows. His brother Callum walked toward him, his smile tight and serious, then he enveloped Rory in a hug. One of the techs, Sanjay, held his arm, blood seeped through his clothing at the shoulder. Antony, his face pale and sweaty, held the reins of two startled, but settling, animals.

Siobhan!

Rory ran to the edge of the loch. She must've heard him coming for she raised herself from the dip in the shoreline. A surge of relief flooded through him. She appeared unharmed, but her eyes widened as he got closer.

"Rory, you're bleeding!" She pointed to his shoulder.

Long drips of blood coloured his shirt. His scalp stung so he placed his hand on the top of his head and came away with damp, sticky fingers. Blood covered his hand, and his neck and collar.

"I'm fine," he said. "Scalps bleed a lot, Mum always said."

"Sit down somewhere. Let me look at it. Where's the medical kit?" Siobhan's tones were officious. Commanding.

"You'll be the nurse now?" He lifted an eyebrow at her.

"I do know some field first aid. Let me see it," she demanded.

Rory sat on a log by the shoreline, then she peered at the back of his head. Xian, Angus and Callum crowded behind him.

"Ooh, brother. Does nae look good," Callum commented.

"Marring your beauty, boss." Kendra walked from behind him and stood in front of him with a smirk on her face. "Women love a man with a scar." She crossed her arms and looked at Siobhan. A bag with a shoulder strap dangled from her hand. "Well, patch him up then." She dropped the medium-sized medical kit at Siobhan's feet.

"Okay, everyone," Rory said. "Give Siobhan some space. Are we sure those bastards have left? Where are the horses?"

"Antony held them," Callum said, then leaned in closer to Rory and whispered, "Did nae lift a finger to fight, ken."

"I did see that," Rory whispered back.

Siobhan glanced from the open medical kit and looked over to Antony, who still held the horses' reins. She let out a slow breath, then dug into the medical kit.

"Send Sanjay over." Rory blinked away the sting on his scalp. "He's wounded too. What happened?"

"Got his wing clipped." Callum walked over to the young tech who still held his arm, blood soaked his top at left shoulder level.

"Where's ma' Boy?" Rory scanned the scene.

His stallion wasn't in the small clearing. He whistled. Hooves thudded on the path ahead. His black horse trotted back leading the other loose horses. He made his way through the group and walked right up to Rory then nudged his shoulder, softly nickering.

"I'm okay, Boy." Rory lifted his hand and stroked the soft muzzle near his head.

"Wow. He's tame." Siobhan had a gauze in her hand as she stood back, eyeing the large stallion.

"Well, we grew up together," he said.

Siobhan pressed the cold, wet gauze to the raw section of his scalp. Whatever she'd used to clean his head, stung like blazes.

"Ah, mmm, *ow!*" he hissed. "You could have given me warning!"

"Oh, sorry," she said.

The others moved away, but Boy stayed close, nickering softly.

"You'll be pleased to know it's not as bad as it first seemed." Siobhan spoke above his head. "You're correct. Scalps bleed a lot, and it should heal well, except..."

"Except what?"

"The hair may not grow back." She dabbed again.

"Makes nae difference to me," he said.

More stinging.

"Kendra's right. It mars your appearance somewhat," Siobhan commented. "Might put the young ladies off."

"What young ladies?" he grunted.

"Well, I suppose Kendra hasn't been put off at all." Siobhan picked a bandage out from the first aid kit.

What was she meaning? Him and Kendra? No, he had to put her right.

"Kendra is with our Doctor, Christine, not me," he said.

"Oh. The lady doctor."

"Aye."

"There are plenty of young women in your compound though," she said after a pause. She wound a bandage, keeping the dressing to his cut in place.

"Aye, there is but I don't necessarily need a young woman," he said. "Age means nothing."

"Nothing?"

"Aye, nothing." He tried not to sound impatient. It seemed to bother her. "My parents—well ma faither was eighteen and my mither thirty-seven when they got married."

"What?" Siobhan stopped bandaging.

"You heard me. Age means nothin'," he said. "Love means everything."

Siobhan resumed bandaging his head. He couldn't turn to see her expression. The silence was empty, interrupted only by the thudding pulse in his ears. He had thoughts. They were becoming words he couldn't hold in, no matter how much he was certain it could never be the time nor the place. Not on this journey. But he would say it anyway.

"Relationships. Isn't that what life is all about? Family. Friends... the man-woman thing?"

Siobhan's hands paused in their task. She took a breath to speak but stopped herself as Callum returned with Sanjay. The tech sat next to Rory.

Sanjay was quiet. Pale.

"You okay?" Rory asked the young IT tech.

Sanjay nodded. Siobhan began to inspect his wound, not lifting her eyes from the young man's shoulder, avoiding eye contact with Rory. Rory stood and walked with Callum to Xian and Kendra.

"They're playing with us," he said to his crew, then gazed around at the receding mist. He counted two more dead lying on the hillside. "Leave them." He pointed toward the bodies. "Give those bandits something to do instead of bothering us. As soon as Sanjay's good to go, we'll move on."

"This is yours." Callum held out a long sword with a black leather-bound handle.

"Is this what he cut me with?" Rory asked.

"Here is its scabbard." Xian handed it to him.

A criss-cross of the same black leather, which wound around the handle of the sword also decorated the scabbard. The blade was one sided. He held the weapon, hands trembling. It looked Japanese, if he wasn't mistaken. *Beautiful.*

"A Katana." Xian had read his thoughts. "A reproduction, but the owner has honed the edge sharp, as you well know."

"Magnificent," Rory said.

He held it out and rested it on his fingers just below the hilt. It went blade heavy, so he moved his hand along till he found its centre of balance at almost six inches from the hilt.

"Yes, it's a good blade," Xian said.

"Then it's yours, my teacher." Rory held it out in both hands and bowed, presenting it to Xian.

"No." Xian held his hands up before him. "I couldn't."

"Aye, you can. And please do." Rory remained bowed and holding out the sword. "I mean it. In appreciation for all you have taught me."

Xian blinked and reached out to take the sword. The others stood in silence as he replaced it in its scabbard.

"Thank you." Xian held the sheathed sword and bowed.

Rory bowed in return, then glanced over to Sanjay. Siobhan had finished bandaging his shoulder.

"Mount up. We must get going," he said. "This nuke won't wait for us."

Chapter Seventeen

Horses nickered and whinnied as everyone remounted. Around Siobhan, riders spoke in soothing tones and patted broad necks, settling their jittery mounts. Siobhan sat on Rory's stallion as he rummaged in the saddlebags behind her. Kendra assisted Sanjay to get into the saddle.

Her own relief on the discovery of only a friendship between Rory and this warrior-like woman surprised Siobhan. Sanjay winced in pain as Kendra pushed under his uninjured shoulder to get him onto the horse. Siobhan chided herself. She should have put Sanjay's arm in a sling and determined to do so when they stopped next.

Antony was quiet as he mounted, and he'd not said a word since the attack. This was unusual for him as he always had a comment to make. Antony's colour had returned, and it was possible, and most likely, his silence was because he'd never seen real action as the Community Militia had.

Real action, not manoeuvres and hypotheticals.

"Ach, mustn't have packed one," Rory mumbled into the saddlebags behind her.

Siobhan turned in the saddle and followed his progress to the loch-side. He shed his blood-stained shirt, stiff with dried blood, as he went. Lined with musculature, his bare back rippled. The muscles in his arms flexed and relaxed as he wrapped the shirt in his hands. Tattooed Celtic artwork covered his entire right arm up to and including his shoulder. Unbroken lines wove in and out and back upon themselves. She recognised the Endless Knot tracing a circular path as a band around his mid-upper arm covering his biceps and triceps. The triskele swirled its way on his deltoid near his shoulder. The Celtic Trinity knot was prominent on his forearm. Swirls surrounded them all, plus more intricate weavings in ink. Dried blood covered parts of it.

Rory approached the water and stooped low, wetting the clean section of his shirt and then washing the blood off his body. Fine freckles dusted his fair, almost white skin. His bandage looked more like a headband, giving him a hippie appearance.

Rory finished his wash, turned and made his way back to where she waited on his horse. Rory's torso was a study in anatomy. Large pectorals sat below sturdy shoulder muscles. His abdomen taut, and muscles pure definition. At the top of his pelvis on either side, a thin line traced its way along the muscle's edge to his soft buckskin trousers where...

Stop Siobhan!

Rory glanced up at her and held her gaze. She faced the other way as heat rose to her cheeks.

Had he seen her ogling him? She bit her lip.

No time for that. There were more important things to focus on!

Out of his saddle bags Rory brought a flap jacket with large flat sections, and he shrugged into it.

"What are you wearing?" she asked.

"SAPI vest. Did nae bring a second spare shirt."

"The way things are going you'll need an armour-plated vest *and* a helmet." She pointed to his bandaged head.

He smiled then put his foot in the stirrup and mounted behind her. The metallic scent of blood lingered around him.

The day cleared further as they moved off with the loch to their left. Kendra brought her horse close.

"Haven't seen any of the bodies we saw last time, boss." She glanced to the other side of the loch and back again.

"Been picked clean, I suspect." Rory's exhaled breath caught the wisps of hair on Siobhan's neck.

She let out a quiet gasp, trying to ignore the warmth and the feelings it stirred.

Kendra looked directly at Siobhan.

Has Kendra noticed my reaction? Ooh, I need to get a handle on this.

"We still have to keep clear of anything we pass. Radioactive," Kendra said.

"I ken," Rory answered.

"You found the bodies?" Siobhan glanced around to Rory.

"Led us to the submarine like a trail o' breadcrumbs," he said.

Kendra rode off, leaving Siobhan gazing far ahead to where the clearing fog revealed the river flowing out of Loch Maree. They rode alongside the three islands in the middle of the loch. Rory twisted in the saddle, then wheeled his stallion around for a closer look behind the group.

Only tree branches moved in the wind on the path they'd come from. There was no sound except the sighing of the wind through the leaves. Then an osprey circled overhead, emitting short, sharp, high-pitched whistles in quick succession at their intrusion into its territory, the irritated, angry call a reprimand to their trespass. It circled back to its nest high in the tallest pine where it now roosted, protecting its young.

Rory breathed heavily behind her. "Ach. I'm gettin' jittery now. *Hmph.*" He steered the horse back to the others who'd stopped as well.

"Nothing. Yet," he said to those ahead. To Siobhan he whispered, "This day is nae over and I'm sure we've no' seen the last o' that lot. You be ready, okay?"

The old road beside the loch took them through the overgrown garden of an abandoned house. The trees grew thickly where the garden nestled by the lake.

"Right, everyone off your horses. Time for some lunch," Rory ordered.

The group dismounted, and Kendra rummaged in the saddlebags of a packhorse and brought out bread and cheese. Angus got out his home-made book, sat on a stone and continued his study.

"I'll be over by the water. I need to... you know." Siobhan's cheeks warmed as Rory gave her a blank look. "I need to relieve myself," she said as she marched toward the loch.

The breeze blew cool off the water's edge. Finding an old rowan tree, she glanced around to ensure no one from the group was looking at her. It was the part of camping she didn't like.

Footsteps came behind her. She turned, with a sharp remark ready for whoever of the group was rude enough to disturb her. A hand engulfed her mouth and gunfire began by the old house.

Stale-human smell accompanied the rough hand. She yelled behind it.

"Quiet," a gruff male voice shouted in her ear as his arm came around her waist and tightened.

"Where's Siobhan? She went to the loch to pee," Rory's voice came from near the house. "Anyone seen her?"

Through the rattle of bullets, no one answered him.

The smelly man who held her breathed heavily into her ear from behind. With his hand clamped over her mouth, getting air was difficult. She pulled short, sharp inhalations, trying to stave the panic rising within her. She freed a hand and dug her nails into the man's hand at her mouth. He grunted.

Horses whinnied and shrieked while the people yelled, but Rory hadn't spoken for a while.

Had they shot him? Is he okay?

An electric shock of alarm ran along her spine.

The smelly man grunted again. His arm around her jolted, then he thrust her away. She could breathe again! She ran into the garden's overgrown shrubbery, but the man didn't pursue her. She hid behind the foliage and glanced back at the grunts and noises of effort coming from the direction she'd just fled.

Rory tussled with her ex-captor. He had the man's arm in a hold, which brought him close in, with Rory's back to him. He was holding the man's hand in both of his, in a lock, trying to remove the hunting knife from him. Its sharp blade glinted dully.

Siobhan swallowed. *That guy had a hunting knife?*

Rory kept his hold on the man's arm. The man punched at Rory's back with his free fist. Rory grimaced and grunted with every pounding to his back and shoulder, the muscles in his forearms stood out with the strain.

The knife soon dropped, and Rory kicked it away. He elbowed the man in the stomach then spun. The man had doubled over but now thrust himself forward, pushing Rory onto the ground. Rory landed flat on his back with the man on top of him, grabbing for his throat.

Siobhan's lungs burned as she held her breath.

Rory kicked and spun his legs, lifting his body by arching his back. The man above him lifted off the ground and Rory flipped him over onto his back. Rory was now on top of the man, punching him in the face. Siobhan let out a wordless cry.

Rory's arms lifted high, one after the other, and landed with force onto the man's face. The man grunted at first, then was silent. Blood covered Rory's knuckles. Siobhan's stomach wrenched.

"Rory, stop! He's unconscious." Siobhan ran from the ancient shrubs and stood beside Rory, who straddled the man whose face was now bloodied and broken.

Siobhan's stomach twisted.

Rory stepped off the man, his chest heaving.

"You okay?" he asked, his brow knotted. "Did he hurt you? Did he stab you?"

"No." She glanced at herself.

No blood.

"Check yourself," he ordered. "Sometimes when people get stabbed, they don't know it at first. Dinnae feel it till later when the numbness wears off." He ran his hands over her arms and back then hesitated. "Ah, you can check the front."

"I'm okay, Rory. Are you?" she asked. "Your hands are bleeding."

"What was that all aboot!" Callum ran through the trees. "The others have gone. What did you do to this guy, Rory?"

"He had Siobhan," Rory said.

"Siobhan. Are you all right?" Antony followed Callum through the trees, his expression full of concern.

Too much concern.

"What happened?" Antony asked. "Why were you over here on your own?"

Siobhan tightened her mouth. Antony looked sincere, but he wasn't. She'd enough experience of Antony to know the difference. Why was he being so fake? And why did he not truly care that the bandit had attacked her?

She looked from Antony to Rory. Rory held her gaze, with a look that said he also recognised the falseness of Antony's reaction.

"Ooh, what are we going to do about this guy?" Antony pointed to the injured attacker.

"Leave him. His pals will find him when we go," Rory said. "Hopefully it will hold them up a bit. Although, it didn't stop them for long last time." Rory stormed to the loch and washed his hands.

Siobhan followed. His knuckles were raw from his bare-fisted fighting.

"I'll get the first aid kit to—" she began.

"No, lass, I'll be okay," he said.

"Thank you, Rory."

He nodded and glanced up from the water's edge.

"How well do you know that man?" His voice was quiet as he pointed his chin toward Antony who was tramping back to the horses.

What did he mean? There was animosity between Rory and Antony, but was he accusing him of something?

"I have known him all my life," she said. "I grew up with him."

Rory stood and faced her. "That does nae answer ma question." He strode toward the horses.

Siobhan walked beside him but stopped at the unconscious man with the battered, bloody face. Rory stepped ahead a pace then halted. She couldn't help her expression as she stared at her attacker—disgust and accusation would cross her face. Rory's vehemence and aggression had surprised her.

"Siobhan." His voice was low. His stare intense. More intense than it had ever been so far. "He had you. And he had a knife. No question as far as I'm concerned." He gave a short nod, turned, and continued to the horses.

After eating, the group remounted and resumed their journey by the loch. They soon passed it by to their left. Siobhan sat in front of Rory, the silence a thick wall between two people sitting so close. She glanced at his skinned knuckles.

He'd do that for me? Severely hurt another to prevent harm to her? Rory *was* a physically powerful man, but she'd never had cause to fear him.

She still didn't.

The small seaside town of Poolewe came into view ahead of them. White houses with grey roofs dotted the coast, and as the sun shone brighter, brilliant blue water lay enticingly ahead.

Idyllic.

If only her circumstances were different. How she'd love to go for a swim or a sail. Not that she could do either, but she'd try. She jiggled in the saddle. It wasn't only the danger they'd already faced that made her jittery, but she desired to be at the loch and see the ocean close up. She barely remembered what the beach was like.

A vague recollection of a seaside holiday at St Andrews when she was very young, flitted into her mind. A strong wind blew off the water and across the wide, long beach. Her mother stayed by the sandcastle they'd made, her hat-strap tightening under her chin as her broad-brimmed sun-hat strained against the breeze coming straight in off the North Sea. Siobhan ran along the sands at full pelt, the cathedral ruins were on the cliffs ahead of her. She pretended to be Eric Liddell and the other runners in that movie. *What was it called?* Her father was young and fit but allowed her to overtake him and win the race.

As fathers do.

The horse nickered and pranced.

"What are you doing?" Rory asked.

"Nothing."

"You're kicking ma horse," he said. "I'm in control of this animal, remember? You're confusing him."

With her daydream, and her desire to be at the loch and see the ocean close once more, she had jiggled her feet. Her growing impatience added to her edginess. She willed herself to calm down and focus. They'd be there soon, and they had an important job to do.

Important!

That was an understatement.

If they failed, they would all die and most of Scotland with them. She glanced at Rory's hand holding the reins. What would become of him?

The afternoon passed and the sapphire-blue water glistened in the brilliant summer sunshine. The sun warmed her front and Rory warmed her back.

They passed the inlet where people moored small sail boats and larger motorboats. The tide was out and boats near the shore on wet sand lay tilted to one side, appearing abandoned and helpless. The tides. The phases of the moon. These were phenomena she had only read of in her early science studies. Now she experienced the effects of them all.

Sometimes this whole expedition was *overload.*

Gunfire popped. Bullets whizzed past them, and Rory tensed behind her.

"Move!" he shouted, kicking the stallion into a gallop.

On either side, Rory's crew urged their horses in behind him. Siobhan held tight to the pommel of the saddle as they rode hard through the small village; close-packed houses flashed by her. At a gravel lane just after the town, Rory turned Boy sharply and led them behind a single storey stone-building, an old, dilapidated garage.

"We'll make our stand here," Rory yelled to the others.

He slid from the saddle, reached up to her, and dragged her down. "Stay low," he commanded.

Siobhan squatted against the wall.

Callum flew off his horse. "There's about half a dozen of them," he shouted to Rory from the corner of the building then peered around the side of the garage again.

Kendra jumped off her horse, lifted her bow off her shoulder, and notched an arrow. She joined Callum at the far end of the building where the gunfire was loudest.

Siobhan glanced around the laneway. Antony had a handgun and made his way to the end of the lane with Angus and Geoff. Sanjay and Sundeep were with him as well. Antony paused, then stepped out.

"Antony," she whispered hoarsely. "What are you doing?"

Gunfire blazed from the opposite direction, where Callum and Kendra defended, whizzing bullets close by. Rory pressed Siobhan to the ground, lying her flat, face down. The gravel grazed her face and stung. Rory lay on top of her, covering her head with his head and arms.

"Don't move," he said into her ear, his weight heavy on her.

The volley of gunfire from the bandits slowed. Callum's returning fire petered out. Kendra panted by the corner of the building.

The clatter of horses' hooves filled the lane. Rory lifted his head off Siobhan and turned. Still laying over her, he fired his submachine gun. His body vibrated as the *thud, thud, thuds* rocked through him, knocking Siobhan's back with each release of a bullet. Siobhan's ears rang with the noise.

The lane filled with the crack of returning gunfire. Horses screamed.

"Get her!" an unfamiliar voice yelled amongst a cry of pain.

Rory fired again, the snap of his gunfire matching a bang from Callum's handgun.

"Oh, shite!" a deep voice cried as a body thudded on the gravel of the lane.

The acrid scent of propellant hung low in the air, stinging Siobhan's nose.

"Stop. Stop!" an unfamiliar and weak male voice came from the end of the lane.

The weight of Rory lifted from Siobhan. A bandit threw his gun to the ground, it clattered in front of him, then he raised his arms in the air. The bodies of three of his comrades lay in distorted positions to his left. A groan came from one, then not another sound. At the other end of the lane, two more lay dead. Next to them, Antony stood, along with the rest of the team except Sundeep, who lay immobile near the one remaining horse who hadn't fled but skittered around, wild-eyed.

Siobhan ran to Sundeep. Bullet holes had ripped through his jacket, and he groaned as she turned him over to face them. Sanjay crawled closer, silent. He placed a hand on his brother's arm, then after a short time, closed his brother's eyes.

Xian tied the hands of the surrendered bandit. Callum and Kendra kicked the legs of the immobile or prostrate bandits, ensuring they were in fact dead. Angus and Geoff peered around the corners of the building to make sure there were no more.

"It wasn't meant to be like this," the bandit shouted, anguish in his voice.

Rory spun. "Wasn't meant to be like what?" Rory followed the bandit's stare.

It led to Antony.

Rory made his way to Antony, who stood fidgeting with his gun.

Antony had an expression Siobhan recognised—a tell. Something only someone who had been as close as a lover could see. She should have noticed it earlier. He was jealous of Rory.

Hated him.

For his robustness, his leadership talents, and the love his people had for him—everything Antony desired but lacked. She was certain his fidgeting hand holding the gun wouldn't stop.

"No, Antony!" Siobhan ran and stood in front of Rory. "Put the gun down!"

Rory placed his hand on her shoulder, his strong fingers digging deep into the muscles near her collarbone, shoving her away behind him.

"Coward!" The shout came from the bandit at the other end of the lane, who directed his accusation at Antony.

Xian flew out from behind the building near where Antony stood. With his legs extended, he kicked the gun from Antony's hand then landed to hold the drawn Katana to Antony's throat. Antony raised his hands, his eyes narrow and mouth a thin line. Callum raced forward with a rope and yanked Antony's hands behind his back, tying them securely. Antony never flinched, his eyes remained staring ahead, focussed on no one.

"I'll get the horses that ran," Angus said. "They've got the equipment we need." He left the lane.

Rory stood silently staring at Antony, nodding slowly.

"I knew there was something about you," he growled. "But we dinnae have time for this at present. We need to collect our gear, prepare our dead for transportation," he pointed to Sundeep, "and get to the sub. Then we'll hear the whole story." He took his gaze from Antony and addressed the bandit. "Can we expect any more surprises?"

The bandit shook his head, his long, matted, greying hair falling around his face and his torn leather jacket.

Siobhan walked to Antony, whose arms were now firmly tied behind his back. She faced him full on, her disgust and anger burning in her throat.

How could he?

"Consider yourself under the arrest of both authorities. Government and Community," she snarled.

"Your wild-boy there has clouded your mind, Siobhan." Antony pointed to Rory with his chin, his expression full of disdain.

She held her open palm to his face. "Not now!" she said.

He opened his sneering mouth to speak.

"Save it for later," she said. "You *will* give a full account of yourself and your actions." She turned and walked back toward Rory.

Rory watched her approach him, blue eyes never leaving hers. She made to walk past him, but he reached for her upper arm and held it with a gentle, warm grip then drew her close.

"What was *that* all about?" he whispered so low, only she could hear.

"He's been up to something, that's for sure," she said.

"No, not him. *You?*" He shook her arm softly, his blue gaze riveted to hers.

Words of explanation didn't come. What *was* she doing? *Why* had she stood in front of Rory when she expected Antony would shoot him? Then, there was a sudden thump in her soul as a revelation hit her.

She would protect Rory with her life if that was needed.

His stare remained on her, and the slow shaking of his head began once more.

"Never do that to me again, Siobhan," he whispered.

The *clip clop* of a horse's hooves and a whinny with a nudge at his back broke the moment.

"Aye, Boy, I ken you always come back." Rory reached behind and grabbed the stallion's reins.

Chapter Eighteen

After wrapping Sundeep's body in his bedroll blanket then loading him over a packhorse, they remounted their horses and continued the journey. Siobhan had placed Sanjay's arm in a sling, as he'd cradled it with his good arm and blood had seeped through the bandage at his shoulder. She would take a closer look at it when they finally arrived at Drumchork, or as near as was safe.

The blue sky was cloudless and the loch's water sparkling.

This is so incongruent.

Callum had bound Antony and the remaining bandit who was under arrest, a packhorse stood-in for a hearse, and the whole party made their way to an unstable nuclear warhead or two.

A pleasant afternoon's outing in the Scottish Highlands.

Rory was silent behind her. She had little to say, her mind whirring with the day's events. He'd shielded her twice, beaten a man almost to death to protect her, and had the gall to reprimand her, all-be-it in a gentle way, for attempting to do the same for him. He was a chauvinist.

Or is he just protective?

Rory shouldered an unusually large burden of responsibility, not necessarily warranted. She had heard he was like his father, a man who seemed to be a superhero in many peoples' eyes. Not only those in the Community. Antony held the man somewhere between awe and disdain.

Did Rory believe he had to fill his father's boots completely? His father's death had deeply affected him. His responses to her insensitive questions yesterday were evidence he was still working through his grief. According to Antony, Rory's mother died six years ago, and his father soon after.

What had happened there?

Rory was definitely protective of his family members and had a genuine concern and active interest in the welfare of his community. It was just good leadership, wasn't it? Or did it go deeper? A hero complex maybe?

They followed the road; the party quiet. Most of them probably directed their thoughts to their task ahead—and Sundeep's death. In addition, the recent revelation of the deception and possible betrayal by Antony. Was it a shock to them?

Oddly, it wasn't a shock to her.

Something about his behaviour of late had niggled at her. Unexplained absences. Furtive glances. When questioned, Antony always had an excuse and an alibi if asked. A guard saw him *here,* or he was off on his own *there.* No, nothing he had done on this journey had surprised her. She only wished she had been smart enough to put it together and deal with it before people had got killed. She glanced at the horse in front, carrying her friend's body. Her eyes filled with tears.

Poor Sundeep.

Beside the road, the loch was a serene calm. Seagulls called as they soared on the sea breezes. The wind blew across the loch, rippling the surface and bathing her face in fresh, cool, salty air. It reminded her it was a sea loch, and the big wide ocean was just out there ahead. Past the far entrance of the loch, was a body of water they called The Minch; it sat between mainland Scotland and the Isle of Lewis. Places she'd only ever seen on a map were now so close she *could* reach out and touch them. Her arms would be long enough.

"It's beautiful, Rory." She turned to face him, expecting to see an expression of awe mirroring hers. Instead, his eyes were hooded, and lines furrowed his brow, his jaw muscles tensed, and no smile hinted at his mouth.

He blinked and looked at her. "It is. And we must do all necessary to keep it that way."

"Of course. It's why we're here," she said.

"Aye, it *is* why we are here." His answer had a philosophical note to it.

What are you up to, Rory Campbell?

The edge of her hearing caught the grunt of an engine. Rory reined Boy around to look. A small, pale-blue motorboat, with the word *Spirit* painted on its side, chugged along the loch. It caught up with them and travelled close beside until they reached a place soon after a sign which read *Loch*

Thurnaig—a small calm inlet of Loch Ewe. Rory and the members of his crew were unperturbed.

"You are familiar with this vessel?" she asked him.

"Oor friendly fisherman," Rory said. "Murdo MacDonald."

As if on cue, a shout of "*Ahoy*" came from the boat now closer to the shore. Rory waved, and they made their way to a small outcropping of land where there was a floating pier. The captain of the boat drove it near then threw a rope to the small pier. Callum jumped off his horse, ran to the pier, and tied the rope to a pole. The fisherman disembarked from his boat and headed toward them as Rory dismounted. Siobhan got down from the saddle after him.

Murdo's eyes never left Rory while he walked toward him along the pier to the grassy area where they had led the horses. A broad smile filled the old man's face. It seemed inappropriate in the circumstances.

Wasn't this a dire situation? Wasn't he our only help up here? Siobhan wondered. He should behave more seriously. But he didn't. Murdo Mac-Donald embraced Rory with an enthusiastic, tight bear hug.

Were those tears in his eyes? It was hard to tell in the weather-beaten face.

"So good to see you again, young Rory," Murdo said, his voice as gravelly as Siobhan had expected.

He gave Callum a hug as well and shook hands with the rest of his team. Yes, there were definitely tears.

"This is Ms Siobhan Kensington-Wallace," Rory said. "From the Scottish Government." Rory drew her forward and Murdo shook her hand with vigour.

"Lovely to meet you, Ms Kensington-Wallace." His smile lingered, and he glanced between her and Rory, several times. She blinked, and Rory scratched his bandaged head.

"Yes, so nice to meet you." She needed to take this old man's intense stare away from them. "I'd introduce my colleague, but he is in disgrace." She inclined her head toward Antony still mounted on a horse. Murdo's gaze slid briefly to the mounted prisoners.

"This distance is safe enough for us." Rory gave a sharp nod. "We'll set up camp here on the grass and begin our preparations. And how shall I put it? Our *discussions*, with Major Antony McLellan."

His crew sprang into action; the government team members followed suit.

They soon erected tents, set out the computer equipment on camp tables, opened metal boxes containing detonators and timers, emptied the larger saddle bags that held the radiation protective equipment, then seated the restrained members of the party under guard.

Murdo gave Rory a shirt, which Rory examined with eyes wide.

"Och. The label is still in it," he said. He took his stiff and bulky SAPI vest off then put on the flannelette shirt. "I have nae seen one like this for years."

The afternoon sun angled beams of light through the trees which skirted their makeshift campsite. The continual soft lapping of waves against Loch Ewe's shoreline was a constant background noise, and a breeze, cool as it came off the water, stirred Siobhan's hair. Her face was hot and tight. So were her arms where her shirt hadn't covered them.

Sunburn?

She leaned against the small portable table on which Sanjay had set up the laptop computer. He held his arm and grimaced as he looked at the screen. Angus stood close behind, peering intently at the computer screen, observing everything Sanjay did.

"We need to get a closer look," Sanjay said, wincing.

He gently grabbed his shoulder. Apart from his wound, he'd rallied remarkably well, and was incredibly brave, in Siobhan's eyes, for continuing after the death of his brother.

But they had a job to do, and nothing should stop them. And her friend knew that.

"Ye'll have tae believe me." Murdo was emphatic. "It's a Russian 677 Lada with AIP. Diesel fuel cell. The radiation must be from one or more unstable nuclear warheads attached to the missiles in their bays. Nae body's tae go near the thing unless it's tae fix it." The fisherman's head was at an angle, broaching no argument.

Sanjay turned, glanced at Murdo then grimaced again. Beads of sweat had formed on his brow. He studied his computer screen, typing to bring up more information.

"Are you okay, Sanjay?" A shiver travelled along Siobhan's spine. If Sanjay wasn't up to the technical part, they could be in difficulty—to say the least.

In front of the tents, Antony sat to the left of the bandit. Murmurings had come from their direction since Kendra had forced them to sit crossed legged on the ground.

"Well, I'm telling them!" The bandit's hoarse loud voice stopped the activity surrounding them.

"Quiet, you two." Kendra slapped the back of the heads of both men with a firm hand.

Rory placed the silver radiation-protection suit he handled back in its bag then walked over to stand in front of the two men.

"Now is as good a time as any, don't you think, Siobhan?" Rory glanced back to the computer desk where she stood, inviting her to step forward as well. "You need to be in on this."

She left the table with Sanjay at the computer and Angus standing behind him watching his every move. Antony's frown was a straight line matching the line of his tightly closed mouth. The bandit looked weary, and his dirty face wore the streaks from his tears. His chest rose and fell rapidly, interspersed with heavy sighs.

"Who wants to go first?" Rory asked.

"I do!" Regret tinged the bandit's broad Scottish accent. His torn and dirty leather jacket hung off his shoulders. He mustn't have washed for days, and a stale man-smell wafted into Siobhan's face.

"First, what's your name?" Rory folded his arms as he looked at the middle-aged man.

"Rabbie MacPherson, sir," the bandit replied.

"Where do you come from?" Rory asked.

"Ardmillan, sir," he said.

"And why would you be chasin' us through the Highlands then?" Rory asked.

Rabbie's brows lowered, and he turned his head to Antony. "Ask him," he growled.

At the makeshift computer desk, Sanjay leaned back in his camp chair and bore his stare into Antony. Angus looked up from the screen as he stood behind the IT tech and turned his attention to the interrogation. Geoff, standing by them at another portable table, stopped assembling the CB radio kit he'd brought. Murdo stood with his arms crossed and tugged at his beard while the rest of the team gathered behind Siobhan and Rory.

Antony maintained a stony silence.

"Well?" Rory addressed Antony.

"You wouldn't understand if I told you." Antony briefly glanced up at Rory then resumed his examination of the grass in front of him.

"Ach! Ye cowardly bastard, McLellan," the bandit spat. "You caused the death o' my men and ma baby brother! Ye should rot in hell! And I sincerely hope ye do!"

"Well, you'll be there to enjoy it, won't you?" Anthony sneered back.

"Okay, gentlemen," Rory said. "MacPherson, please?" Rory nodded his encouragement to the bandit.

"A few weeks ago, this man here"—McPherson inclined his head toward Antony— "comes around our place, like, where we spend oor time seein' what's what. He asks us what we think of a liberated Scotland since England remains in a mess and cudnae bale us oot financially even if they wanted tae. Level playin' field, he says." He paused as he glanced at Antony.

"Go on." Rory's fingers lightly tapped his upper arm as he stood with arms crossed.

"Well, we did nae see him much after that," MacPherson continued. "Some of us got all excited aboot a totally independent Scotland, aye. Now was the time, ken? Ill wind that blows nae gud, an' all. I mean, we had nae heard o' the government for years, aye? British, English, Scottish or whatever. If things came back"—his eyes lit up and his voice deepened— "we could be *Scotland* again." His hand raised in a fist. "Last week, four days ago, this shyster comes back, and buttonholes me. Kenning I had a group o' men I worked with. Told us tae follow and give trouble tae the vehicles that would soon come oot o' the Government compound. 'What Government compound?', I says. He then telt me all aboot the bunker under Arthur's Seat, ye ken? So that's where they'd been holed up for years, ken?"

Rory nodded once more, his silent attentiveness allowing McPherson to find his words.

"So, we did," MacPherson went on. "We pretended to harass the armour-plated vehicles that came out the concrete yard at the back o' the hill. Kept our distance once we'd given them a scare."

Antony fixed his gaze to the ground. Siobhan's heart raced. It was all becoming *so* clear.

"You put us in danger right from the start, Antony!" She stepped toward him. Rory placed his hand on her arm, preventing her from moving closer.

"If *he* had stuck to the plan, we would have never been in danger." Antony spoke at last, directing his vitriol at his neighbour.

"Aye, but *your* plan changed, man." McPherson spat back. "Ye still wanted harassment but ye were nae in yoor armoured vehicles any longer once ye left the Community Compound in the Highlands."

"You can thank Mr Wonderful, who *knows-all-about-it* here for that!" Antony lifted his chin up at Rory. "I had no way of letting you know we weren't using them anymore. You didn't have to come so hard, though."

"Aye, but it had tae look realistic," McPherson said. "Thems were your orders, ken. Then those men at the compound fought back. Ye said they were barbarians who kenned nothing. Well, they kenned how tae fight. And they did. Plus yoor 'ain men gunned us doon! Lost Jamie, ma wee cousin, in that debacle. Did ye no' tell them we were on yoor side, like? We still wanted the money ye promised, so we followed."

"We are well aware of the rest—" Rory began.

"Och, I dinnae think so," the bandit spoke louder. "For last night, he comes to us in the forest and says we have tae—"

"Quiet, man!" Antony growled.

"What did he ask you to do, Mr McPherson?" Rory released his grip on Siobhan and straightened his shoulders.

"Quiet!" Antony snarled.

"You!" Rory leaned over and yelled into Antony's face. "Be silent."

"He says we were to take *her*." McPherson indicated with a nod to Siobhan.

Siobhan stood stock still, her body rigid as her heart rocked in her chest. *Antony would put me in danger?*

She turned her head to meet Rory's stare. His nostrils flared, his face reddening, and his hand moving toward his gun.

No! She slowly shook her head. "Let justice take its course, Rory," she whispered.

The muscles in his cheek tensed as his eyes narrowed.

'Please,' she mouthed.

His shoulders lowered slightly. "Verra well," he said to her, his voice low.

"So here we are," Rory addressed the men sitting on the ground in front of him. "One of our number is dead and another injured. Two important technical people for our task. And I am sorry for your losses," he directed this statement to McPherson. "Seems you have been used."

Rory stared at Antony without comment. He had given Rabbie a chance to explain and had exhibited compassion and understanding. But there was an enmity between Rory and Antony.

Would he be as kind to Antony?

Antony stared at the ground.

She was furious at Antony for what he'd done. Teeth-grinding, fist-clenching furious. He knew how important it was to everyone that they dealt with the nuclear danger. His treatment of McPherson, a loyal, patriotic Scot, was abominable. And his total disregard for her own safety...

She couldn't keep it in anymore.

But coming from her it would mean little.

"Mr MacPherson." She turned to the shabby, dirty man before her. "I believe the duplicity of your employer, as we shall call him, goes beyond what you can envisage. It is the truth that, from about eight months after the Stock Market Crash just over forty years ago, and aided by an issue history named *Brexit*, Scotland has in fact been an independent country, governed totally separate from the rest of Britain, which indeed can no longer call itself the United Kingdom. The Scottish Government chose to keep this knowledge from the Scottish people until they deemed the time suitable."

The silence was only momentary. MacPherson, still restrained by the ropes Callum had tied around his wrists, let out a roar and lunged for Antony. His head connected with Antony's cheek, and he bit. Kendra leaped forward, but too late. Xian came from behind and pulled Antony away from MacPherson as Kendra got a grip on the bandit's shoulders and pulled the other way. A yelp of pain came from Antony as a chunk of his cheek remained in MacPherson's mouth and blood cascaded down his face.

"Keep them apart!" Rory moved forward to assist Kendra with the enraged bandit, now spitting the flesh from his mouth.

"Ahh!" Antony continued his cry in between shallow, shocked breaths.

"Why are ye so surprised?" MacPherson spat through a blood-filled mouth. "Yoo have caused the death of those dear to me because of your *lie*. What was it all for, man?"

"Get him over by the far tent and clean him up, Kendra!" Rory ordered. Kendra, with Xian's help, moved the man away.

"What *was* it all for?" Siobhan asked Antony once they had removed the bandit.

"Aren't you going to clean me up?" Antony cried, his eyes wide, then he grimaced.

"Not until you tell me why." She couldn't stop the tremble of anger rippling through her.

Rory's warm hand tightened on her arm once more.

"We deserve an explanation, don't we?" Her voice rose in pitch. She took a breath to calm herself.

Rory nodded and turned his gaze to Antony, an eyebrow raised.

"I needed to show the Government the futility of joining with the Communities out here." Antony spoke through gritted teeth and spit flew out of his mouth with every word. "I needed to show the First Minister how barbaric and dangerous the people *up top* are. That you're not capable of what of our educated, intelligent, and skilled members can do. And joining to govern with those *up top* would be a disastrous mistake. A preposterous notion. *We* need to rule. Not you hippies with armies. You Doomsday Preppers who think you've got it all sorted and need to protect the average citizen from the *control* of the Government. We're the ones who know how to do it—*not you*. You'll cause a bloody revolution. We should stamp you out before you even try!" Antony directed his vehemence totally at Rory.

Everyone looking on were silent, and like Siobhan herself, immobile—paralysed with shock.

How could Antony think *it*, now he'd met them all? Good, sensible, honest, resourceful people. Brave, organised, skilled people living in peace amongst themselves. Protecting themselves from those who would do them harm. They risked *all* to make their part of this crazy world safe! Without hesitation or questioning! She shook her head.

"No," she said.

It came out softly at first. Then became louder as she repeated it through halting breaths, as the spring of emotion sitting in her, welled up and she couldn't contain it.

"No. No. No!"

Antony turned to her, his expression like a fist down her throat, stopping any further comment.

"Siobhan, I knew you coming would be a mistake. You've always had a soft spot for those *up top*." He sneered the word out of his mouth as if to chase it all the way to hell. "I knew you'd latch on to one of them with your romantic notions of the *wonderful world* up here. I hoped all this violence would make you realise how fanciful and unrealistic your imaginings of life outside of our safe bunker really were. Instead, you latch on to John Connor like a limpet. The boy's young enough for it to be illegal. Just look at yourself, woman!" Antony continued breathing heavily as blood dripped down his face and pooled at his collar.

Siobhan covered her face, blocking out the accusation and hatred fired directly at her. Hot tears soaked her fingers, her shoulders shook as emotions exploded within her. They muted her words, rendered her speechless, and kept her face buried in her hands.

Chapter Nineteen

Invercharing Community

Murray buzzed. The Community's old computer now had more RAM and Gigabytes. He'd written a couple of programs. The calculations, completed in moments, flew past his screen.

He was in heaven.

They now had more data on file, larger storage, more historical records, engineering and agricultural information, music and electronic instruments, and enough maths programs to keep him very happy for a while.

The Government's computers had a million times more data though. They communicated with each other, and apparently, in the Government Bunker they had an *intranet*. Murray sat back in his chair, his eyes dry from peering at a screen for hours.

The control-room was quiet. The Government people sleeping on camp stretchers now began small stirrings.

Is it morning already? Have I been at it the entire night?

Murray nudged Stan beside him, his head dropped off his folded arms resting on the table.

"What! Oh." Stan's mouth hung open and one eye stuck closed with sleep.

The aroma of warm food wafted past Murray's nose.

Hmm, bread.

"Breakfast," Ceilidh called as she stepped her way through the awakening bodies and placed plates of warm bannocks and a large pot of porridge on the table in the middle of the control-room.

Murray nudged Stan again then walked over and took a bowl from the pile.

"So, you've got a taste for it now, Murray?" MacIntosh stood next to him.

"What? Oh, yes," Murray said. *MacIntosh doesn't mean the porridge, that's for sure.*

"So, you'll come back with us?" MacIntosh's voice was encouraging, with a determined edge to it.

"Seriously, I have to ask Rory first," he said. "I can't give you an answer until then."

Man, he really wanted to go, but this guy's insistence was getting... well. Murray hunched his shoulders, trying to suppress a niggle of anxiety tweaking the edges of his reasoning.

"How is everyone this morning?" Angela's voice was cheery as she approached the breakfast table. Definitely not her norm. She dressed in a blouse and a straight skirt with her long red hair loosely tied behind her. "Has everyone recovered from our excitement yesterday?"

Murray scowled at her. She was making light of it. Like it happens every day, and they were experts at dealing with that kind of onslaught. He doubted it would have been resolved so quickly if the Government's machine cannon wasn't here.

Angela stood closer to McIntosh, offering him bannocks and her arm brushing against his.

She'd been very friendly with the visitors.

Too friendly.

Obviously friendly, and *more*, in fact, if yesterday's incident was anything to go by. Wow, he hoped he'd never see *that* again. The heat rose to Murray's cheeks.

He walked back to his chair in front of the computer and opened an Excel document. Anything to take his mind off *that* memory. His attention flicked back to Angela. She was up to something.

"Mr Macintosh—" Angela pushed stray strands of hair behind her ear.

"Please, call me William." The man placed the finished bowl of porridge on the table.

"William," Angela said. "You have been so busy with the computer geeks, if that's what you call them, you haven't had a look around our compound, now have you?"

Uh, oh. What if this guided tour gets as personal as the last one? Murray thought. *How embarrassing.* Angela looked desperate—cringingly so.

What was she after?

Murray would have to keep tabs on his ambitious big sister today.

After Angela had finished breakfast, she escorted MacIntosh out of the control-room. Murray ditched his unfinished porridge and followed, keeping his distance. Angela walked MacIntosh to the room where the Chief Council met.

Would she show off their tables they line up to look like a boardroom?

"And in here we make all our important decisions regarding the governing of our community." Angela waved MacIntosh into the meeting room, then followed him in. Murray stood outside the still open door, out of sight.

"I, myself, have been on the Chief Council for the past six years," Angela said, "since my mother passed away."

"Oh, I'm sorry," MacIntosh sounded respectful.

"Caitlin Murray-Campbell, my mother," Angela went on, "was a founding member of the Community. And indeed, of the Community way of life and system of government. She groomed me for leadership from a young age, having seen my potential. They say I am very like her."

Yep, except Mum was humble.

"Here we adjudicate disputes and make informed and important decisions affecting the Community." Angela's voice wafted through the doorway. "And as you know, we are also concerned about those who live outside our Community and any incidents which may impact us and them. The present situation with the nuclear problem is an example of our dedication to the welfare of Scotland."

"Hmm," MacIntosh replied.

It was hard to tell if it impressed MacIntosh or not.

"Let me take you to our meeting hall, where we assemble the whole Community." Angela strode out the door.

Murray ducked back into the doorway behind him. When Angela and MacIntosh moved off, he continued his tail.

"For a young person I have a great amount of experience in governing and making important decisions." Angela's voice echoed in the hall. "The other members of the Chief Council find my leadership skills impressive. They would be the first to tell you I am an asset to this Community and, indeed, would be an asset in any form of government.'

What does she want?

"I heard you speaking to my younger brother, Murray," Angela said. "You mentioned taking him back to the Government Bunker."

"A young lad with those skills, it would be a shame to waste them." MacIntosh sounded enthusiastic once more. "We could teach him a great deal."

"So, you want him to visit the Government Bunker?" Angela asked.

"Yes, that would be wonderful," MacIntosh said. "But he feels he needs the permission of his older brother, Rory."

"I may be able to persuade Rory." There was a suggestive note to Angela's tone.

"Oh, I'd appreciate it greatly, Miss Murray-Campbell," MacIntosh said.

"And you would want someone with governing experience to return with you?" Angela resumed her spiel. "Surely the Government needs someone who has experienced life out here and knows how to survive, and has a deep knowledge of the people *up top*, as you call us?" Angela's voice dropped. "A valuable resource, a team member who would be an ideal representative of the Communities when the Scottish Government rules overtly, once more."

"Well, those sorts of decisions are not up to me," MacIntosh said.

"But you could put a good word in for me, couldn't you?" Angela's tone was unusually soft.

Silence came from the room as Murray stood behind its door.

What's goin' on?

"Miss Murray-Campbell!" MacIntosh's startled voice came out the door. "I'm a married man!"

"Oh! Okay. Beg your pardon." Angela's sharp authoritative voice returned. "Let me show you our science facilities."

Angela's clicking heels, followed by MacIntosh's footsteps, made their way out of the assembly hall. Murray dashed inside and through the hall in time to see MacIntosh disappearing into the barn where they stored the scientific equipment, meagre as it was. Compared to the equipment the Government brought, it was an embarrassment. Why would she want to show MacIntosh that?

Murray snuck along the corridor into which Angela had taken her guest. Why was she showing him their archaic computer equipment in the almost bare technical room? Well, at least the old computer had more RAM now.

Still so unimpressive.

Murray ducked into a side room once more as Angela guided MacIntosh out of the small room and led him along the corridor to... *oh, no!*

Angela strode fast and the large man behind her easily kept up with her pace. Murray caught up as they entered the room where they housed the Time Machine.

"Angela, no!" Murray's voice rang out in the high raftered barn.

MacIntosh stepped over the cables taped to the hard-packed earthen-floor and cast his gaze over the console containing the controls for the Time Machine.

"What do we have here?" He ran his hand along the metal console then glanced up at the fibreglass cubicle that had once been an old shower recess.

"Angela. No," Murray said.

MacIntosh's eyes flicked up to Murray's, they held curiosity. MacIntosh faced Angela.

"Tell me—" he began.

"Only if you promise to let me come to the Government Bunker." Angela's response was lightning fast.

"No, Angela!" Murray's voice rang out in the barn.

He ran over the cold, dirt floor to where the power cords connected to their electricity supply and pulled them out.

"Okay. He's all riled up. You've *got* to tell me." MacIntosh's tone was suddenly greedy, his left eye twitched as his stare bore into Murray.

"No, Angela." Murray's nails dug into his palms as he faced them both.

"Quiet, brother. You don't know what's at stake here." Her eyes were wide as she turned to him.

"Angela, *you* don't know what's at stake here. Don't!" He shook his head so hard his neck hurt.

"Time Machine." Angela barely spoke, her throat convulsing in a swallow.

"What?" MacIntosh's hands paused on the control console.

"Nothing." Murray fought to calm the adrenalin surge. "Just something we've been playing with."

His throat tightened with an anguish and an anger at his sister, like nothing he'd ever experienced.

Shut up Angela, leave it at that.

"It's a Time Machine and it works. My brother Rory has used it twice." Angela gulped as she stood straighter.

Yep, and that same brother, Rory, is going to kill you.

"You can have permission to examine it if you promise to take me with you when you return to the Government Bunker." Angela's eyes narrowed.

Murray's breath began to falter. She'd done it. She'd *really* done it. Sold everyone out for her ambitious desires.

Oh, hell.

Chapter Twenty

Loch Ewe

Rory sat beside Siobhan on a log by the water's edge. A sea otter played nearby, his splashes and dives stirred the water and caused more ripples as his miniature waves hit the shore. At any other time, his antics would have been quite amusing.

Siobhan had stopped crying but still looked distressed. Her face, rosy from sunburn, was now even redder. Rory had held her close, hugging her to his side and feeling every sob shaking through her body. He'd followed Siobhan when she retreated to the loch's side once Antony had finished his little speech. His cutting, accusing, embarrassing speech.

Bastard.

Traitor.

Madman.

Rory was now convinced years of living underground had warped the man's mind.

Rory had to get on with it. Time was wasting.

"Siobhan, I've got to speak with Sanjay about this nuke." He sounded apologetic as he took his arm from around her shoulders.

"I'm so sorry and slightly embarrassed—" Siobhan's moist eyes looked into his.

"Don't be," Rory said. "I think the man is unwell. Well, it's what I'll say for now, anyway."

Rory stood and walked across the grass to the table where Sanjay looked at a computer, the screen light reflecting on his face hid none of his pallor. Angus hovered over him.

"Sanjay, are you okay?" Siobhan had followed Rory and now rushed to the IT tech's side.

Sanjay shook his head and grimaced. "I need to let whoever will sort out the nuke"—he grabbed his shoulder and gasped— "I need to let them know what to do."

Beads of sweat dripped down his face. Siobhan placed her hand on his forehead.

"He's boiling," she said.

'Infection?' Rory mouthed over Sanjay's head.

Siobhan nodded. "I'll go get some antibiotics." Siobhan half turned to go.

"No. I need to tell you *all* this now, please." Sanjay looked to Rory with pleading eyes.

Rory moved closer to view the computer screen. Footsteps came behind him and he turned to see Xian, Kendra, and Callum standing there.

"Oh, no," he said. "You three are on guard duty."

"No, we've handed that over—" Kendra began.

"Guard duty and no arguments!" Rory said, his voice as loud and firm as he could make it without yelling.

He would yell at them if he must. Callum blinked. Rory gave him a look, then Callum turned and walked to the tents. Kendra still had her mouth open and a hand on her hip. He narrowed his eyes at her. She closed her mouth, turned, and followed Callum.

Rory looked at Xian.

Xian shook his head. "You may just need me, man."

Angus' shoulder brushed against Rory's as he peered at the screen.

"So, we board and set the timer on the detonator," Angus said. "We may have to do it on each one."

Angus' green eyes were wide, either from excitement or fear, Rory wasn't sure. But he was sure Angus would join him in wearing a silver suit.

"You must remove a missile from its torpedo bay, one from each rack, and change it from contact detonation to timer detonation." Sanjay took a few breaths. Speaking seemed to exhaust him. "There can be up to sixteen missiles, depending on how many have already been deployed."

"Sixteen!" A shiver passed along Rory's spine. *Unbelievable.*

"How much time do we need?" Xian asked.

"Enough time to clear the sub from mainland Scotland and the Isle of Lewis," Rory answered.

"And more." Sanjay took another deep breath. "You need to be well away from the landmass to not disturb the fault line which runs almost horizontally right through Scotland."

"What fault line?" The cold shiver in Rory's spine was getting icy.

"The High Boundary Fault line which traverses Scotland through Arran," Sanjay said, leaning forward a little and taking a long slow breath. "It runs along the Firth of Clyde and Helensburgh in the west, runs through Perthshire near Dunkeld, to Stonehaven in the east." Rivulets of perspiration made their way down his face.

"Oh," Rory swallowed.

"To sail past Lewis is almost one hundred miles," Murdo said, having joined the line-up surrounding Sanjay and his laptop. "Submarines travel at forty miles per hour. That's nautical miles. You'll need to set the timer for about eight hours to get into the North Atlantic Ocean."

"But the sub will have to be under before we can detonate the nuke or nukes," Angus pushed his glasses further up his nose. "So the ocean absorbs the impact *and* the radiation."

"Do they have automatic dive?" Xian asked.

Murdo screwed up his lips and looked at Rory. "Not really," he said. "It's an old Russian sub, remember. Och, and dinnae forget anyone could ha' made those nukes. North Korea bought them, after all. They could be Pakistani, Indian or any of the non-NATO countries."

Rory pursed his lips.

Someone may have to drive it. And dive it.

"I'll taxi ye tae it." Murdo offered. "I'll leave ye with a dinghy."

"Well, show me how to set the timers, Sanjay," Rory asked.

He leaned closer to the screen as Sanjay brought up the illustrations and explained to Rory, Angus, Murdo and Xian.

Rory squinted. "Ahh, could you also show me on the detonators we have? In case the nuke is nae the same as in the illustration. Then we'll use those." He turned to Xian. "Can you go get me the gadget, so he can show me on the actual timer and detonator, please?"

Xian turned and walked toward the equipment piled near the tents. Rory, watching him go, caught Siobhan's expression out of the corner of his eye. She blinked away tears and swallowed. Their eyes locked.

Siobhan's expression was one of 'why you?'. He gave a brief shake of his head. She turned and walked away. To get medical supplies for Sanjay, he guessed.

Xian returned with a detonator and timer then placed them on the table in front of Sanjay. Sanjay lifted his hand to the detonator; his movements were slow as he showed the sequence for disengaging the 'on-impact' mode. He winced often.

"And then the timer," Sanjay said, his voice husky as he explained the procedure.

Along with Rory, Xian and Angus leaned over Sanjay's shoulder, watching every detail. When he finished, Sanjay sat back heavily in his chair, his arms limp by his sides, a grimace fixed on his features.

"You won't have to do all sixteen. Probably only two." Sanjay's chest rose with an inhalation. "One on each rack should be enough. Those going off will simulate impact causing the others to detonate. But you still must activate the others. Switch them on if they aren't already. Sort of thing..." he let out a slow, ragged breath.

"Let's get you lying down to rest now, Sanjay," Siobhan said.

Rory and Siobhan supported Sanjay as he walked to his tent. On the way she grabbed a small container from her supplies. Once in the tent, Siobhan undid Sanjay's bedroll and, after laying him on it, gave him anti-biotic tablets.

"Where did you get those?" Rory asked. "We have nae seen antibiotics, well real ones, for years."

"We have a small pharmaceuticals lab in the Bunker. I'll get something to cool him down." Siobhan put the tablets back in her pocket and went toward the water's edge with a facecloth.

Rory walked back to the others who had remained at the computer.

"Short straw?" Xian asked.

"No question," Angus stated matter-of-factly as he pushed his spectacles up the bridge of his nose. "I'm the scientist. I'm going."

"Well, it's a two-man job so I'll be with you," Rory was just as adamant.

"No, Rory," Xian crossed his arms and faced Rory directly.

"Xian, dinnae argue. It's my job. I know it," Rory said.

"But we need you," Xian said.

"I've no intentions of not returning," Rory replied. "You sound like I'm going tae die."

"But how will the sub dive?" Xian asked.

"Automatic pilot I think they call it." Rory shrugged and twisted his mouth.

A cry came from Sanjay's tent.

"Help!" Siobhan screamed.

Rory and Xian sprinted to the tent where Sanjay lay with Siobhan kneeling beside him. Sanjay's breath sounded like wind whistling through a narrow tube. He looked like he struggled for air. Murdo brought a torch from out of the Government's kit lying nearby, and lit Sanjay's face. He was red and swollen, his neck thick, his tongue even thicker and poking out through his lips.

Angus came up behind them. "He must be allergic," he said. "Where's your Adrenalin?"

Siobhan ran back to the supplies to get a resuscitation kit. Rory turned Sanjay onto his side, but it had no effect on his breathing.

"But that's what you do, isn't it? Put them in the coma position?" Rory said. There was desperation in his own voice. He usually left the serious first aid to others.

"No, clear his airway. Tilt his head back," Angus said through the doorway of the tent.

Rory did as Angus directed. In the torchlight, Sanjay was now turning blue. Rory started pressing Sanjay's chest and did it the whole time they waited for Siobhan. Sanjay hadn't taken a breath for a few moments when Siobhan finally returned with a kit.

She took out a tube-like instrument and pressed it onto Sanjay's thigh. It clicked. Sanjay remained still, not attempting to take any breaths.

"What's meant to happen?" Murdo asked.

"He's meant to start breathing again." Siobhan pressed the Adrenalin gadget once more into the IT tech's thigh. Still nothing happened. She took his pulse. Rory compressed Sanjay's chest again a few times. Siobhan shook her head.

"No pulse. No breaths. Oh, I took too long finding it." She sat back on her haunches, covered her eyes with her arm and shuddered.

Rory placed his hand on her shoulder, wanting with all his heart to hold her, but not daring. Siobhan's shaking shoulders calmed, and after a few moments she raised her head and wiped her eyes with the heel of her hand.

"He said he'd had penicillin before, and he wasn't allergic." Disbelief filled Siobhan's voice.

"That's how it works." Angus' grave statement came from behind them. "You need exposure to it to develop an allergy. Just because you've had it before and were okay doesn't mean the next time you will be. Well, that's what I remember from when we had real anti-biotics."

Rory let go of Siobhan and turned "Thank you for the morbid piece of information," he said into Angus' face. "You and I need to go and prep."

He pushed Angus out of the small tent, as easily as he pushed aside the hollow ache developing within him—he'd lost another team member. He was being callous. But what could he do for Sanjay now? Sanjay was dead. We all behave like we are immortal.

But we're not.

No one can cheat the grave. His father was the proof of it. A wry smile touched his lips. Rory shook himself. He and Angus needed to get going so they *all* wouldn't be dead.

If they were lucky.

Antony's activities had delayed them. He'd thwarted them from the start with his team of bandits, and then his award-winning performance!

Rory left Siobhan and the others in the tent to deal with Sanjay.

At least he's with his brother now.

Rory grabbed Angus' arm and marched him through their campsite to the equipment.

"Ye must sail afore the tide goes out or ye risk running this sub to ground." Murdo followed giving his expert advice. "And ye must nae do that! Breech the hull and ye'll expose us all. I'm thinkin' the sub's contained the radiation so far. I'm sure the submarine is intact. As it is, ye will have tae sail her out while she's up and not submerge her until oot in The Minch."

"We're running out of time. Let's do this while they are distracted," Rory said.

He hated the thought of goodbyes. His throat tightened at the prospect of a *goodbye* to Siobhan.

Angus and Murdo collected equipment as they passed the computer where the detonators were, and crossed the grass, heading for the fisherman's boat. Once on board and the motor revved, Rory looked toward their camp. Siobhan was running to the boat.

"Stop," he ordered Murdo. "Please."

Siobhan ran onto the makeshift pier at the same time he jumped out of the boat.

Rory stepped toward her and grabbed her around her waist. He bent to reach her face and pressed his lips firmly onto hers, then she leaned her body into his. His hand slid behind her head into her tight French roll, and his fingers loosened her hair out of it. He'd imagined himself doing this so many times while riding behind her on their journey here. Her soft, honey-blonde tresses floated around his hand. Her trembling mouth was warm under his and gave back everything he put out.

If this was to be his only time with her, he would let her know how he felt. He broke off their embrace to speak. She grabbed his hair and part of his bandage and pulled his mouth back to hers. His words squashed in her mouth, mingled with her breath.

"No, don't," she said around his mouth.

He pressed his lips harder, pulled her body into his more firmly. Her whole body shook. She smelled of flowers, the same perfume that was *her*. Her breasts pressed into him, soft, warm, and definitely feminine. Her heart pounded through her ribcage and beat against his own.

He would treasure this hint of *all that may have been,* for a lifetime, even if the rest of his would be short.

She broke off their kiss again. "Don't do it," she said.

He shook his head. "I have to."

"No, *you* don't." Her voice caught in her throat.

"Aye, *I* do." He nodded then rested his forehead on hers, warm and soft.

"I know this sounds stupid, but I love you," she said. Her fingers brushed the whiskers of his short beard. "I want you to come back."

"Cannae promise that." He rubbed her nose with his. Her sapphire-blue eyes, so close, were even darker in the dimming light of day.

"You don't always *have to* be the hero, Rory." Her voice was a whisper.

Rory didn't answer. Just drew in her scent, drank in her eyes, and let his body lean against hers.

How could he tell her he had *seen* this—his silver-suited trip with Angus?

And that he *knew* he and she were meant to be together.

How would that work now?

Maybe the vision of the future was a gift to keep him going. To give him hope of love and a future. But now, it seemed impossible. There was a sub to dive deep. He didn't know how it would work and he wouldn't hold out false hope to Siobhan—or to himself.

The urgency of the moment returned to him.

"Got to go," he said and reluctantly released her. "You know there is a greater need than ours, Siobhan."

Gently, he pushed her away, turned and ran back to the boat.

Chapter Twenty-One

The Sub

The dark form of the North Korean submarine moored at Drumchork Pier loomed opposite them in the starlight. Rory and Angus stood with Murdo on the private peer outside Murdo's cottage. Their equipment lay at their feet.

"The hatch has been open for a week," Murdo said. "I'm not too sure if anyone is in there." Murdo stood facing the vessel, his hands at his belt. "I can tell ye the fuel gauge shows ye have enough to take this boat about one hundred and fifty miles out if ye travel at your forty mph." Murdo turned and stared straight at Rory, his face half illuminated by the lights of his boat.

"How do you know that?" Angus asked, the words coming slowly out of his mouth.

"You haven't been in it, have you?" Rory asked, a flash of cool emerging on his brow.

"Och, no, lad," Murdo said. "The fuel tank's hatch is on the ootside."

"The gauge indicating the fuel levels *is* on the inside," Angus observed.

Murdo remained silent in the half light.

"You've exposed yourself!" Rory said.

An icy sensation hit his gut. This old fisherman had effectively sacrificed himself. A hurt in his chest accompanied a sudden acknowledgement of Rory's fondness for him.

"Aye, well," Murdo said. "I've had my life and now ye have enough fuel. But dinnae tell the other fishermen I've raided oor secret stash." The cool night breeze stirred the old man's hair. "Ye'd better suit up. I'll no' tak ye any closer without your fancy-dress."

Rory sighed heavily, then turned to his kit and put on his radiation protective suit. Beside him, Angus did the same. They climbed onto the boat, carrying the rest of their gear.

"You're not suiting up...?" Angus looked at Murdo who, with a brief shake of his head, stepped into his boat.

Rory picked up the headgear for his suit and looked inside it. Embedded in it were an earpiece and a small microphone. Plus, the speaker pack with aerial modification for CB radio which Geoff, the Government communications guy, had added. Angus showed Rory his was the same. Droplets of sweat dribbled down Rory's back. Now a wash of relief flowed through him. At least communicating with Angus would not be by hand signals. They couldn't even lipread through the respirators. Murdo started the engine and set off for the submarine's starboard side.

"We've set our radios to your Hertz, Murdo," Angus said above the engine's chug. "We'll be able to keep contact with you for a while yet."

"Get your headgear on the noo," Murdo said.

Rory secured his headgear then tested the microphone. Rory gave a thumbs up when both Angus' and Murdo's voice came through clearly.

Once near the vessel, Murdo cut the engine and the small boat drifted closer. The wash from the motorboat lapped against the side of the submarine. The smaller vessel's lights illuminated the flat deck area of the submarine, then clunked to a halt as it connected with the boat. Rory stepped out of the gently rocking motorboat onto the narrow deck and turned on his own torch. Angus followed him. Murdo threw the rope attached to the dinghy to Rory. He caught the rope and tied it to the handrail near the hatch, then Murdo let the dinghy drop into the water. Rory grabbed the bags of equipment from Murdo and handed one to Angus.

"Farewell, boys," Murdo nodded, his eyes lingering on Rory. "I'll be on the radio for as long as you're within range."

The old man stepped to his wheel and drove his motorboat away. Rory waved, then turned to Angus.

"You first," he said.

"Aye, aye, captain." Angus gave a mock salute and, carrying a bag of equipment, began his one-handed descent down the ladder of the hatch into the submarine. Rory followed, carrying a bag of equipment as well, and landed on the sub's floor with a clank.

A dull red light-source illuminated the long narrow corridor. Pipes ran from one end to the other. Everything was metal. Rory turned his torch off and hung it by the clip on his belt. He had to crouch beneath the low ceiling.

Submariners must be short people.

"Internal power's still working," Angus said. "Murdo must have got it going somehow." Angus switched off his torch and hung it on his belt. "Which confirms to me the leak is a warhead."

Rory followed Angus along the corridor that led to the business part of the vessel. The low ceilings and narrowness continued. Ahead, the space opened up to consoles and desks covered in switches, dials, and lights. Meters, gauges, knobs, buttons, and small screens filled the room. It was neat and compact, tidily holding everything Rory imagined required to sail this underwater vessel. And more.

On a narrow seat at the end, which had a dashboard of sorts, sat a small man in a dark-khaki uniform wearing an ornate hat. Another sat next to him.

One held a handgun. A Daewoo K5, if Rory was not mistaken.

Rory dropped his equipment bag, raised his hands and bowed to the man he assumed was the captain of this North Korean vessel. Beside him, Angus bowed too, then Rory raised his head.

Both men in uniform stood and bowed. The one in the fancier uniform placed his hand on the console in front of him. He leaned heavily against it, his legs shaking. Rory took a step closer. In the red illuminated light of the submarine, he could hardly tell the state of the man's skin, but something told him, that in the light of day, it would be as red as the light on his bridge.

The submariner faltered. Rory closed the space between them and steadied him. The man dropped the handgun, its clatter loud on the metallic floor of this compact space. He looked into Rory's face. The man had no eyebrows or lashes, and no hair protruded from underneath his cap. He spoke in a thick voice a language that meant nothing to Rory. His companion stood up beside him, and shaking also, helped Rory with the more senior submariner. He also had red peeling skin and scant hair but appeared a little stronger than his colleague. Only just.

"We are here to help," Rory said to the submariners. "They may know some English," he said to Angus, then turned to face him.

Angus stood immobile, staring at the men who were victims of radiation poisoning.

"Help me get him seated again," Rory asked.

Angus shook himself out of his stupor then assisted Rory to where they could sit the man more comfortably. His companion followed, and with slow laboured movements, sat beside him on the bench seat.

"I will try to explain," Rory said to Angus across the weak and dying man.

"He won't hear you very well, Rory," Angus said. "We have internal speakers. He'll only hear what comes muffled through the headgear."

Rory lifted his hands toward his headgear.

"Don't take yours off, Rory!" Angus shouted. "Be safe. You never know. We may get out of this yet."

"Okay." Rory frowned his doubt.

Can you boys still hear me? Murdo's voice came through both their headsets at once.

"Yes," they answered in unison.

"We've found the captain of the vessel," Rory said while smiling at the captain who had looked up on hearing Murdo speak into their helmets. "He looks near to death. He's got a first mate, if that's what you call them."

Och weel. That's ideal, Murdo said. *He'll know. Ask him.*

"Great idea! But I don't speak Korean." Rory tried to keep the sarcasm out of his voice.

Well, ye have a Chinese friend, do ye no', Murdo said.

"Aye, but he does nae ken Korean," Rory answered. "He told me so."

Maybe your Korean speaks Chinese.

Angus' eyes opened wide, mirroring his own.

"Get Xian, please!" Rory asked.

"While Murdo's getting Xian," Angus said, "I'll get the timer out. They may recognise the equipment and deduce what we want to do from it."

Angus walked back to the bags and pulled out the gadgets.

Rory helped Angus place them in front of the captain and first mate, then pointed. The captain lifted his head and looked at the equipment, the strain of these slight movements evident on his face. Angus made a supplicating gesture with his hands, then the first mate watched everything he did.

"What're you doing?" Rory asked.

He watched Angus while he listened to the conversations coming from his earpiece. Murdo had reached their camp and was shouting for Xian.

"They may get what I mean, and direct me to the missile bays," Angus said.

"He's pretty weak." Rory pointed to the captain. "Hope he lasts long enough to help us. His first mate seems a little stronger."

Xian here, Rory. Xian's voice came through the headphones. *You know I don't speak Korean.*

"But he may well know Chinese," Rory said. "You'll have to shout so he can hear."

Rory stooped over the captain and Xian began to speak. The submariner's eyes lit up and he answered Xian. A breathless conversation on the Korean's side continued for about five minutes. Rory placed his head almost to the mouth of the Korean when he replied to Xian. The Korean and Xian both seemed to only miss a few words of the conversation.

Then Xian and the Korean stopped talking.

"Well?" Rory asked.

His Mandarin is way better than my Korean, man, Xian said.

"What'd he say?" Rory asked.

He said he and his companion are the last survivors of this sub's crew. His friend is a helmsman. Which means he can drive the thing. He is a 'Torpedo-man's mate', the equivalent of a nuclear-gunner, on this vessel. He knows exactly what to do to sort the nuke. He recognised what Angus showed him and he said they'll help him do it for as long as they have the breath.

Chapter Twenty-Two

Rory switched the radio to Angus' headgear. Angus, the gunner, and Xian had a three-way conversation while Angus assisted the ailing man along the narrow corridor to the missile bay, under the Korean's direction. Rory followed with the bags of gear.

"Shut the hatch, Rory." Angus' voice crackled through Rory's headgear.

Rory placed the bags on the floor of the missile bay, turned and ran up the ladder and grabbed the hatch handle. He glanced across the loch in the camp's direction.

Silhouettes of his people, small in the distance, lined up in front of their campfire. They faced the submarine. Siobhan's figure caught his eye. He waved, and she waved back.

Might be the last time I see her.

He slid down the ladder and passed the other submariner, the helmsman, who now sat behind a small wheel-like steering contraption next to what seemed to be a gearstick. The boat's steering mechanism—one for side-to-side and one for up-and-down. They looked familiar from the glance he'd managed of the *how-to-drive-a-sub* manual Murray had printed.

Angus strode toward Rory, making his way back to where the knobs and dials were. "The hatch is closed?" he asked.

Rory gave a thumbs up.

"You sure?" he asked again.

"As sure as I can be, not being a trained submariner," Rory replied.

"Good. Now I need to set the co-ordinates to get us through the narrow opening and start our journey out of this loch," Angus said. "We need Xian again." Angus raised his voice and spoke into his headgear. "Xian, please ask the helmsman to get us out of the loch and into the ocean."

Angus traipsed to the submariner and the conversation in Mandarin resumed. This time the helmsman relayed the co-ordinates to Xian who gave them in English to Angus.

"Okay, I know from the manual," Angus said after Xian's latest message, "one of us has to be in the engine room to man the engines and be the accelerator to get this boat moving."

"I'll go," Rory volunteered.

"No, I'll go," Angus said. "I want you to navigate. Once I've accelerated, we should be okay, and I can go back to working on the detonators." Angus viewed the array of knobs and numbers at the navigation panel. "I can't read the symbols. They've stuck Korean over the Russian knobs. I need the helmsman to put in the numbers. Come here, Rory." Angus indicated to the helmsman. "Help me get him to this console where he can punch them in."

Rory helped the man from his narrow seat and walked the short paces with him while Angus got Xian to ask him to set the co-ordinates. The helmsman pushed a couple of buttons then Rory supported him back to his post where he resumed guiding the vessel out.

"Come over here, Rory," Angus said. "You've got a job to do,"

Rory moved closer to Angus who pointed to another screen on the console. The lit screen was green and had a lighter green line which moved around in a circle, like a clock with a crazy hand spinning constantly. There was a large section of lighter green to their right. The screen emitted a *pip* sound.

"The radar's still working. If we get near any big blobs, alert him." Angus pointed to the helmsman. "Or call me, okay?"

"What about that?" Rory put his finger on a blob on the right of the screen.

"It's the pier we just left," Angus said.

Angus turned and ran back to where the other North Korean sat. Angus and Xian's conversation filtered through Rory's headphones, and he could faintly hear the submariner's voice travelling along the narrow corridor which led from the bay.

Rory concentrated on the radar. After a few moments of conversation, Angus came back to Rory.

"I'm going to the engine room to accelerate and get this vessel moving a wee bit faster." Angus stepped down a steep ladder to a lower section of the submarine.

Soon everything began to vibrate, and Rory became aware of a sensation of forward motion.

"So, there's only two missiles," Angus said through Rory's headphones. "I don't think I want to know where they sent the others. Surely, we would have heard if there were any nuclear strikes nearby. Scotland and the UK, that is. The Geiger counter tells me only one is crackling to the max. The other is probably from the radiation surrounding it. Rory! Can you hear me?"

"Aye," Rory shouted into his mic, "I'm trying to not take my eye off this screen for long."

"So, I only have to convert one," Angus said.

"Oh, good. What does that mean?" Rory asked.

"I have to change one from impact detonation to timer detonation. I'll wake the other one up and it will go off with this one." Angus' words whooshed through Rory's headphones like the wind over Bhienn Fionn. "I'll set it for eight hours. That'll get us out of The Minch and well into the North Atlantic before she blows."

"Speaking of The Minch and geographical things such as that," Rory said, "there is a big blob on either side of us coming up. I think we need our submariner; he can navigate. He can do that, can't he? Och, I'm sure it needs two of them to drive this thing, unless my friend the helmsman can give me a crash course."

"Help me bring him back then," Angus said.

Angus came up from the engine room then ran with Rory to the Korean in the torpedo bay. Two tubes from the wall were open and a definite missile-looking object was half out of the top one.

"Is that safe to leave?" Rory asked.

"Oh. Right. I'll put it back in its bay. Help me, would you?" Angus reached up to the missile in question.

Rory helped Angus gently push the missile back into its tube then Angus shut it tight.

"Once we're through the heads of Loch Ewe, I'll work on it," Angus said. "Let's get Dae-Jung back to the bridge for this part. You okay to help?"

"Yeah," Rory said. "First name basis now, are we?"

Angus grinned.

He's enjoying this. Gave him purpose, maybe.

Rory helped Angus assist the North Korean back to the bridge. They both almost carried him.

"Oh, by the way. The nuke is made in Pakistan," Angus said from the other side of Dae-Jung.

"And that means?" Rory asked, navigating the narrow corridor and trying not to snag his suit on any of the nobs and pipes that lined the walls.

"It's dodgy," Angus said. "Don't know if the timer will work when I set it."

They entered the bridge with Dae-Jung's weight distributed between them.

The helmsman was pointing the previously abandoned handgun at them. Dae-Jung spoke short and sharp to the grim-faced and weakening helmsman. He replied to Dae-Jung in between faltering breaths, still pointing the handgun in their direction. Their conversation continued with orders, alternating with pleading, from Dae-Jung.

Rory's pulse thumped in his ears. Sweat trickled down his back as the interaction between the two Koreans continued. If only he spoke Korean. He imagined the man felt he would betray his country if he helped them. Or maybe he wished to die in his own way, a way which didn't involve being blown up.

Get a grip, man. We're all in the same boat.

Rory's cheek tightened with the start of a wry smile, but he suppressed it. Not the time or the place for humour—of any kind.

The Korean helmsman lowered the handgun, shoulders shaking and tears falling down his cheeks. Rory released the breath he'd been holding and crept toward the man. He slowly reached for the pistol, smiling and nodding as he did so. The man surrendered the weapon.

We risk death on this mission, but these Koreans have already begun that final journey.

Rory's heart rate accelerated as he placed Dae-Jung in front of the navigation equipment. Dae-Jung, with the help of the helmsman, set about negotiating the underwater terrain and moving the submarine through The Minch. The submarine hadn't submerged yet and Rory supposed it was similar to sailing a boat through headlands. A very big boat which was mostly underwater.

Dae-Jung had perked up a little. Probably due to their presence and the fact they were going to solve his, and Scotland's, serious problem. Possibly. His helmsman was now fully co-operating.

Sweat dribbled into Rory's eyes. He blinked it away, unable to wipe his face in the headgear.

"How are we going to be sure it goes off, then?" he asked, dreading the answer.

"I'll make sure." Angus was matter-of-fact.

"No." Rory shook his head.

Angus looked at him through his visor. "Yes," he said firmly. A tone like it had never come from Angus. He was almost impolite.

"No," Rory countered. "The Community needs you and your brains, Angus."

"And it *doesn't* need you and your *leadership*, Rory?" Angus yelled.

"There's always another soldier," Rory said. "Not everyone has your intelligence, Angus."

"Rory, you don't have to be the hero and sacrifice all," Angus said. "You're not your father. No one expects you to be. And you're not just another soldier, Ruairidh. You are a leader. *Our* leader. People would follow you to the death if you asked them."

Rory shook his head. He'd heard the *don't have to be a hero* speech once already today. Angus was getting serious with his estimates of him as a leader. He'd used the Gaelic word for his name, which meant king. What Angus hinted at... he shook his head once more.

"Your life is good now," Angus continued. "Think of Ms Kensington-Wallace. You love her. She loves you. Any fool can see it. Even a person like me, to whom love is *off-the-radar*, can see it."

Rory twisted his mouth. Why should Angus think *he* has to do it? Why should anyone? Wasn't a leader meant to face sacrifice and choose it, if it could possibly save his people, the ones he loved? Wasn't it *his* duty as the leader Angus says he was? To see it through to the end, no matter what *the end* is?

Doesn't the captain go down with his ship?

Another wry smile tugged the corner of his mouth.

Angus continued his determined stare through his visor.

"How could it work?" Rory asked. "She'll go back to her bunker. She's never lived outside of it."

"She'd do it for you, Rory. I'm certain of it."

Chapter Twenty-Three

Rory assisted Angus to take Dae-Jung back to the torpedo bay. Loch Ewe was now behind them. Angus opened the torpedo hatches, pulled the one in question out, and started to work on its nuclear device.

"Do you need help here?" Rory asked.

Angus shook his head, absorbed in his task.

"I'll go watch the radar then," he said.

Angus nodded.

Dae-Jung gazed at Rory. He seemed more fatigued all of a sudden, the recent activity having exhausted him. Rory gave a slight bow and went to leave. The Korean bowed in return and spoke, his voice croaky. Rory made nothing of the meaning of the words, but the sentiment was obvious. The man was grateful and relieved. Rory bowed once more, turned in the narrow corridor and walked to the radar screen. The other Korean sat at the helm.

On the radar screen, the crazy arm spun around, over, and over.

In his headgear a static buzzed.

"Rory." Angus' voice came through his headgear. "I'm switching your frequency. Someone wants to speak with you."

Rory? It was Siobhan's voice.

"Aye, Siobhan?" His words caught in his throat.

We need an update. What's happening? she asked.

"Angus is changing the detonation mechanism over as we speak. There's only one faulty nuke and Angus says setting it off will get rid of the other one."

There was only two?

"Aye."

Where are the others? There was dread in her voice. *I can find out from my assistant in the Bunker. But there had been no reports of nuclear warheads released near us before I left.* After a pause, she continued. *So, there was a North Korean on-board?*

"Aye, two, and they're not well," Rory said. "I don't think they'll last much longer. The gunner only had enough energy to tell Angus what he needs to know."

So, he'll set the timer, and you can put the sub onto autopilot? To dive?

"It appears it takes more than one to drive this thing," he said. "And there's the question of who closes the hatch."

Silence.

Rory. Her voice held pain.

"I love you, Siobhan," he said. "It doesn't help you now, I know, but I needed to tell you. I... is anyone listening apart from you?"

Not on this frequency, why? Her voice was husky, as though she held back tears.

"I just wanted privacy to tell you if it were another time, in another situation, I ken we'd be together."

Should he tell her he saw their future?

He was doubting that now. How could the future with her happen now he was going to...?

I love you Rory, Siobhan said through the headset. *I always have. I remembered you from when I was a child. A tall, handsome, deep-red haired Scotsman who wasn't afraid he'd look silly playing dolls with a little girl. A kind and strong man. You were always the man I dreamed of when I was growing up. Oh! That's so stupid... I'm sorry—*

The radar continued sweeping its constant arc.

Angus walked into the bridge and passed the helmsman.

"I'm amazed we're still within radio reach," Angus said, then looked around as if searching for something.

"You okay?" Rory asked.

"Yeah, forgot where I'd put... Where are those—? Oh, there they are." Angus walked past Rory toward the ladders.

"Let me know if you need me," Rory said.

"Okay." Angus spoke over the static in Rory's headgear.

"Siobhan, are you still there?" Rory asked.

Yes. There were tears in her voice.

Rory hated that she'd been crying.

"It's not stupid," Rory said. "I knew I loved you from before I met you, as a child or as a grown woman. You see—" A sharp crack sounded at the back of Rory's headgear and a heavy thud reverberated within his own skull.

Through the blur of pain, Rory peered out his visor. Angus wasn't wearing headgear and there was a monkey wrench in his hand. Then Rory's world went blank.

***

Waves slapped rhythmically against the side of something, accompanied by a rocking motion, waking Rory from a groggy state. Pain clenched the back of his skull as though a fist tried to drag his grey matter to the outside of his head. His chest was tight from the vice surrounding it and he could hardly breathe. He opened his eyes; it was foggy. No, his visor had misted, and he was flat on his back in a squidgy-rocky thing. He tried to wipe his visor and two gloved hands came into view in the starlight. The stars were above him and his feet were elevated on the edge of the dinghy in which he now found himself.

Rory brought his feet down and struggled to sit. The fist was now thumping inside his skull. His head told him to stop moving or it would behave as badly as the worst hangover he could ever imagine. He ripped off the tape that held his gloves to his sleeves, freeing his hands. Next, he removed his headgear and respirator mask.

He sucked deeply on the cool night air. The fresh saltiness and distinctly ocean scent filled his nostrils and settled the pain—somewhat. He rested his head back on the side of the dinghy.

Ow!

Rory reached his hand behind his head and felt an egg-shaped lump.

Night birds flew overhead, their cries mournful. It meant he wasn't too far from land, didn't it? The loud humming of an engine came underneath and ahead of him, then the splash of waves hitting together. A wash rocked his small craft wildly. Spray, from the impact of waves on the side of the dinghy, hit him in the face, shocking him with its chill, stinging his eyes with its salt. He was wet now.

Rory scampered forward to view ahead of him. In the dark night he could barely make out the top of the submerging submarine, the tall, thin radio mast the last thing to disappear under the ocean.

"What!"

His convulsive exclamation sent a shooting pain to his forehead. He laid back and observed the stars for a while.

So, Angus had knocked him out and set him adrift in the dinghy. He shook his head a wee bit, the pain returned, and he stopped.

Talk about hangovers!

He could do with a scotch right now.

Angus.

Rory bit his lower lip as he gazed at Pleiades.

Angus.

He picked up his headgear and tried the radio. Dead. Damaged by the bash to his head.

The dinghy continued a gentle rocking after the wash subsided.

Where am I? He lifted his head, risking pain, and scanned the horizon. Behind him in the distance was a land mass.

The Isle of Lewis?

He was out in the North Atlantic Ocean. How the hell was he going to get back?

Didn't think of that, did you, Angus?

Damn.

He rested his head gingerly back onto the side of the dinghy. He'd been telling Siobhan he had seen the future with them in it together. It had made little sense then. If he didn't get back, it would make none now.

There used to be *Search and Rescue*. He'd read of it once, and he could do with it now.

The waves gently rocked the dinghy, and the stars continued their journey around the North Celestial Pole. A motor chugged in the distance behind him. He turned and waved his headgear and then remembered his torch hanging on his belt.

Maybe the battery would last.

Chapter Twenty-Four

Shores of Loch Ewe

S iobhan sat on the floor of her tent. The light from lanterns placed outside the circle of tents dimly illuminated the radio handset she held. Rory's voice had cut off mid-sentence, then static hissed. Now the handset was as silent as death.

"Rory?"

No response.

"Rory!" Siobhan turned the shortwave radio dial through the Hertz to try to pick up Rory on another wavelength.

Nothing.

Xian was on the radio set up outside on the camp table, with the others crowded around him. He hadn't spoken for a few moments either. She dropped the handset on the tent floor then ran across the grass to them.

"The radio's gone dead," Xian said when she reached him.

"They're probably out of range by now," Geoff explained. "Or they've submerged already."

No one spoke. The lapping waters of the loch thudded against the shoreline.

"That's it then?" Kendra's voice was entirely question. "They've got the dinghy, right? They can jump out once they've got the sub diving, yeah?"

Xian shook his head. "The nuke was dodgy, made in Pakistan. The timer may not work. They had to be there to ensure it did." He added under his breath, "And you can't jump out of a submerging sub."

Siobhan's knees lost their power to hold up her body, despite her understanding fully the mechanics of a diving submarine. She sat hard on the ground by the loch. Behind her, Kendra wept uncontrollably, and Xian spoke softly to her as he walked her to the tents, their voices receding in the night. A silent Callum walked with them, leaving Siobhan alone.

Callum. Rory's twin. *How would he take this?*

The loch's water continued its lapping against the shore. The cold from the ground underneath her thighs seeped into her skin. Night birds called in the starlit sky. She looked at the celestial display above her. Rory had helped her appreciate the night sky—truly appreciate it for the first time.

Angus and Rory would set the timer for eight hours. When they were in the middle of the North Atlantic Ocean, far away from Scotland's outer isles, Iceland and Greenland. And the smaller islands—what were they again? The Faro Islands.

Through her numbness she noted her thoughts were too clinical.

Rory would still be alive for another eight hours, possibly.

The wind blew her hair around her face. It had been loose since he took it out of her French roll and had run his fingers through it. She could still smell him on her, and feel his tight body pressed against hers. Warm and taut muscle the whole length of him. His scent, the aroma of the Highlands—horse and heather—was in her blouse and on her face.

On her lips.

Life was not fair. In fact, it truly stank.

She'd found him, the man of her dreams—literally. And she didn't care how juvenile or pathetic it sounded, like something out of a soppy romance novel. People in the Bunker often mocked those novels. Why had they kept them in the archives if they weren't for reading? There was nothing wrong with love and romance. She now realised that before Rory, she thought she'd had both, but in actuality, she'd experienced neither.

When he was gone, in eight hours, what would she do? A thick lump came to her throat. She took calming breaths.

Then a burning anger appeared, scorching her chest, threatening to sear her soul.

Bloody Antony!

If all that rubbish hadn't happened with *him,* then Sanjay and Sundeep would be alive, and *they* would've done it. They were both dead. They *would* have died anyway. Wouldn't they?

She put her face in her hands.

What am I thinking?

Poor Sanjay and Sundeep. What was she going to tell their mother, Rajnandini, back in the Bunker? A brilliant biochemist from the original

Brains Trust and a dignified matriarch—a generous-hearted woman whom she could call *Aunty*.

Siobhan's heavy breathing continued for a time. Her jaw clenched, joining the tension in her curling fists. She would go and hit Antony on the head. They'd tied him up. He couldn't stop her!

It wouldn't make any difference to Rory not being here, or anything that had happened in the lead up to him going. Her tiredness helped calm her.

Then the realisation struck her, as hard as a thump to the back of her neck.

It would have come to this, anyway. Rory, being Rory, would have made sure *he* was the one to go. She hadn't known him for long, but this one thing was certain: for that man to be true to himself, he *had* to get into that sub.

Damn him!

"Damn you, Rory Campbell!" she yelled at the top of her lungs.

She threw a rock at the sea loch. Its heavy *plop* into the water echoed in the night. A startled night bird flew off, calling its warning to others. Midges swarmed above her head.

That's it.

She let her tears pour down her face then laid on the grass. It was exhausting being angry and the effort of sitting was too hard.

***

Siobhan's face was as cold as her back and legs. She looked at the sky. The stars had turned on the North Celestial pole, their night's journey forwarded while she had slept by the shore.

Her hearing caught the chug of a motorboat across the loch. Siobhan sat up. Lights were at the pier that sat outside the old fisherman's house, on the Isle of Ewe in the middle of the loch. It was quiet for a time, then the motor started again.

She followed the chug of the motor moving across the water as the boat made its way to the makeshift pier to her right. Then, footsteps thudded on boards as someone landed on the pier; somebody tied a rope to the pole; more footsteps headed in her direction.

"Ms Kensington-Wallace?" It was the old fisherman, Murdo MacDonald.

What on earth did *he* want?

"Yes?" She stood and took some hesitant steps toward him.

"Could ye please fetch yoor wee first aid kit?" he asked. "I have someone with a head injury who requires yoor attention."

She didn't reply, quite reluctant to go with this man who was practically a stranger.

A strange stranger.

"Ye'll want tae come and tend his wounds," Murdo said, "believe me, lass."

Chapter Twenty-Five

Isle of Ewe

S iobhan stepped out of the rocking motorboat onto the pier, the medical kit over her shoulder. Murdo trod behind her as she walked along the pale gravel path in the starlit night. The fisherman hadn't said a word since asking her to come with him and remained mute in response to her questions. A sense of unease swirled inside her, stirring up the numbness. She may as well be a *nurse* as do anything else at this point in time.

Light shone from the window of the cottage at the top of the incline. Once there, Murdo opened the door.

"Welcome to ma' wee cottage," he said. "Ye'll ken the man inside."

Murdo stayed by the open door and gestured for her to enter.

Siobhan stepped into a lamplit, one-roomed crofter's cottage. An old solid fuel stove stood against the wall to her left, and a bed was against the far wall behind the gingham-covered table directly in front of her. Someone on the bed groaned. She stepped around the table as a tall man raised himself from the bed and stood.

"Rory?" She dropped the medical kit and hurried to him, wrapping her arms around his waist, and hugging him to herself. Her heart pounded as his heart beat loudly in her ear pressed against him. "I can't believe it." Her whisper muffled into him.

Rory's arms surrounded her. His cheek rested on the top of her head; his breathing loud above her.

"Mmm." His deep voice rumbled in his chest against her ear. "Siobhan..."

She could have held him forever, but she recalled Murdo's comment of a head injury.

"You're injured?" Siobhan pulled herself back to look him in the face.

Rory's eyes were full of tears. He wiped them away.

"Ah... I've had a wee bash to the back o' ma head," he said.

He raised his hand to place it behind his head. His bandage was off, and his loose curls sat in an unruly manner about his face.

"Dinnae think there's any blood this time." He blinked away more tears and wiped his cheek with his hand.

He held her face and his mouth descended, with his eyes locked on hers the entire way. His warm, soft lips engulfed hers as he pressed hard. Rory ran his fingers once more into her hair and cupped her head. He broke their kiss.

"Och, I thought I'd never do that again," his said, his mouth centimetres from hers.

He gently kissed her upper lip, then her lower lip. He pressed her to himself once more and held her there.

Horse and heather.

They hugged in silence. The Aga stove clicked, heating the small room of the cottage, and the night breeze blew in through the still open door.

"Ah, will ye be needing anything, Ms Kensington-Wallace?" Murdo said with one hand on the door. "To tend to the man's wounds, like?"

"A head injury. Hmm. It depends on if you lost consciousness, Rory." Siobhan disengaged herself from Rory's embrace.

"Angus knocked me out cold." Rory continued to focus on her, his blue eyes pooling with moisture.

"Angus?" Siobhan blinked. "Wouldn't have thought he had it in him."

Rory raised his eyebrows. "Och, he was determined."

Murdo coughed from the doorway.

"Yes, well, if that's the case," she said, "I must ensure Rory's all right concussion-wise, which means I will have to keep him awake for a while." Siobhan turned to Murdo.

"Aye well, I leave ye to it then," he said. "I'm verra sure ye'll find a way tae do that, lassie. Goodbye." The old man tilted his head to Rory and shut the door.

Siobhan turned back to Rory. He had one eyebrow raised quizzically.

"Well, sit down. Let me look at your head then," she said.

Rory sat on the edge of the bed and pointed to his injury. Siobhan inspected the back of his head and found a large swelling but no cut.

"You're right. No blood." She sat beside him. "Where's Angus?"

Rory looked at his hands in his lap. "Somewhere past Lewis. That's where Murdo found me in the dinghy." He swallowed. "Angus has taken it upon himself to sail a submarine out to the middle of the North Atlantic and personally ensure the nuke goes off." He looked into her eyes then. "I was very mad at him when I came to. But now that I see you, I'm just thankful."

He raised his hands to her face and pressed his lips to hers once more.

Siobhan felt the strength of the man now restrained as he held her face in a gentle grip, his fingers trembling. Siobhan inhaled; his scent was comforting. His warm skin touching her was the evidence he was alive and real, and here with her now. His ardent lips moved away, then he rested his forehead on hers, his breath caressing her face.

"Good old Angus." Rory's voice was gentle—sorrow mixed with something else.

Relief?

"How did Murdo know where you were?" she asked. "Did Angus tell him where he dumped you?"

"No." He shook his head, then gathered her into his arms and held tight. "And Murdo would nae tell me anything about how he knew. Only some vague 'he'd guess we should be at such-and-such a place by whatever time it was'. He must've been following us."

Rory leaned back, loosening his hold, and stretched then flinched.

"Och, after the day I've had I'm going tae need to lie down." He stood and took off his shirt and placed it over a chair beside the table. "It's Murdo's. A factory-made one. Still with the label in it," he said. "Don't want to ruin it any more than I have already." He turned back to her and made his way to the bed where she sat. "Am I allowed to lie down? Promise I won't go to sleep. On purpose, anyway."

Siobhan smiled and moved to allow him to lie down. The bed creaked with his weight. Rory laid back, gingerly placing his head on the old pillows covered in flannelette. With each lift of his head, each tiny adjustment, his abdominal muscles tensed, defining six sections. The lamplight illuminated his sleeve of Celtic tattoos.

Siobhan sighed to herself. "I hope you now understand you don't own the sole rights to the *hero* title."

Her words came out as a reprimand. But she'd sensed his struggle and how he believed the responsibility of *fixing it* lay on him, whatever *it* was to fix—even a nuclear warhead.

"My father owns the rights to that one." Rory swallowed.

"You're not him, no matter how many people say you're like him," she said. "Don't put so much pressure on yourself, Rory."

Rory's nostrils flared. "I miss him," he said. "I was with him when the slaver shot him. We were rescuing my mother and wee sister. And then, he died. Bled to death in my mither's arms. She did all she could, but it still was nae enough." His words trailed off. "Och, I've said too much." He placed his arm over his eyes, covering his tears.

An ache in sympathy with his started in Siobhan.

"Oh Rory," she said. "That's such a traumatic thing to have lived through."

His forearm remained over his eyes. He sniffed. "Come closer, Siobhan."

Siobhan shuffled closer and leaned over, placing one hand on either side of him. Her hair fell over her shoulder onto his chest as she laid her head on him.

She listened through his ribs to the sound of his breathing for a while.

"You must stay awake," she said. "I need to know you only have a concussion. Oh hell, what if you're having a cerebral bleed?" Siobhan lifted her head.

"Do you always think the worst?" he asked. "I'm okay, Siobhan. I've got a wee headache, 'tis all." Rory's tears had dried, and his tone was now teasing.

"I think I should check your pupils." Siobhan looked into his eyes. One of his brows arched. "I need a torch," she said.

She scanned the room. Behind the door lay his radiation suit with a utility belt attached. She walked over and picked up the torch.

"I'd be surprised if it still worked," Rory said, then shuffled himself further over on the single bed, making room for her.

"Look at me." She shone the light into his eyes. His pupils reacted briskly. "That's okay," she said. "Don't ask me what I'd do if it wasn't."

"I'll be fine," Rory said.

"How do you know?" she asked. "You don't know what the future holds."

He opened his mouth to speak but stopped himself.

Rory lifted his hands to her face and pulled her down to him. The torch clattered on the floor. Their lips met, warm and urgent, his beard tickled around her mouth and brushed against her cheek; his russet-ginger, Highlander's beard. He broke off their kiss.

"We *are* together, aye?" he asked.

"Yes." She nodded. "If you're okay being with a much older woman."

"That again?" He huffed. "Did you *not* get it? Your age does nae matter to me! Does it matter to you that I'm a wee bit younger?" His gaze was intense.

"Doesn't matter to me," she replied, "as long as you don't accuse me of being a cougar."

"A what? A big cat?" His brows drew together, and his head shook in confusion.

"No, it's ... doesn't matter. It won't matter. It's nobody else's business."

"Exactly." Rory gave a short nod.

He sunk back into the bed, relaxing. A mat of hair grey between his defined pectorals. Siobhan couldn't resist the urge to run her fingers in it and found her hands had made their own way there and were now playing with it. His chest rose and fell, and his breath blew past her hands. The dim light of the only lamp in the room fell on him, his cheeks glowed softly where they were bare of beard and a glint reflected in his softening eyes.

Rory raised his face to hers and kissed her lips, encouraging her onto him. His strong arms surrounded her, and large warm hands traced their way along her back, resting on her buttocks, pressing them onto him. His kisses continued.

Siobhan lifted her lips from his and placed her hand on his chest, palm down.

"What are we doing?" she asked.

Rory raised his eyebrows, eyes wide. "What do you think we're doing? Nothing either of us does nae want to."

"What do you mean?" Sudden indignance flashed through her. Did he just assume she'd be okay making love to him?

Boy, would I be okay.

But... she didn't want to get pregnant. Not now, that's for sure. There was so much they had to sort out. She doubted he had contraceptives. Or maybe he did. He *was* a very sexy man. And she was sure he wasn't with anyone… until now. And he didn't seem the kind of man to sleep around. So…

Rory was looking at her, his eyebrows still raised. "I mean… Let me say it better," Rory said. His voice was deep and even, certain of every word. "I'll no' do anything you dinnae want to, Siobhan. And I for one will nae make you my wife, until you are my wife."

She blinked a few times. "Meaning?" she asked.

His head tilted to the side; his eyes soft. "Let me show you."

Rory slid his hands from her buttocks and around to the buttons on her camouflaged-patterned shirt. He undid them then slipped off her shirt, assisting her to remove her arms from the sleeves. He let the shirt slip to the floor. He put his hands behind her, deftly undid her bra, then pulled the straps over her shoulders, never taking his eyes away from hers. His fingers tracing their way along her arms left a shiver of touch-memory in their wake.

Siobhan lifted her trunk and slid out of the bra. Rory pulled it away and she lowered herself back down, her bare torso now touched Rory's in its entirety. Rough chest hair tickled her front; her nipples sensitive to every part of him they contacted. He touched his mouth to hers, gently pulling at her lower lip.

Rory broke away and lifted himself, turning to his side, he placed her on her back. He was now on top of her; sturdy arms holding his heavy body centimetres above hers. His lips began a journey from her mouth to her throat and down between her breasts. Soft sensuous caresses. Tickling.

Rory's mouth moved to her nipples, taking one at a time into his mouth, the hair of his beard adding to her awareness of his touch as it brushed the surrounding mound of her breast. Wet and warm, his mouth enveloped each nipple, sucking, he brought them to a point and released, discharging a sensation between her legs with each turn.

Siobhan's breathing escalated, her heart pumped, and *so* much was going on between her legs. His mouth made a bumpy journey to her waist as her abdomen rose and fell with each breath. Rory's loose, long hair flowed closely beside his face and trailed behind, resting on her bare skin, repeating each sensory stimulation in its quiet passage across her body.

Then Rory knelt, and a smile came to his lips.

"You okay?" he asked.

"Am I okay? Yes!" She hadn't meant to sound so breathless. Or so eager.

His smile reached his eyes.

He moved his hands to the top of her cargo pants and undid the button and the zip, his eyes never leaving hers. He grasped her cargo pants at the waist and slowly peeled them off her legs, then tossed them on the floor. Rory's hands travelled up the sides of her thighs and connected with her underpants and held them.

"Still okay with this?" he asked.

Siobhan nodded, unable to speak; her mind racing ahead and her body not too far behind it.

Rory was focussing on her and *her* pleasure, ensuring she was not uncomfortable with any of it.

No man had ever been so intent on *her*.

Her desire for Rory heightened. Her heart raced, her skin registered every connection with his, and a gentle pulsation accompanied the increasing dampness between her thighs.

He pulled her underpants off and threw them on the floor before he placed his hands on her inner thighs and spread her legs.

"Wait. What about you?" Siobhan asked.

She sat up, her legs now either side of him, and placed her hands on the waistband of his buckskins. His gentle lovemaking had obliterated the memory of his alluding to *no sex*. And there was an obvious bulge in his trousers.

"No, Siobhan," he said. "I cannae remove those. Remember, I'll not make you my wife until you *are* my wife." He leant forward and kissed her hard, lying her back down as he did so.

He moved his mouth along her front as before. She grasped his soft russet-red waves, not too sure how much more of this she could take. Every touch sparking a fire growing in intensity low in her belly—and other places.

This love-making with Rory was so different from anything she'd ever experienced. This wasn't just sex, even if he wasn't going to...

It *was* love.

Rory made his way to her pubic hair with his mouth, slow and caressing. Here he lingered, then plunged to her depths.

Chapter Twenty-Six

The blond, curly-haired boy holds the toy bow in his left hand. The arrow hangs loosely from the other, dangling from the bowstring.

"It will nae work!" His shoulders sink, and the arrow drops to the ground.

"Come here, son. Let's have a look at what you're doing."

The young child comes close and leans his small body against his leg. Rory squats and puts his arm around him.

He takes the boy's left hand in his and holds the toy bow. With his right hand, he helps the boy hold the arrow.

"Now, you rest the arrow on your finger, like this." Rory nocks the arrow into the bowstring and shows the lad how the shaft rests on the archer's hand.

"Oh, that's it! I was nae doing that, Daddy."

He lets the boy release the string and the arrow darts from the bow. It skips over the ground and clatters to a halt a long way before its intended target.

The boy's lips pout.

"Aiming is another lesson, son." He hugs the boy, then turns.

Siobhan walks toward them.

The wind blows across the moor and the loose dress she wears presses close to her form.

Her growing belly shows.

She walks straight to him and presses her body to his as their son collects his arrow.

She smiles.

"You look happy," he says.

"I am." Her mouth stretches to a grin. "Christine says I am a walking miracle. Way past my prime, yet pregnant for the second time. Must be the virile man I have regular sex with."

Rory's mouth tugs with a smile he cannot repress.

Rory woke. The early morning sunlight streamed across the room from the window behind him and lit the paintings of Murdo MacDonald's family.

It must be about four o'clock, sunrise this far north in the middle of summer.

Nearly time.

Siobhan lay on her side in front of him, his arm around her waist and his hand cupping her flat belly. He drew in her scent.

Always flowers.

Siobhan stirred, and as she did, her bare skin shifted beneath his hand and her curly pubic hair brushed beneath his fingers, tickling.

She rolled over to face him, her eyes so close were their usual sapphire-blue in the daylight—the same colour as the loch outside on a sunlit day.

Rory kissed her lips, and she returned it through her sleepiness.

"Hmm. You umm... taste like..." she said, screwing up her lips.

"Wonder why that is." He raised his eyebrows. "And please dinnae be so romantic first thing in the morning, like."

Siobhan snuggled into his side and draped her arm over his chest.

It was so good. So right.

"Rory?" she asked.

"Aye."

"You're a young man—"

"Dinnae start that again," he said.

"No, please hear me out. It's important." She lifted herself onto her elbows, so her deep dark-blue eyes peered into his.

Siobhan chewed her lip.

"I'm past my biological prime," she said. "And we may not have any children and I know you'd make a great father and you should be one and it's not fair if you don't." Her words ran together, and the tears had started.

"Now wait, wait. Ssh ssh," he said. "It's okay, we have children. Two at least."

She sucked in a faltering breath. "What do you mean?"

"Just that," he said. "We have at least two children. The eldest is a boy." Rory put conviction into his voice.

She frowned then her face lit. "Oh, you've time travelled to the future, and you know all this?" she asked, then frowned again. "You knew I'd fall in love with you from the start? Like it was inevitable. Where's my free will in this?"

"Whoa, whoa, now." Rory put his hands up to stop the barrage. "No, I did nae time travel to the future. I... ah... see things."

May as well be totally honest from the start.

This was her chance to call him crazy. To have her suspicions that he was odd confirmed and make her way out of this... whatever *this* was for her.

Rory held his breath and searched her eyes. What was she thinking? Forget time travel. If only he could mind read!

After a silence, and a lot of frowning, she opened her mouth but said nothing.

Uh, oh.

"Speak to me, Siobhan."

"What exactly do you see?"

"Snippets from the past and the future. I can't make it happen," he said. "It just does. Rarely, though. My aunty is a doctor, and well, she says it's because I've travelled to the past and back, twice, I'm able to see time, ken?"

Siobhan raised one eyebrow and held his gaze. "You've done it twice?" A hint of incredulity lingered in her voice. She blinked a few times, the attempt to comprehend his explanation plain on her face, and she wasn't winning.

"I had to retrieve my father from the past," he said. "But it did nae work out." He bit his lower lip.

"What happened?" she asked. "You weren't hurt, were you?"

"No, but that's when my father died." Rory sighed. "It's a long story, but our father stole a time journey to the past to protect our mother. It was after we were born here in the future. Or the present, which is now the past, or whichever way you want to look at it."

Siobhan blinked and shook her head at the same time.

"There is history there that you need to tell me," she said, "but later, if you'd prefer it, okay?"

He nodded, relieved he didn't have to go into all the detail now.

"Being into physics, I've often pondered time travel." Siobhan's mouth curled up on one side as she looked into his eyes, her gaze piercing. "I've always wondered when a person travels through time, do they step out of it momentarily? Does it mean they are in timeless eternity? What do they experience? Whenever I've discussed this with my fellow scientists, and even once with a theologian, we concluded it may send someone mad. Do you think you're mad?"

"Um..." he said.

How do I answer that one?

"I did at first, but Aunty Bec's explanation about being able to view time works for me," he said. "I don't remember the 'during' of time travel, only the before and after."

"Well, I know you aren't mad, if that helps any. *Viewing time*." Siobhan's voice held a thoughtful wonder. "How did I come to fall in love with a time traveller and a sage?" She leaned onto him more, almost winding him in her eagerness. "So, you saw us?"

"Aye, but I did nae ken it was you."

"Huh?" She tilted her head. "You'll need to explain that."

"Well, I knew I would marry a beautiful, honey-blonde woman," he said, "but I did nae ken it was you until..."

"When?" The word stretched out of her mouth.

"When I first smelled your perfume." Rory blinked.

"But that was—" she began, but a deep, distant boom interrupted her, rattling the cottage for twenty seconds.

Books fell off the shelf behind the door. A spare cooking pot tumbled off the metal rack above the solid fuel stove and clattered to the floor. Rory held Siobhan close, and she gasped as she pressed her head to his chest.

"It will all be okay if he was submerged," she said, lifting her head to him.

"Unless things changed any," Rory said, "last time I saw him he was diving."

They held each other in silence.

Siobhan blinked at him. "If he wasn't, this hut will blow away and us with it. Very soon."

"He was under," Rory said with certainty.

There was a knock at the door. Siobhan pulled the bed-clothes over herself.

"Come out when ye are ready, Rory." Murdo's voice came muffled through the closed door.

"Okay, we'll just be a moment, Murdo," he yelled.

Rory jumped out of bed and put on Murdo's shirt. Siobhan found her clothes on the floor and dressed. Rory opened the door where Murdo sat on an old chair, just to the right and facing west.

"Did you see anything with that boom, Murdo?" Rory asked.

"Nothing. And there would hae been if..." Murdo didn't finish.

"Aye," Rory said.

"Young Angus. God rest his soul." Murdo bowed his head.

"A hero," Siobhan said.

She was beside Rory, and she slipped her arms around his waist.

"And Dae-Jung and his helmsman; brave North Koreans." Rory indicated with his chin to Murdo. "This man here is a hero, too."

Murdo looked up from his chair, squinting in the morning sunlight. Siobhan faced Rory, waiting for him to say more.

"He filled the sub's tank with fuel to make sure it cleared Scotland, well and truly," Rory said.

Siobhan gasped. "When did you do that, Mr MacDonald?" she asked Murdo.

Murdo gave a shaky grimace and didn't answer.

"I don't know when it was, but he did nae have a suit," Rory said to Siobhan. "Do you have anything for him?"

Siobhan blinked, her mouth open, recalling the contents of the first aid kit, no doubt.

"Can you make things easier for him?" he whispered.

She shrugged, walked back into the cottage and rummaged through the medical kit.

"I'm fine, Rory. Dinnae bother." Murdo's gruff voice seemed even more so. "I feel fine."

"But you may not for long," Siobhan said from inside the cottage. "It depends on how much exposure you had." Siobhan had the medical kit at her feet and rummaged more. "Here's all the antiemetics I have and... some sleeping pills. Morphine tablets too." She held them out to him, but he didn't take them. "I'll put them on your table." The bottles rattled as she placed them on the checked cloth.

"Thems over yonder dinnae ken yet that you did nae actually finish yoor ride on that there submarine, ye ken?" Murdo looked to the campsite by the shore.

"You mean you haven't told them he's alive?" Siobhan asked, shielding her widened eyes with her hand, the risen sun now hitting them with its full light. "We'd better get over there!"

Rory and Siobhan collected the depleted medical kit then walked to the motorboat. At the camp, people moved around and shouted, also disturbed by the boom, no doubt. Their journey over to them with Murdo was a quiet one. Rory held Siobhan's hand in his. He needed the reassurance of her presence beside him. It had been a close thing.

So close.

Murdo steered the boat to the pier nearest their camp. Rory jumped out and tied the rope to the pier for Murdo.

"Make a seaman of you yet, Rory." Murdo grinned at Rory as he walked back to the motorboat.

"I haven't thanked you properly," Rory said. "You saved my life, Murdo. And have risked your own."

"Och weel, I did what I came for to do. And you have saved mine many a time, brother," he said. Murdo's crinkled eyes seemed to glitter.

"What do you mean?" Rory frowned.

Murdo held Siobhan's hand and continued helping her out of the moored, but still rocky, boat.

"Does she ken about your travels, Rory?" With a nod, Murdo indicated in Siobhan's direction.

"What do you mean?" A chill collected at the back of Rory's neck as he repeated his question.

What does this man know?

His crew at the camp had noticed the boat. They were calling his name, their whoops and cries coming closer.

"Rory, I'm your wee brother, Brendan," Murdo whispered into Rory's face.

"But how—?" Rory began.

Murdo put a finger to his lips and slipped a small piece of paper into Rory's hand. "Make sure your wee brother gets this, okay?"

Behind Rory, his crew were cheering. Xian raced up to him and slapped him on the back.

Chapter Twenty-Seven

A lump formed in Siobhan's throat. Soft, deep sobs mingled with sighs of relief surrounded Rory as Callum embraced his twin in a bear hug. Rory's crew had tears in their eyes and broad smiles on their tired faces. Siobhan swallowed and turned to the loch while the reunions continued behind her. It was early, but the sun was well above the horizon. If she recalled correctly, tomorrow was the summer solstice. As it would be the longest day of the year, the sun would not set until very late. Murdo's boat chugged back to the other side of the loch where a row of fishing boats moored to a pier. Seagulls circled above their masts.

"Let's pack up and get going. I just want to be home." Rory said to his crew and Siobhan's Government team behind her.

Rory touched her shoulder, then his hand slipped around her waist.

"I hope you're okay that it's common knowledge we're together," he said. "I cannae keep anything from my crew. They knew about us before we did, as they say." He grinned beside her.

Her mouth tugged at the corners. "Yes. Let's go home."

What did she mean by that? Where was home now? In the Government Bunker, or here, *up top*, with Rory? It was as though she was in the *in-between*. Something deep inside told Siobhan she was on the precipice of a new beginning, and a *knowing* saturated her. She was with this man now, and there would be no turning back from Rory—not ever.

The crews reloaded the remaining equipment onto the horses after striking camp. Sundeep and Sanjay's bodies, wrapped in dampened camp blankets to keep them cool, lay on either side of the sturdiest-looking pack-horse. Antony and McPherson mounted, then Callum tied their hands to their saddles.

Standing next to Rory, Siobhan fiddled with straps of her duffle bag as he loaded the pack horse with her gear.

"Do I ride with you again?" she asked.

Rory arched an eyebrow. "Well, you need to learn how to ride," he said. "But as I'm wanting to get home without any mishaps, I suppose I must endure you sitting in front of me all the way."

She opened her mouth to reprimand his cheek.

"Rory!" Callum's deep voice called from where he stood with his horse. He faced the hills behind them.

Siobhan turned with Rory to the direction in which they would travel back to the Invercharing Community. Overlooking the loch, a group of people, some mounted on horses, positioned themselves on the side of the hill. Guns and swords glinted in the sunlight. Their clothes were shabby, and lank hair stirred in the breeze.

"Who are they?" she whispered to Rory.

"Bandits," he said, his hand twitching at his pistol tucked into his belt. "Mount up as soon as we can, everyone. We'll veer to our right as we start our journey. No use sitting here like ducks."

The group were soon riding their horses at a walk back the way they had come, and the bandits stayed to their left. Siobhan looked at their audience regularly. Rory, Callum, Xian, and indeed everyone in their group, did the same. The bandits hadn't moved an inch. Their weapons remained at their sides, and they seemed content to watch them journey past.

Once they had reached Poolewe, Callum cantered up to Rory's horse.

"What was that all aboot, do ya think?" he asked Rory.

Rory shook his head. "They did us no harm." He looked his brother in the eye then. "I'm not sure. Stay alert, eh?"

A silence had descended on the party, thanks to their unwelcome observers.

Rapids roared beneath the arched stone bridge they crossed on their way through the quaint, small village of Poolewe. The village had appeared empty on their way up to Loch Ewe, but now families stood in their doorways and stared at them as they rode through their village. Some waved. Young children giggled. Rory shifted in the saddle behind her and remained quiet. He nodded at the adults who acknowledged them.

Once through the town, Siobhan faced Rory. He wore a frown.

"Why the audience?" she asked.

"Dinnae ken." Rory's frown never lifted.

His puckered brow continued for most of the morning. It was there every time she glanced around at him.

They stopped for lunch a third of the way along Loch Maree and sat opposite the first of the three islands in the middle. Siobhan ate the stale bannocks and dried beef, scanning the countryside. The grey-stoned, green-grassed mountains beside Loch Maree sat in quiet reflection in the waters of the still loch, the loch itself mirroring the bright, sunny day.

Still so beautiful. How wonderful to live here. If only it was safer. Siobhan swallowed the dry meat. Her nerves had been on high alert since the morning's spectators. Once again, the beauty of the wilds of Scotland were tempered with its dangers—the people.

Siobhan eyed the landscape once more. It truly was magnificent—tall, grey mountains, out-croppings of rock, clumps of darker-green forests. Her eyes flicked back to a lone figure. She gasped.

"Rory." She couldn't keep the alarm from her voice.

Be calm Siobhan, or you'll make everyone jumpier than they already are.

"What?" Rory was by her side in an instant.

"Ah, I'm not sure, but is that a person way over there?" She pointed.

Rory took out his high-powered binoculars and looked in the direction. He shook his head.

"No. A standing stone. Maybe one of the standing stone circles that are all over the Highlands."

"But it's only one," she said. "That happens?"

"Aye," he sounded unperturbed.

Siobhan continued chewing the tough meat. She didn't recall any standing circles on their journey to Loch Ewe, but then they'd had other things on their mind.

They finished their food then remounted. Rory, at the head of the party, turned Boy so he faced them all.

"We're making good progress, due to our early morning's start, but I wish to camp beside Loch Maree," he said. "The same spot at the loch-side near the woods as we camped on our way here, okay? It will be ideal." He turned the horse and kicked him to a walk.

"Ideal for what, Rory?" Callum asked, riding right behind his brother, as always.

"You'll all find oot when we get there," Rory said, waving his hand dismissively.

They reached the place and set up camp with efficiency. A campfire lit for cooking was soon on the blaze when Rory approached Siobhan as she sat on the log beside it. He carried his long range rifle and smiled for the first time since leaving Loch Ewe.

"Callum, Xian and I are going hunting, and we'll have a celebratory feast of sorts tha' night," he said. "Need some fresh meat. Have nae eaten well for a few days, eh?" Rory kissed her on the lips before walking off with the other men.

He spoke orders to Kendra and Geoff as he passed. Ensuring their vigilance, no doubt.

There was a definite strange feeling surrounding the camp and a prickling on the back of Siobhan's neck, but not as in a threat. After all they'd experienced with an underwater nuclear explosion nearby, everything was giving her the *heebie jeebies*. But the people who'd stared at them earlier in the day seemed benign, even curious.

Siobhan wandered to the loch side, stood among the grey pebbles and stones, and filled cooking pans with cool, fresh water for heating over the campfire. Camping was becoming another skill to add to her repertoire. Rising from her task she inhaled the crisp mountain air. The grey, triple-headed monolith on the other side of the loch wasn't wearing such a cloudy halo today. The sensation of being watched remained. Maybe it was the grey monster over there.

Siobhan laughed to herself at her explanation. Her first laugh in a long time. Yes, the previous days of stress were lifting. Let them. More stresses would come. Such as what to do with Antony.

And what to do about her and Rory.

How would it pan out? She pushed the problem aside for the moment. Celebrate, then think through the difficult things. Just be here; here and now. Life was too short to worry about tomorrow. Yes, so short for some. She still had to tell Aunty Rajna of the death of her precious boys.

Warm tears trickled down her face. She hadn't allowed herself to cry until now. She wiped the moisture off her cheeks. She wasn't being disrespectful, only practical. Celebrate first. The boys would have understood she needed a break from all this intense emotion.

Siobhan walked back to the fire with the water then helped around the camp, avoiding Antony as much as possible. She did *not* want to have any confrontations with him at present. And *any* interaction with him would be a confrontation.

She sat on the log by the fire for another hour; with no wind, the smoke hung around the camp. She would smell smoky, along with everything else. She was looking forward to a shower. Male voices and foot-tread came through the forest. Rory and Callum each carried a brace of rabbits while Xian followed behind with the guns. The rabbits had split bellies, already gutted.

"We'll take them over near the loch and skin them," Callum said.

The others devised a spit.

***

The evening meal of spit-roast rabbit was the most delicious Siobhan had ever eaten. *Ever.*

After their meal, Rory stood from his seat beside Siobhan. He had a flask of whisky in his hand, and he poured a dram into everyone's mug, then held his high.

"To our heroes and dear friends," he said. "May we never forget them. Scotland is indebted. To Angus. To Dae-Jung and the helmsman. To Sundeep and Sanjay. To Murdo MacDonald." Rory lifted his mug in a toast.

Those around the fire replied to his toast, holding their mugs high and repeating the names.

Rory removed the lid of another flask, a silver-metal hipflask from his kit. Holding it high, he began to pour out its contents onto the ground beside him. He blinked often and his brow crinkled. The group held a respectful silence for a while. Even those restrained, who'd had their bonds loosened to eat their meal, remained silent.

"*Slainte Mhor.*" Rory raised his mug again.

"*Slainte Mhor!*" Echoed around the circle, then they all drank once more.

The smooth whisky warmed Siobhan's throat. She glanced at Rory. His mouth formed a tight smile as his gaze rested on her. He tilted his head back and swallowed the last of his whisky.

"A Highland single malt. *The* best Scotch," Rory said as he sat beside her.

"But you've poured it out on the ground," she said. His libation in honour of the fallen was somewhat of a mystery to her.

Rory stared at the silver hipflask in his hand. His broad shoulders rose with a pensive breath.

"It's no' a sacrifice if it cost me nothing." His intense gaze connected with hers.

Yes, Siobhan thought, Rory knew what that truly meant, and had almost sacrificed his all to save others—people he didn't even know—to ensure the safety of Scotland. Angus had taken the task from him, though without his consent. Siobhan fought with waves of emotion. Sadness mixed with guilt at feeling so grateful Angus had prevented Rory from fulfilling the role he believed was his—almost a birth-right.

Callum walked to his tent with Kendra and returned soon after. Callum held a whistle and Kendra a small bodhran. The music started, Callum sang and Rory's crew, plus those from Siobhan's team who knew the songs, joined in. Rory sang softly next to her, his deep masculine tones following the melody tunefully. Callum's voice was just as masculine but held more musicality.

Most of the lyrics eluded Siobhan but some tunes were familiar, as they had played them in the Bunker. After a time, people's voices required a rest, so Callum played his whistle for a few musical pieces, its haunting low-pitched notes echoed around the campfire and flew off into the night. Then Kendra sang, her female voice lilted and breathed through the lyrics in the Gaelic tongue.

Siobhan's chest warmed. They were singing Scotland. The whistle was the wind through the Highlands. The bodhran the steady beat of the mountains, the continuation of the season's cycle, year in and year out. Voices singing in the Gaelic belonged to the animals—the deer, the grouse, the osprey, the sea otter. The lyrics themselves were the lives and thoughts of the people who have inhabited the Highlands for millennia, for generations and generations—some of them *her* ancestors.

The music spoke to her very soul—touched it. The scene around the campfire blurred.

"The human soul responds to music. You're made that way, aye?" Rory's deep voice was gentle in her ear. "The one who made all, sings to us through the wind, the forest, the animals of his world. Each life is a song to sing. You hear the lives of those who have gone before you in the music."

"How?" Siobhan wiped away her tears then frowned at him.

"You're a scientist. You ken you carry the genes of your parents and their parents, and so on. You're no' just *you*. You're part of everyone who came afore you. You are a flesh and blood part of everything that is, which only has its being through the one who made us."

"You believe that?" she asked. She was seeing yet another side to this man.

Rory didn't answer, only returned his gaze to the fire. The music continued to surround them and flowed to fill the loch to her left and the forest behind her.

"*You* hear the lives of the ones who have gone afore you," Rory said at last.

"I do?" Her tone was as incredulous as the idea was to her.

"Aye, you do. When ye asked me how I time travelled," he whispered close. "You did nae doubt the possibility but mentioned *portal* as a way o' doing it. That's no' scientific, is it? Yet you asked me if it was a method I used. A portal to travel through time is something your ancestors would have believed in, lass."

She squinted at him. He raised his brows at her.

"So, if not a portal, then you have access to a time machine or a wormhole," she whispered hoarsely into his ear. "Though the latter seems most unlikely."

"Och, no, I've said too much already," he said. "Conversation over."

Chapter Twenty-Eight

Rory spent the night covered in a blanket beside the fire with his arms wrapped around Siobhan. Her hair smelled of her flowers mixed with beech and rowan smoke. He held her tight as the morning light awoke him. She stayed asleep for a while.

They would be back at the Compound today.

And then what?

Cold metal touched his right cheek. Rory remained immobile.

"What do you want?" he asked the tall, masculine shadow that hovered over him and Siobhan. She woke, eyes wide. He gave her a sharp squeeze, ordering her to stillness.

"I want you and all yoor people to wake up and stand over there." The man whistled as he removed the gun from Rory's face. "And do not make any sudden moves or I'll ruin the face of the exceptionally beautiful woman you have been holding in your arms all night, laddie."

Rory stood very slowly and indicated for Siobhan to do the same.

"I'll just order my people before they get jumpy, okay?" Rory asked.

The quietly spoken, calm but aggressive, older man nodded. He wore a long coat over brown-grey trousers and a homespun jumper. His tanned, weather-beaten face had dirt ingrained in his wrinkles. His voice wasn't one of the old man he appeared to be.

How had this man got past the night watch?

And it was daylight now. No, it wasn't the fault of the one on watch. Rory himself had encouraged festivities. He'd only wanted to celebrate being alive. And being with Siobhan.

He'd let them drink... and drop their guard.

It was his fault, and his fault alone.

People materialised from behind the camp. They bore the marks of living rough in the wilds of Scotland with untidy clothes and unwashed bodies. They walked from the forest with purpose toward the camp. Each held a knife or carried a firearm pointed and ready. A group headed for the horses, others strode to the tents where his crew and Siobhan's Government people emerged.

So many?

"Everyone stay calm now and do what these people ask, okay?" Rory said, using his voice of command.

In the entrance to his tent, Callum reached for his handgun.

"No, Callum," Rory ordered.

Callum dropped his gun, and Kendra placed something back in her tent.

They stepped to the line drawn in the pine-needle covered ground, which the man had made with the heel of his boot.

"Hmm. Interesting. You have captives," the man said, tilting his head toward Antony and McPherson.

"Those people are under arrest, and we will take them to be tried," Rory explained.

The man raised his eyebrows and said nothing then he turned to his people.

"Horses, weapons and some food would be nice," he said to them.

Three of his men untied the horses' reins from the line Rory's crew had secured the animals to. The horses whinnied and nickered nervously as the strangers led them toward the far end of the camp. Rory's chest tightened as they led Boy past him. The tall black horse let out a neigh, reared, and pulled against the man leading him. Rory swallowed past a drying throat.

The women of the group rummaged through their food supplies, taking what they could hold in the empty cooking pans.

"There isn't much o' the roast rabbit left, Webster," a salt-and-pepper grey-haired woman with dark eyeliner said.

She wore faded black clothing and walked toward the leader with her kohl-outlined gaze fixed on Rory. Webster stood near him.

"So, now you are all lined up," Webster said. "Who do we have here?"

Webster turned and faced Rory and Siobhan, who stood in the middle of the line-up. They remained quiet.

"You know we have been following you since you made your way to Loch Ewe?" Webster said.

Rory raised his head. He must have missed their tail on their forward journey. Too busy with McPherson's clan.

"And we saw the trouble you and yours gave them." Webster walked to McPherson and bent low to look into McPherson's down-turned face. "Then we saw all the *hoo ha* around the submarine. And earlier today, a sonic *boom!*" His hands mimicked an explosion as he returned to Rory and Siobhan.

"So, who are you?" Webster asked, his face inches from Rory's and his foul breath wafting into Rory's nose.

"My name is Siobhan Kensington-Wallace," Siobhan said, "and I am from the Scottish Government."

Rory glared at Siobhan for breaking the silence. She looked straight ahead and didn't flinch.

"I'm Rory Campbell from the Invercharing Community and these are my people. We're on our way home from dealing with the nuclear issue caused by the submarine."

"Aye, nuclear issue. The sonic *boom.*" Webster did it again, his wide-open eyes accompanied the hand actions.

He then stepped closer to Siobhan.

"The Scottish Government. For an independent Scotland, I presume. A noble notion." His voice held sarcasm. "Wouldn't we Scots love that?" Webster nodded to his companions. They smiled back while McPherson lifted his head. "But the Government," Webster continued, "and I use the term in quotation marks, has not been heard from for years." Webster's Edinburgh accent held a scholarly tone.

"That will change," Siobhan said with conviction. To Rory, Siobhan's well-spoken English seemed devoid of any Scot's accent at this moment. "We wish to have a meaningful dialogue with the people of Scotland."

"*Meaningful dialogue.* Another grand notion, lassie," Webster said. "And how are you going to do that?"

"We will meet with the people who run communities"—Siobhan glanced at Rory— "and others."

"Oh, and we are the *others*, eh?" Webster asked.

"Yes, sir," Siobhan said. "We'd be very glad to meet with yourself and any other leaders of the different groups who are—"

"Siobhan! Stop making promises you can't keep!" Antony yelled from the far end of the line-up.

Siobhan tensed beside Rory. She sucked in air then turned to Antony.

"Would someone please gag that man?" she asked. "He does not speak for the Scottish Government!" Siobhan turned back to Webster, visibly calming herself. "I promise you, Mr Webster, if you wish a voice, we will grant you one. The Government is planning to exert its powers and fulfil its responsibilities to its people. Soon we will function as a government should, and we wish all those concerned citizens who want to be part of it, to join us in getting Scotland back on its feet."

"Very noble and grand sentiments, Ms Siobhan Kensington-Wallace," Webster said. "But I'm sorry to admit, I have lost all faith in a government who runs into its rabbit hole at the first sign of real trouble and decides it's time to pop out its wee bunny head forty years later. Sorry lassie, 'tis nae good enough. And we dinnae want anything to do with it." He grinned tightly at Siobhan.

Siobhan held her head higher.

Rory's heart beat for her. Siobhan was a nuclear physicist, not a politician. She spoke well, but not well enough for the tough heart standing in front of her. The educated tough heart who lived with several people who, this incident aside, Rory was reluctant to call bandits.

"Who are you then, sir?" Rory asked, looking the man straight in his grey eyes.

The man chewed his lip and squinted his stare back to Rory. "Let's just say we are a group of people who don't wish to be part of Community life and want nothing to do with formal government. You could say we are nomads and scavengers."

I would definitely call you scavengers.

"I ken *you*." The woman with the greying hair and dark outlined eyes pointed at Rory. "Rory Campbell, did ye say?" Her accent was broad Highland.

Rory turned to her and nodded mutely.

"I kenned your faither, Scott Campbell. Och, he was a *man*." She smiled to herself. "And ye have nae done too badly from his siring, either laddie." Her eyes traced a journey from his head to his toe and back again, then she turned to Webster. "His faither was a good yin. He wiped 'oot that mob o' slavers near Fort William a few years back, ken? Well, a *good* few years back, aye." She looked at Webster and tilted her head at him.

"What?" he asked.

She flicked her head toward Rory. "Give the lad back his horse," she said. "Fur the sake of his faither's memory. The man died riddin' us o' them slavers, ken."

Webster's shoulders slumped. "Och!" He looked resigned. "Women!" He turned and lifted his chin in the direction of the man who held Boy.

Rory whistled and his horse broke free and trotted to him.

"Thank you, ma'am," Rory said to the strange woman as he grabbed the reins and Boy nudged him with a soft muzzle.

The woman smiled and tilted her head in the direction in which they would head home. "Ye live in Invercharing, ye say?"

"Aye," Rory said.

"But yoor faither and his funny wee wifey lived in Glencoe, aye?" she asked.

"Aye." Rory wouldn't say more in case he triggered her memory of himself in another time, looking exactly as he did today. Rory remembered her—the black market pharmacist.

"Ye ken that old farm hoose lines up with the stone over yonder?" She nodded toward the top end of the loch; the direction of the standing stone Siobhan had noticed yesterday.

Rory pushed his eyebrows together. Where was she going with this information?

"Well, they're on a Ley line, ken?" She seemed to answer his unspoken question. "It's the summer solstice tha day, aye. Be careful. Ye never ken what may happen."

"That's enough of your old Druid talk, Deidra," Webster said. "Let them go if they must. Aye, on ye all go. The rest o' your things are ours. Away with yoo." Webster dismissed them with a flick of his hand.

Rory waved his people to start walking then helped Callum and Xian hitch the bodies onto Boy's back. They marched away, empty-handed.

Not for long.

First thing he would do on his return, after seeing the Government off, would be a mission to retrieve their goods. He wouldn't let wild people like *this man,* no matter how well spoken, have the horses and weapons he'd commandeered from them.

And they had his father's rifle.

Chapter Twenty-Nine

Invercharing Community

The Compound was a welcome sight after their day's journey. Rory sighed. It had been a long walk. They'd tied Sundeep and Sanjay's bodies over Boy's back and periodically stopped to take them down and place them in a chilly burn to keep them from deteriorating too quickly. The odour of dead human was obvious, and Boy's unsettled nickering became more frequent the closer they got to home.

George stood waiting at the gate. Having surrendered their CB radios to their early morning guests, Rory had no way of informing him of their soon arrival. The lookout in the watchtower would have told George of their approach—and their lack of horses.

Bullet holes pock-marked the walls of the compound's buildings. They'd have to patch them up before winter. The smell of baking bread permeated the air. It was always the aroma of home. Government personnel walked between their vehicles carrying the large boxes that stored their gear. Vehicle doors were open, and Government staff loaded the equipment into them.

Packing up already? But, aye, they would've felt the reverberations of the underwater blast from here and decided their mission was completed.

"You look like you have a story to tell," George said.

He stepped toward Rory, eyeing those who walked behind him, crumpled and dusty, dragging their feet and most looking up as they smelled the bread and sensed their hunger.

Rory nodded wordlessly. George looked past him, noting the bodies on Boy and the two restrained men, one of them Antony.

A tall man in camouflage gear walked toward them, followed by Brendan, Mandy and Christine, who had come out of the front building and now strode past him. Brendan approached Rory, and he grabbed his little brother in a tight hug.

"Ow," Brendan said. "Good to have ye back, but dinnae break mine, aye?"

"Here, this is for you." Rory handed Brendan the folded piece of paper Murdo had given him. "Memorise it, then eat it," Rory said.

"What?" Brendan laughed.

"No, seriously. Memorise it." He nodded at his wee brother as a smile tugged at his cheek. Brendan frowned and unfolded the paper.

"It's just numbers," he said.

"Memorise. Eat," Rory said then mimed putting food in his mouth.

"You're weird," Brendan said through a laugh.

Behind Rory, Kendra and Callum hugged their women. Every journey out posed the question of return, and every reunion was like a resurrection.

"Ms Kensington-Wallace, we are packing ready to return to the Bunker," said a government man. "We thought you wouldn't want to delay once you arrived. Well done, everyone, on your successful mission."

The Government man directed his congratulations to them. Rory read his name badge: *William MacIntosh.*

"Thank you, Bill," Siobhan said. "As you see, we have less than we left with." Siobhan's gaze slid to Boy. "We lost Sanjay and Sundeep." Her voice broke.

Rory placed his arm around her shoulder and MacIntosh stiffened at his open affection to Siobhan. They'd yet to inform those in the Compound and the Government of their relationship.

What could be the political fallout from that?

George peered behind him, his eyes squinting over his glasses. MacIntosh followed his gaze.

"Yes, it is me," McLellan stated from the back of the group.

"Well, *you* can remain quiet!" Siobhan had composed herself. "Major Antony McLellan is under arrest. Mr Stobbart, would you please find a place to keep Major McLellan and Mr McPherson detained?"

"Aye, Miss," George answered Siobhan then looked questioningly at Rory.

"I'll fill you in, George," Rory said.

"And I will fill you in, Bill," Siobhan said to her now second in-command. "But please may we all have a rest and a freshen up before we attend to those unpleasant tasks?"

Siobhan watched Antony and McPherson as they walked past, escorted by Militia to a secure place.

"Ms Kensington-Wallace." MacIntosh stood in front of Siobhan, as if to bar her way. "May we leave as soon as possible? It's barely midday and we would make it home to the Bunker before dark. It's midsummer's day and we'll have plenty of daylight."

"Ms Kensington-Wallace needs time to recover from her journey, Mr MacIntosh." Rory held Siobhan's arm and ushered her past the large man. "What's his hurry?" he whispered to Siobhan as he walked her into the main building.

Rory led Siobhan along the corridor to his rooms.

"Have a shower, Siobhan, then we'll sort out what we need to." He kissed her gently on the lips. "I'll be back soon." He left.

Rory looked for George and found him in the now empty control-centre. The tables were back in their original positions prior to the Government visit. George noticed him the second he entered.

"Rory!" George strode across the room to stand next to him. "We have a problem," he said into Rory's ear. "Your big sister has divulged secret information."

"What!" Rory couldn't keep the anger out of his voice. "Where is she?" he roared.

"Rory, lad. Calm doon." George's gaze flicked to the two remaining Government personnel who were picking up the last of the supplies to take out and load onto their vehicles. "The Government is packing *it* up," he said.

Rory blinked. "They're taking it with them? *That's* why MacIntosh is in such a hurry to leave."

Rory stormed through the hall and made his way to the back of the Compound to his sister's rooms. He bashed on her door with his fist.

"Who is it?" Angela's voice concealed none of her alarm.

"Your brother!" Rory yelled, his chest heating with his rising anger.

No sound came from behind the door.

"Let me in, Angela!" he shouted.

A member of the Militia who had taken the detained men to a secure section of the Compound, was passing. "You okay, Mr Campbell?" he asked.

"I'm fine," Rory answered, curt and sharp.

Angela's door creaked open. Rory took another breath to stop the wave of anger about to break shore. It wasn't working. He thrust the door open. Angela stood back, her wide eyes narrowing again to her lofty stare.

"What do you want, Rory?" she asked.

"What have you done?" Rory stepped forward, mentally pulling himself back from grabbing her.

He warned himself to not lay a hand on Angela. It would only give her more ammunition.

Angela stood taller and flicked her long, red hair over her shoulders. She remained silent.

"You told them?" He spat the words in her face.

Angela blinked at his vehemence. "Of course, I told them," she said. "It's a scientific discovery we need to share now we have an understanding with the Government."

Rory shook his head in disbelief. "What are they doing with it?" he demanded.

"They're only looking at it," she said.

"No, they're not," he said. "They're taking it!"

"What?" Angela seemed genuinely surprised. She stormed past him. "Let's go see," she called over her shoulder.

Rory caught up. "What made you do it, Angela?" His voice thudded in his throat in time with his footsteps.

"I'm going to the Government Bunker," she said.

"And you sold us out for *that*?"

Angela stopped dead and Rory had to scamper back to be face to face with her.

"You cannot understand how much it would mean to me, Rory, to be part of the Scottish Government," she said. "To be part of Scotland's *restoration*. To be away from this middle-of-the-bloody-nowhere-Highlands Compound!" Her breathing shuddered.

Rory shook his head. "You don't get it either, do you? They have a time machine. They can change the past now. What *will* they do?" he asked. "Do *you* know? Can you trust them?"

Angela didn't speak at first, breathing heavily through her nostrils.

"It's too late now," she said at last. "How am I going to get it from them?"

"I don't know," he replied.

Even his relationship with Siobhan may not help him get the Time Machine back.

Rory continued his brisk walk side by side with his sister to the barn in silence. The earthen floor was clear of the cubicle and two Government men packed up the console. Murray stood to one side with MacIntosh beside him. Rory strode up to them.

"You cannot take it. I do not give my permission," he yelled into MacIntosh's face.

MacIntosh stiffened and held his head higher.

"Well, Mr Campbell," he said. "Your permission has nothing to do with it whatsoever. Apart from being a monumental scientific advancement, the Time Machine is an important resource for the Scottish Government."

"No, it's not." Rory shook his head. "I'll speak to Siobhan." He turned aside to Murray. "What are you doing here?"

Murray opened his mouth.

"He's coming to the Bunker with us," MacIntosh spoke for him.

"No, he's not," Rory said. "I definitely do not give my permission."

"Your brother is over eighteen. He doesn't need your permission." MacIntosh took a step closer to Murray.

Rory blinked. "What do *you* want, Murray?"

"I wouldn't mind seeing the computers and stuff at the Bunker." Murray sounded hesitant.

"Can you wait a wee bit?" Rory asked. "Go later on?"

"Sorry, but he's going now." MacIntosh again.

"Why can't it wait, MacIntosh?" Rory asked.

"We are here, we'll take him with us."

"No." Rory was adamant.

MacIntosh pursed his lips and gave his head a slight shake. "Well, it's not a request. It's actually an order from the First Minister herself. Murray is coming with us."

"Why?" Rory narrowed his eyes. *Something is really up.*

"They want me, Rory," Murray said, "because I'm good at maths and I know what to do for the calcs for the Time Machine."

Rory sensed in his brother's tone that they'd put him under duress.

"Tell me," Rory asked in the Gaelic.

"They'll no' ensure the safety of the Compound if I dinnae go," Murray answered, also in the Gaelic.

Rory spun on his heel without a word. He ran to his quarters and slammed open the door.

"Siobhan!" His yell filled the old farmhouse.

Siobhan came out of the bathroom wearing only a towel; her wet hair dripped on her shoulders, her eyes wide and blinking.

"What's the matter, Rory?"

He took some breaths to calm himself. It wasn't her fault. Siobhan would know nothing of it. It had only been Angela and that MacIntosh guy.

"They've discovered the Time Machine and are dismantling it to take back to your Government Bunker. They are forcin' Murray to go 'cos he knows how to operate it," he said, his voice firm, and trying not to yell.

Siobhan's eyes never blinked throughout the time he spoke, and her mouth remained opened.

"A Time Machine." Her voice was awe-filled.

"Aye! Siobhan you cannae let the Government have it. Please speak to your First Minister. She's ordered it!"

Siobhan shook herself. "Okay, let me get dressed and I'll speak to Bethany Watts on CB radio."

Chapter Thirty

*I*s *that understood, Siobhan? Over.* The voice of Bethany Watts, First Minister of Scotland, came through the handset of the CB radio.

"Yes, First Minister. Over," Siobhan said.

Very well, Bethany said. *We trust you will have a safe journey home. We will be waiting for you—and the Time Machine. Over and out.*

Scooting the chair out from under her, Siobhan let out a long sigh. Her still wet hair had dampened the fresh blouse she wore, which now stuck to her shoulders. Walking along the corridor from the communications room to Rory waiting in his quarters, Siobhan pushed away the mild sense of dread swirling within her.

Rory would not be happy—*understatement* of the century.

Siobhan opened the door to his quarters and stepped in to find Rory rummaging in a kitchen cupboard. Bottles of preserves lined the bench underneath it.

"Well?" Rory stepped back from the cupboard, empty-handed, as she closed the door behind her.

"First Minister Bethany Watts was adamant." Siobhan pressed her lips together as Rory's stare became angry. "You can't take it back by force, Rory."

Siobhan put her arms around him. He was tense, every muscle in his long torso tight, and he had an air of desperation about him. He leaned back against the cupboard doors painted the *mission brown* of the nineteen-seventies.

"Oh aye, I can." Rory's voice was deep and firm.

Siobhan shuddered.

"No, Rory. Don't. I'd have to arrest you," she said. "Don't make me. The First Minister has ordered us to return with it."

The tight muscle in Rory's jaw relaxed a little.

"Don't let them use it, Siobhan, I *beg* you," he asked.

He was so intense. She'd never encountered this level of desperation in him.

"I will do all I can to ensure that MacIntosh and his team do not make any time journeys until you and your people here have a full say in it, and all the input you want. Okay?" she said.

"They can never use it, Siobhan. *Never.*"

"But *you* have."

"I'm sorry, but I don't trust the Government," he said. "Too many loose cannons."

Siobhan blinked, taken aback, and frowned.

"Oh, Siobhan. You cannae think me unfair. Look at your pal, Antony. You must've seen it coming. You used to be with him, aye?"

How did he know that? "Who told you?"

"You did," Rory said.

She blinked her disbelief.

"You can tell when a man and woman have been, you ken, intimate in their relations," he said.

"It was over, ages ago."

"Hmm." Rory lifted his eyebrows. "I'm still no' happy about the Time Machine leaving here. Nor ma' wee brother, Murray. They, I mean the Government—no, actually that MacIntosh—has threatened us if he does nae go."

"What?" she asked. *That is unbelievable.* "That can't be right."

"Well, it's what ma wee brother says." Rory breathed through his nostrils.

"I'll check it out, Rory." Siobhan placed her hand on his chest and felt his heart pounding through it. "I'll ensure he doesn't carry out any threats against this Community. Or make any in the first place."

She tilted her head back to see his expression. He appeared to be calming, his heart beating under her hand steadied.

"Did you recognise Murray? He was the lad with me when we visited you and your father." Rory's smile was tight. "Who can you trust in the Bunker to look out for him?"

Sweat dampened her hand resting on him, and his eyes narrowed as she hesitated. She'd struggled with a question all the long walk back to the compound and had finally decided in the shower. But what she would tell Rory now, wouldn't please him.

"Rory, *I'll* keep an eye on him."

He took a deep breath in and gripped her shoulders, his warm, large hands like tight clamps on her upper arms.

"You're no' telling me you're going, Siobhan?" he asked. "We're together now, are we no'? You'll no' leave me?"

"Rory." *Where should I start?* "I have things to clear up at the Bunker. I need to sort out Antony's and MacPherson's prosecution. I am a key witness."

Rory looked at the stained ceiling with a pained expression on his face. She'd struggled with her plan, but her certainty of its logic overrode the cool sweat now forming on her upper lip.

"I have so much to tell the First Minister about life out here," she continued. "And people like you, who are wonderful leaders and would be part of it all—the New Scottish Government, I mean. I have my personal belongings to sort out. Rory," she said as he began to speak. He'd returned his gaze to her, and his eyes were now slits. "I can't just leave it all. I have a role to hand over. And going in convoy is the safest way to return."

"Don't leave me, Siobhan," he almost moaned.

Siobhan's throat ached. "Rory, I'm not leaving you for good. I am leaving so I can come back and be with you for good."

"Marry me now," he said.

"What?" She inhaled but couldn't breathe out.

"We have a minister," Rory said. "He'll marry us."

"But I'm about to go." The air in her lungs finally moved. "They're waiting for me, so the convoy can leave."

"Don't go from here *not* my wife."

Rory was dead serious. Was he afraid he'd lose her?

"Rory, you know I'm yours."

"Aye, but I want you to *be* mine." His blue-eyed gaze bore into her.

"We won't have time to... consummate it," she said.

Rory shook his head. "Dinnae care. Please don't leave here until you are mine."

Siobhan blinked. The man before her was earnest. He loved her. She loved him. Those in the Government Bunker may not approve. They may misinterpret it. They may regard her as a traitor, not a peacemaker. Not a woman in love with a man—a great man.

Rory waited for her answer. There was love and longing in those intense eyes. How could she deny them each other?

Damn the nay-sayers. She'd show them what Community people were really like.

And MacIntosh could wait.

"Yes," she answered.

"Aye?"

"Yes."

"I'll go get the minister then. Dinnae move!" He kissed her firmly on the lips then ran out the door.

***

The ceremony was brief and fulfilled the legal requirements.

Talk about whirlwind.

The whole Invercharing Community and the Government contingent were present. Rory's family were happy for them, if somewhat surprised. There was genuine acceptance in the hugs Siobhan received from each of his siblings.

Siobhan placed her duffle bag in the back of the armour-plated vehicle. Murray jumped in the back seat with her, and Angela would ride in the front with MacIntosh. Rory leaned on the vehicle and fiddled with something in the pocket of his buckskins.

"Siobhan, we did nae have rings," Rory said. "I'll see to it for when you are back here. But in the meantime..." He held out the object he'd been handling, took her right hand, palm up and placed a navy-blue velvet jewel box on it.

Siobhan looked at the small jewellery box and blinked.

"What's this?"

"Open it," he said. "They're for you."

She opened the box. Inside was a set of diamond-stud earrings. Twin miniature multi-prisms refracted light a million-fold. Tiny rainbows emitted the seven colours of the spectrum. Her mother's words came to her—a rainbow signifies a promise—sunshine after rain; good times after hardship.

He didn't have wedding bands, but he had these rocks!

"Rory, they are incredibly beautiful."

"They were my mother's. The only thing of hers that survived the looting after The Stock Market Crash. And now they are my wife's." His large hands engulfed hers holding the box in her palm.

Siobhan lifted her face and pressed her lips against his. Then he wrapped his arms around her and brought her close to him.

"Dinnae be gone long, heart of my heart," he whispered into her hair.

"Don't be in a hurry to be a hero at your own expense, Ruairidh Campbell," she whispered back.

"I'll think twice now I have so much more to lose."

A member of the Government's Defence Force marched Antony and MacPherson past them.

"So, did you tell your *husband* about the nuclear fallout cloud?" Antony said when he came level with them.

It was as though the world stood still while the people present absorbed his question. The conversation by the doorway to the main building ceased. Those involved in the last-minute loading of the vehicles stopped their activity. Rory stood tall and glared at Antony. Then he turned his glare to her.

"It's slow moving, Rory," she said. "And it's possible it won't reach the British Isles."

Thanks Antony, for making it sound as if I was keeping something from everyone.

"When were you goin' to mention the nuclear fallout cloud, Siobhan?" Rory asked.

"Rory, it's not as bad as *he* made it sound."

"What's *not so bad* about a nuclear fallout cloud on its way to the British Isles?" he asked. "What caused it?"

Everyone in the immediate vicinity waited for her reply, unashamedly eaves dropping.

"Tell him, Siobhan." Antony's mocking voice came from a far vehicle, which his guard then ushered him into.

"Shut the door to his vehicle, please," she shouted to the man who accompanied Antony.

And gag him.

"When we left the Government Bunker five days ago, there were reports of a nuclear cloud coming from one of the southern states of the USA," Siobhan said loud enough for those around to hear. "A nuclear attack or a power station incident, they weren't sure. Due to known weather patterns, it was making its way east, and the projection was it would cross southern Europe in three to five days' time."

"So, that's *now.*"

"Our meteorologist ran a program which, with the weather data available from this morning, predicted it would not, should not, spread this way," Siobhan said.

A frown replaced Rory's glare.

"I spoke to my assistant while I was radioing the PM," she said. "Louise has been keeping tabs on the cloud's progress and the weather. So, we should be okay."

"Well, you, Murray and Angela will be okay in the Bunker," Rory said, "but if your wee projection is nae correct, *we* will nae be."

"But it's dissipating all the time," she said. "There should be minimal radiation."

"I've seen the effects radiation can have on the human body, Siobhan—" he began.

"No Rory, it will be minimal. Those poor North Korean submariners were right in it. We will have nothing to worry about."

"And if it's not?"

"Then, we will let you know," she said. "You can come to the Bunker where it's safe."

Rory shook his head.

"Your people are welcome to come to the Bunker if we find the trajectory is over Scotland," Siobhan said. "I'll radio you when the next lot of data is in, and I know the program's results."

Rory continued to shake his head.

"No," he said. "The Government Bunker does nae have room for us all. You ken we are not the only Community in Scotland? We have family in Glencoe. Hell, all communities are our family. Besides, we have animals and crops. And who will defend our compound from bandits looting while we are underground? And don't the bandits and that weird group who live in the wilds, and people like them, have just as much right to the Government's protection in an egalitarian society? Isn't that the kind of world your government will want? It's what those of us who live in Community want."

The Compound was silent, devoid of activity as Rory finished his speech. Her *husband* finished his speech. The sentiments he expressed were one of the reasons why his people loved him.

It's one of the reasons why I love him.

"Rory, I'll let you know," she finally said. "In the meantime, we can give you information on how to protect yourselves from any possible nuclear fallout. And yes, we all want the same thing. And when you are ready, Rory Campbell, please be part of the dialogue with the Government? Be part of the changes to government that will build Scotland once more?"

Rory blinked, then swallowed. "I'll think about it."

He pulled her close and kissed her. They stayed there for what seemed an age then he pulled away but kept his face close.

"Dinnae take too long to sort your things 'oot, aye?" he said. "A wife should be with her husband, even if she has an important job with the Government."

"Yes,, we'll be in contact by CB, and I'll keep an eye on you."

"How?" Rory rested his forehead on hers.

"By drone. Only, please don't shoot this one down."

"What? That was you?"

Chapter Thirty-One

Scottish Government Bunker

MacIntosh raced them home. The Scottish Highlands passed by Siobhan in a blur. Perthshire's high, purple heather-covered hills, sitting behind green valleys chocked full of trees, were almost as blurry. Almost. It was more populated here, and the roads were in a poor state so the convoy couldn't travel at such speeds. The crowds gathered as they moved further south along what used to be the A9. Communities had CB radioed ahead, Siobhan assumed.

Perhaps Rory, or his people, had relayed the information of the Government's intentions to ensure their safe passage. Or maybe she compared it to their forward journey, with McPherson and his crew on their tail. Either way, their journey home was untroubled and well observed.

The convoy reached the Kincardine Bridge just before seven p.m. Three hours to home. If they travelled unmolested, they'd be home for a late supper. Siobhan recalled the three great bridges that used to span the Firth of Forth, and the shock that rippled through the residents of the Scottish Government Bunker when terrorists blew up the three bridges simultaneously with lorries packed with explosives. That was early on, right after the Stock Market Crash. Siobhan had been young, but the memory remained. As a child she hadn't appreciated the beauty in the structures. The Queensferry Crossing had tall upright beams but the elegant flow of the wire cables now sat snapped, and the road was chunks of concrete and support metal. She had viewed it on drone footage. Those bridges would have cut their total journey time home by more than an hour if they'd still spanned the Firth of Forth.

Siobhan's conflicting emotions warred within her as she approached the large metal doors set in the concrete wall behind Arthur's Seat in Holyrood Park. They drove through the enclosed up-ground compound abutting the hill, which formed the only outside section of the Government's base. The doors opened to her home and driving in only increased her discomfort. This had been home for what seemed like her whole life. A place where she'd been secure and brought up with the love of her father and the approval of her teachers and mentors.

Now she returned a different person. Siobhan had lived *up top* and, as dangerous as it had been—and could still be—she longed to be back. Back in the Highlands with her untamed man, Rory—her husband. A small ache began. Siobhan missed him already and now longed to be back with him and feel those loving arms around her. His gentle lovemaking of two nights ago held the promise of a satisfying marriage in the sex department.

Shivers of memory began on her neck. She could sense his soft lips making their way along to...

No. Don't go there.

It would only make it more difficult to be without his love. Who knows how long it would be before she could return to him?

Siobhan had a job to finish. She would officially install her assistant, Louise, into her new position as head of Nuclear Surveillance. And she had to convince the First Minister that her own presence *up top* in the Community situation was ideal for the dialogue and involvement of non-government groups who would have a role in restoring the Scottish Government's rule.

The presence of her sister-in-law, Angela, who seemed an ambitious handful, would help greatly.

Siobhan caught Murray in her side view as they descended the long, dimly lit, sloping tunnel to the heart of the Bunker. She'd had little to do with him so far and she vaguely remembered him from her childhood. Murray was exactly the same then, as she saw him now, thin and nerdy looking. He was excellent at mathematics. Siobhan had promised to keep him safe but what from, she wasn't entirely sure.

Looking out the left rear vision mirror she could see the armoured vehicle that contained the components of the Time Machine, as Rory simply called it. More like a ticking time bomb, if Rory was right. And he was. Rory, she had discovered, was a very good judge of people's character. Siobhan would have to form an ethics committee—ensuring she was part of it herself—that would devise and adhere to protocols safeguarding time and history. They were to ensure no one tampered with either.

Like that would be easy.

The vehicles reached the parking bays of the garage areas and Siobhan got out of the vehicle. She smiled at Murray as he scanned the garage level of the Bunker with wide-open eyes. He briefly noticed her smile and flicked one back.

"Okay, Murray." MacIntosh slapped Murray on the back, causing the young man to flinch. "We're going straight to the labs where you will set this machine up for us. Okay?"

"Ah, okay." Murray chewed his bottom lip then went to the vehicle containing the Time Machine.

"I'll come down in a while, Murray," Siobhan said to his retreating back. "I have to report to the First Minister."

Murray glanced over his shoulder and nodded, frowning; a sheen of sweat glistened on his brow.

She'd better get to him in the lab as soon as she could.

But she must see Aunty Rajna first.

***

Siobhan's conversation with Bethany Watts took an age. Had so much happened in only six days? She had returned a married woman. Married to a leader in an outside Community, no less. And Antony was a changed man. Or maybe, they had finally exposed the real Antony. They would prosecute him as soon as was practical.

"I must get to my new younger brother-in-law, Murray," Siobhan said. "I promised Rory I'd look out for him." Siobhan excused herself from the First Minister's office.

***

Siobhan entered the lab, walking right into an air of tension.

"I'll try it again." Murray's voice came from behind a green metal console.

Thick electrical wires ran along the floor to a strange-looking cubicle. Made of fibreglass, it had three sides. In it was a cat struggling to get out of a transparent brown bag, which looked like it was made of a plastic or resin-like substance. A *pod*, Murray called it.

"Re-do the calculations." MacIntosh's voice held irritation verging on impatience.

"I've recalculated three times now. The final check with my slide-rule gives the same numbers." Murray used a tone as though speaking to a child.

It wasn't lost on MacIntosh who glared at Murray, his mouth a thin line.

"Hi. How's it going then?" Siobhan stepped over the thick cables lying along the floor. She made her voice sound cheery.

"For some reason, the machine isn't working," MacIntosh said through gritted teeth.

"Well, actually, you should only be assembling it, not using it yet," Siobhan said, cocking an eyebrow. "We need to devise a Code of Ethics before we do any time travelling. So, no further attempts at time travel should occur until then. And you'd better free that cat before it suffocates."

The animal ceased its scratching and now its low growls were getting softer.

"It doesn't work, anyway. We've been duped." MacIntosh scowled at Murray then stormed out of the lab, leaving Murray and Siobhan alone.

"I can't understand it, Ms Kensington-W... I mean Siobhan. You *know* it works. And my calcs aren't incorrect. I'll stake my life on it. It's a mystery." Murray shook his head, then turned his gaze to the machine in question, chewing his lower lip under a frown. His shoulders hunched, and he blinked often, his usual amicable expression fading. He was just like the cat in the pod.

"Somebody put gloves on and free that animal!" Siobhan yelled.

Chapter Thirty-Two

Invercharing Community

Rory stood at the gate of the Invercharing Community Compound. The tail-lights of the last Government vehicle disappeared over the hill. The sky clouded and the blue, which had greeted him and Siobhan early that morning, now turned to white and deepening grey as rain clouds blew in from the far coast. The grey, windswept Munros and mountains which surrounded the Invercharing Community kept their silent, ever-present watch over the Compound and the green-brown countryside.

My country.

Rory had often thought of it as his heart and soul.

Oh, how it had changed in almost an instant. Now his heart and soul made her way back to the Government Bunker in Edinburgh.

Had he made a mistake in letting Siobhan go? Would he ever see her again?

Rory was certain, as sure as the sun would rise over the Highlands tomorrow, she would do everything possible to ensure her return to him. But what if something prevented her?

What if Siobhan's boss, the First Minister of Scotland, would not give her permission to relieve Siobhan of her duties in the Bunker. Bethany Watts—he couldn't think of a more pompous name—might believe Siobhan's idea of Communities being part of the New Scottish Government's restoration was rubbish.

It may go well with Siobhan being granted permission to leave, then bandits could attack her on the way here.

He'd go get her personally if he must. As long as he could be sure he got out of that Bunker himself. And with her.

The rain came. Water ran down his hair and dripped on his collar, cold-wet trickled down his neck. It stung where it ran over the graze on his scalp.

"Brother. Come inside." Callum placed his warm, large, and identical hand on his shoulder and shook.

Rory breathed in sharply and turned. "Yeah, no use dying of influenza. Then I'd never see her again, would I?"

"She'll be back, brother," Callum said. "She loves you."

Rory spent the next hour tending to Boy. His stallion's coat needed a good curry and Rory brushed with vigour until the horse's black coat shone. Footsteps came behind him, but Rory continued untangling Boy's mane.

"When you're ready, Rory son, we have some debriefing to do," George said. "I need to know your story and you need to know ours. About the attacks, aye?"

"Aye." Rory continued combing Boy's mane, the coarse hair teased out and became smooth in his hands.

"And I know you would rather spend your wedding night with your bride," George said. "But well, the men wish to cheer you up with a Buck's party of sorts. Ye'd be in that?"

A smile tugged at the corner of Rory's mouth, and he turned to his friend and mentor.

"Sounds grand. I have some chores to do first, though."

"We ken you, Rory. Work before pleasure. Much later, then?" George left him.

Rory spent the rest of the day cleaning equipment, saddles, firearms, and sharpening blades—anything to keep busy.

Anything to stop missing her.

Rory strolled over to the main building and stopped at the medical centre. Aunty Bec was there with Christine attending to those in the Community who had received various injuries from the previous attacks on the Community itself and on those who had ridden out with him.

"Come here, young man," Aunty Bec ordered. "I hear you have some wounds which need tending. A head wound, no less." She spoke in her official doctor-tones.

Rory sat on the trolley in front of her and she began to examine his graze then moved to the injury Angus gave him.

"Hmm, that's quite a bump you have there," she commented.

"Angus was determined," Rory said.

"So, he dived the sub and ensured we were safe. And you especially." Aunty Bec began to re-dress the graze as a silence descended on the medical centre.

"I still cannae fathom why he was so insistent," Rory said. "To the point o' knocking me out and abandoning me in the middle o' the ocean."

Aunty Bec spoke not a word as she secured the fresh dressing.

"He was the same that time"—Rory dropped his voice so only Aunty Bec could hear— "when Murray sent Kelly back. Murray said Angus covered for them. Said our parents saved Angus' life."

Aunty Bec nodded, a knowing in her eyes.

"I need to know," Rory said.

Aunty Bec pursed her lips, then gave a sharp nod. "Yes, you probably do."

She walked away to the office of the medical centre then returned ten minutes later, holding a piece of yellowed paper.

"When the Community first started," she said, "it was our policy to keep a record of every person who arrived. We still ask for a proof of identity from each person who joins us, but not everyone has important documents such as birth certificates or passports. People brought whatever they had. When your father brought Angus to the Community as a young man in his early twenties, this was the only document provided. If you can call it one."

She handed him the fragile paper. It was a scrap out of an old exercise book.

Rory unfolded it; the creases were worn to holes where they criss-crossed. The document was a bill of sale from a Mr Derrick Lloyd. It was a receipt for a male youth. The name *Scott Campbell* was in the place for *purchaser*. Under *goods* was the name, *Angus McAvoy*.

Rory stared hard at the paper in his hand—a secret from a friend's past.

"Angus was ashamed he'd been a slave," Aunty Bec said. "You know he was a handsome lad? He never let anyone know, yet he loved your father and felt indebted to him."

Rory shook his head. "It explains so much." His voice broke, then he bowed his head as the well of emotion in his chest overflowed and came out as tears.

Aunt Bec's arms wrapped around him and stayed there for a while.

"He was the one who set the Time Machine for your father's journey."
Aunt Bec's voice was so low Rory barely heard it. But he had. He nodded
his acknowledgement of that secret.

***

Rory left the medical centre as the late evening sky brightened after the
rain ceased and the clouds cleared. He went to the far barn and made his
way to the old section, which had housed the Time Machine. He wandered
into the empty space that once held the cubicle and the console, now only
bare earth. The diminishing daylight filtered in through the slit windows
of the west wall; a dimming spotlight as the sun began to set on this day of
the summer solstice. The focus of this stage now the place that once held
the Time Machine.

"What're you doing, Rory?" Brendan's cheerful voice echoed in the
barn.

Rory turned. This kid always made him smile—when he wasn't getting into trouble. He shook his head as a memory of an old man with
light-brown hair turning to grey, a face so wrinkled it could be a road map,
and body odour which smelled like a cat's dinner, came to mind. A man
who'd risked his life, and certainly fated his own death, to make sure a
nuclear warhead would detonate well out to sea.

"Trying to not be angry, Brendan," Rory answered.

"I've done nothing!" Brendan sounded defensive. "Oh, ya mean the fact
the machine's gone."

Rory tilted his head.

"It was right here, aye?" Brendan stood near a beaten patch of earth that
had scrapes leading away from it.

"Have you memorised those numbers yet?" Rory asked him.

"Aye," Brendan answered. "Ya ken what they are?"

"No." Rory pretended to hold a morsel in his hand then placed it in his
mouth.

"You're joking, right?" Brendan's contagious laugh rang up to the
rafters.

"No, you have tae eat it. I'm serious." Rory's laugh slipped out. He
couldn't stop it.

"They're co-ordinates. In the middle of the ocean, past Lewis," Brendan said through his chuckles. He stood centre-stage, nature's spot-light casting flecks of gold highlights through his light-brown hair.

Rory stopped laughing, suddenly sobered. "Oh, aye. They would be."

Rory put his hand to his mouth again and chewed on imaginary food as he grinned at his brother, remembering other co-ordinates. He didn't know much about Ley lines, but Webster's woman had said the Community Compound's co-ordinates sat along one.

Brendan laughed once more.

Then he disappeared.

THE END
Reviews are an important part of letting others know about books. If you enjoyed *Saving Time*, please leave a brief review at your online book seller.

Thanks

Acknowledgements

Stories come to me in different ways and a comment made by one of our sons-in-law sparked off the thoughts for *Saving Time*. One evening, his observation of the half-life of a Plutonium nuclear rod snuck into my subconscious and that night I dreamed. When I awoke, I wrote it down for as long as the vision stayed within reach.

The story needed a hero, and Scott and Caitlin's son, Rory, was the natural choice. Thus, *Community Chronicles Book 3* began.

I am grateful to my editor, author Annie Seaton, for her expertise, straight-forward manner and patient direction. Also, your belief in me, your encouragement, and the way you push me to do my best.

I am continually learning from you.

A teacher never stops teaching.

Thanks, Mindy Graham, my ever-supportive critique partner and cyber-friend. We'll meet in person one day.

To my beta readers, our daughter Gill, Jill Williams, Ileana Noble and Natasha Campbell. I'm grateful for the time you've put in reading my rough drafts and all your helpful comments.

Thanks to Fiona Jayde Media for the revamp of all four covers in the series.

Our daughter, Emma, who gave valuable input and has a line editor's eye.

My thanks to the judges of the Romance Writers of Australia's competitions who gave advice on Rory and Siobhan's first kiss and the first 10 000 words. Also, to the judges of Ink & Insights 2018 for their comments on the manuscript.

I would like to acknowledge my long-suffering family and friends who listened to me talking about my book—again.

And wonderful Scotland, you are a constant source of inspiration.

Finally, to my husband, for his patient endurance while I spend so much time with the people in the worlds in my head.

I trust you will see some of yourself in my brave heroes.

Jenn

About the Author

DESTINY RELATIONSHIP COURAGE

Retired nurse Jenn has travelled extensively and lived on three continents. Although Australia is the land of her birth, Scotland has always called her back. This country remains her source of inspiration, where she now lives with her husband, and close family nearby.

Jenn loves walking through a forest and climbing a mountain to experience the view. Or exploring a castle ruin and soaking in the history. Her only disappointment in life is that time travel is not possible... apparently.

Award-winning fantasy author Jenn Lees' latest release, *Of High Kings and Mages: Arlan's Pledge Book Three,* reached the Semi-Finalist stage in the OZMA Book Awards for Fantasy Fiction 2024 CIBAs (Chanticleer International Book Awards).

Of Warriors and Sages: Arlan's Pledge Book Two reached Semi-Finalist in the OZMA Book Awards for Fantasy Fiction 2023 (as the manuscript *The Quest*). Longlisted in the Realm Awards 2025 Fantasy Section. As the manuscript *The Quest* reached the Top 10 in Ink & Insights 2021.

Jenn Lees' Best Selling novel, *Of Myths And Portals: Arlan's Pledge Book One* achieved First Place Award (Gold) in The BookFest Fall 2024 Fiction-Romance-Fantasy, Second Place Award (Silver) in The BookFest fall 2024 Fiction-Fantasy-Magic, Myths and Legends, and Fiction-Christian-Fantasy

The Crossing: Arlan's Pledge Book 1 (re-released as *Of Myths and Portals*) achieved the finals in the OZMA Book Awards for Fantasy Fiction (previous draft manuscript) CIBA 2021. *Restoring Time* (Book 4 of the *Community Chronicles Series*) reached the finals in the CYGNUS Awards for Science Fiction 2021 CIBA.

An Ink & Insights Competition judge says of *Arlan's Pledge*:

'Beautifully crafted, full of rich setting descriptions, tension that caught my attention and kept it, and characters that leapt off the page. This author is a skilled storyteller.' (Melody Quinn. Ink & Insights 2021 Competition Master Category Judge)

Arlan's Pledge Series : *'Perfect for anyone who ever wished outlander had dragons.'* Book for Thought Review

Find out more about Jenn Lees and her novels.

Sign up for the newsletter and receive *Running with the Stags,* a free novella in the *Arlan's Pledge Series.*

www.jennleeswriter.com

Want more of Jenn Lees?   Support Jenn Lees Fantasy Author on Patreon.

https://www.patreon.com/c/jennleesfantasyauthor/members

Also By

**HE IS FIGHTING TO KEEP THEM TOGETHER
SHE KNOWS THEIR FUTURE HOLDS DEATH
CAN A TIME TRAVELLER CHANGE THE FUTURE OR IS IT
ONLY EVER UP TO FATE?**

Scotland, 2061.

Rory (son of Caitlin Murray-Campbell and Scott Campbell *Stolen Time: Community Chronicles Book 2*)anxiously waits for the nuclear fallout cloud to clear so he can travel to the government bunker in Edinburgh and unite with his new bride, Siobhan.

**But Siobhan has disappeared... into the Time Machine. The future state of the world and her own personal life shocks her.
Rory arrives at the Bunker as Siobhan returns, vowing to fulfil future-Rory's wishes while keeping from him a secret of her own.**

Once back at the Invercharing Community, the leadership thrusts Rory into a senior role and his efforts to protect his people cause a rift in his marriage to Siobhan, while she battles for acceptance among her husband's community.

Keeping love alive while struggling to keep their people alive is only half the problem as ambitions rise and natural disasters reign in a Scotland emerging from a dark age.

The love of soul mates is tested in this fourth book of the *Community Chronicles Series,* determining whether love is stronger than fate.
Finalist in the CYGNUS Book Awards for Science Fiction 2021 CIBAs.

Fantasy By Jenn Lees

ARLAN'S PLEDGE SERIES

'Perfect for anyone who ever wished Outlander had dragons.'—Book for Thought Review

'Everything about this is captivating, from the world-building all the way to the enticingly romantic love story that readers feel is unfolding directly in front of them. This novel makes readers want to hold on to the world and clutch every page until the end, simply because it's that good.'—InD'tale Magazine April '23

Of Myths and Portals: Arlan's Pledge Book One
(Previously released as *The Crossing. Arlan's Pledge Book One.*)
DESTINY MUST CLAIME THEM
Of Warriors and Sages: Arlan's Pledge Book Two
THE HEART-QUEST MUST WIN
Of High Kings and Mages: Arlan's Pledge Book Three
A KING MUST DIE

Murtairean. An Assassin's Tale
A Novel in the Dál Cruinne Series
AN ASSASSIN'S TWO HITS:
ONE FROM THE PAST TO HAUNT HIM
ONE TO FREE HIM
A MAGE WHO PERSUES
AND A WARRIOR WOMAN WHO LINKS IT ALL

COMING SOON
THE BOOK OF LIGHT SERIES

A mage acolyte who never toed the line
A wounded, washed-up warrior turned spy
A priceless ancient tome that everyone wants
All Jenn's novels are available in paperback, eBook and audiobooks